OBSESSIONS

AN ANTHOLOGY OF ORIGINAL STORIES

Edited by
MARK LESLIE

Stark Publishing

STARK
PUBLISHING

For Kevin J. Anderson

Thank you, Kevin, for continuing to remind me, through the ongoing example that you set, of those eloquent words of your dear friend that your obsession for writing, for telling stories, in other words your spirit with a vision, is indeed a dream with a mission.

Table of Contents

FOREWORD 7

INTRODUCTION: Caught in the Grip 11

MY PRIZE – Leah Cutter 15

CURSE OF THE GHOULMASTER – Stephen Couch 33

THE LAST JULIAN – Annie Reed 59

A RARE BIRD – Joe Cron 73

AT THE HEART OF IT ALL – Kari Kilgore 91

NOT SICK ENOUGH IN THE HEAD – Robert Jeschonek 109

BRINGING LIGHT INTO DARKNESS – Dayle A. Dermatis 137

A MATTER FOR GOD – Kristine Kathryn Rusch 153

SILVER LININGS – Leigh Saunders 175

BLOOD OF HEROES – Ezekiel James Boston 201

SECOND-HAND CASKET – Kate Pavelle 223

PINK PILLBOX HAT – Julie Strauss 243

FOR LOVE OF RONALD STURGIS – Michael Kingswood 259

EVERYTHING GOT COLDER – Dean Wesley Smith 277

THE TOOTH FAIRY – David Stier 289

EXECUTIVE DECISIONS – Rebecca M. Senese 307

EDITOR'S OBSESSIVELY THANKFUL AFTERWORD 329

About the Contributors 333

FOREWORD

Kristine Kathryn Rusch

Here's what I love about Mark Leslie's editing: It has heart.

When Mark picks a project, he generally goes for the emotion genres—y'know, horror (emotion), romance (emotion), and fear (emotion).

An obsession is an emotion gone sideways. Often, obsessions are rooted in emotion. An obsession with death, because as a child, our protagonist witnessed the death of a beloved person or pet. An obsession with collecting, because things allow that person to bury their emotions under something tangible. An obsession with another person, based on love or rage or hatred or, well, you name it.

The stories in this very special volume cover a wide range of genres, from fantasy to noir, from horror to something resembling love. These stories have only one thing in common—an obsession.

Sometimes the obsession is sketched in ever so lightly, because the protagonist really doesn't want others to notice just how big the obsession is. Sometimes the obsession is vast and creepy and hard to miss.

And that's what makes these stories wonderful.

I have watched Mark edit on a variety of projects. He often takes part in our anthology workshop, which requires a lot of reading before a week of in-person sessions during which we editors discuss authors' stories right in front of them. I consider myself lucky to have heard Mark's takes on a variety of fiction.

Sometimes his opinion makes me reconsider something I've read or notice something I've missed. I love that. (Note the emotion here.)

Mark has great insight into fiction, into what makes it work, and, even better, what makes stories link to other stories.

Obsessions does just that. These stories are different, yes, but they belong together. You might even say they're obsessed with each other.

(Okay, maybe that *is* a bridge too far.)

Mark himself was obsessed with this anthology. When it looked like the anthology was going to be canceled, Mark stepped in to save it. He ran a highly successful Kickstarter to help him pay the authors and, ultimately, to put together an audiobook version of the anthology.

You might want to search for the project on Kickstarter, just to see the videos Mark compiled to convince people to support the project. Which they did, in droves.

You now have in your hands (or on your e-reader or in your ear) this marvelous volume. Enjoy it. No, *savor* it. Once you finish, you'll understand why Mark (and the rest of us) are obsessed by it.

It's just that good.

—Kristine Kathryn Rusch
Las Vegas, NV
September 30, 2020

INTRODUCTION: Caught in the Grip

Mark Leslie

I often liken my role as an anthology's editor to being your tour guide as we take a stroll together past a series of landmark stories that these dear author friends I am privileged to work with were generous enough to share with me.

Along the way, I point out the sights, the sounds, the smells. And we'll both revel in the atmospheric emotions, the highs, the lows, the noise, and the quiet; the magic of how we can both experience the same story, and yet be brought to our own unique and intimate internal reactions.

That's one of the things I adored about the format of Rod Serling's *The Twilight Zone*. Those moments where he stepped out to introduce and end a tale, carefully preparing you for the tale you were about to experience.

And, if you consider imitation to be the sincerest form of flattery, then, picture me donning that same style of persona.

Right now, my role is to prepare you for the wonderful voices of the talented writers that you are about to experience. I know that not everybody reads an anthology from start to finish; some readers prefer to dance around from tale to tale to the pattern of their own internal beat. But for those of you who read things in the order presented I have designed and laid out the tales in a way that I hope you can relish.

It is a path, a course, that I have carefully planned out, designed to move you through the various emotions, genres, experiences, the highs, the lows, that these masterful writers will take you through.

Their voices and tales are each unique, but the theme they have explored is consistent.

Webster defines "obsession" as "abnormal preoccupation with a persistent idea of desire."

Sometimes these obsessions are related to a particular hobby, such as avid collectors of various artifacts. Other times the obsession can be something that drives a person to invent something new, cure a disease or attempt to right a great wrong. And at other times, they can send a person down a dark and disturbing path.

Obsessions can be healthy; they can be born out of love and the desire to protect. They can stem from a need to fix something that is broken or replace something that is missing. Obsessions can be perversive and disgusting, unhealthy and bizarre. They can be mild or quaint eclectic things, or they can be all-consuming and life altering.

The stories you are about to read are about different types of obsessions and how those obsessions drive changes or alterations in a character's life and the lives of those around them.

The authors have crafted stories that dig deep into each character's unique obsession. They explore the trauma, the elements of that person's upbringing or their internal character that led to or feeds the obsession. They explore and examine what it really means, on the deepest level, if they obtain that goal they obsess over.

These stories are so rich and fascinating that I'm confident you will be thinking about them obsessively long after you have finished reading it.

But in the meantime, those stories, and these brilliant authors await us both. Come, take my hand, dear reader, and let us take a stroll together as I have the honor of introducing you to the fascinating characters, worlds, and situations they have each spun along this single theme.

MY PRIZE

Leah Cutter

Leah Cutter still has a journal from when she was eight years old that begins with the words: "When I grow up, I want to be a writer." Something else she had when she was a little girl was the first of a growing collection of Kewpie dolls and Kewpie doll memorabilia.

But we'll get to the Kewpie doll collection shortly.

Leah writes page-turning, wildly imaginative fiction set in exotic locations, such as a magical New Orleans, the ancient Orient, rural Kentucky, Seattle, Minneapolis, and many others.

She writes fantasy, science fiction, mystery, literary, and horror fiction. Her long fiction and books have been published by New York Publishers and small presses, and her short fiction has been published in magazines like 'Alfred Hitchcock's Mystery Magazine' and 'Talebones,' and anthologies like Fiction River.

I have had the distinct pleasure of publishing her story "The Glass Girl" in the first anthology I edited for the Fiction River *series, in the 2017* Editor's Choice *edition.*

You can learn more about Leah, her worlds, and her writing at www.leahcutter.com. But in the meantime, let's get back to that Kewpie doll collection I'd mentioned.

"When I was a little girl, my grandmother gave me a Kewpie doll," Leah tells me. Since she preferred stuffed animals to dolls, this was the only doll she had for years.

Leah's mother was quite the seamstress, making matching outfits for the family; for one camping trip, her mom sewed Leah a sleeping bag and made a matching one for her doll.

"Because other people knew that I adored this doll, they continued giving me Kewpie memorabilia even after I was an adult, such as a hand-painted Kewpie plate, a Kewpie from WWII wearing a German army helmet, and even a rare black Kewpie.

"So, it seemed natural to me to take something that was innocent, like collecting a few Kewpie dolls, and turn it into something much darker. It was better for me to use the Kewpie dolls than something I'm actually really obsessed with, such as coffee or chocolate."

And, I, for one, am glad that she did. Because this story stuck with me for so long after I finished reading it that I ended up theming an entire anthology around it.

Now let us find Megan as she is about to enter the sacred room containing her prize Kewpie doll collection.

Megan took a deep breath and deliberately pushed all her cares away before she opened the door to the room containing her prize doll collection.

The faint smell of old plastic greeted her first, as always. It wasn't the nasty scent of forgotten, moldy toys that came from pawnshops or second-hand stores; no, this was sweeter, meatier, like fresh rubber.

Megan's eyes automatically darted to the hygrometer in the corner, making sure that the room maintained a steady forty-five percent humidity. The thermometer beside it assured her that the room was still exactly sixty-seven degrees.

Only then did she step fully into the room and bask in her collection of Kewpie dolls.

The dolls all smiled at her, making her smile in return. As Kewpie dolls tended to look out of the corner of their eyes, she'd arranged many of them to stand sideways, so they'd be looking at her. They always seemed so wise to her, like they held secrets they only told each other.

She'd dreamed more than once that her dolls would fly around the room at night on their stubby little wings, dancing like the angels they were.

Father had always said Megan was his little Kewpie doll, with her dark eyes and chubby cheeks. He insisted that she was the best prize he'd ever won, sometimes calling her just "My Prize." She hadn't minded, not really, that he'd kept her all to himself all those years, especially since Mother had died shortly after Megan had been born so it was just the two of them.

She missed Father so much sometimes. It had been a little over a year since his death. She'd had to celebrate her sixtieth birthday all by herself. She felt as though there was so little left of her without him. She kept his bedroom just as it had been, frequently sprinkling a little of his aftershave on the bed so it would still smell like him when she laid on it.

Though Megan was far from young now, her cheeks no longer pudgy and pink, her dark eyes faded, she still wore the cute dresses that Father liked, the ones that matched her dolls, that were tight across her chest and flared out around her waist, ending just above her knee. She particularly liked the dresses made out of cotton with white backgrounds and tiny prints of butterflies, pumpkins, or even hearts.

When Megan was feeling particularly daring, she might, on a Sunday after church, when she was certain she wouldn't see anyone she knew, use some mousse on her graying hair and make a little hair lick standing up in the center of her head, just like one of her dolls.

The dark green walls of the room set off the shelves nicely. The shelves themselves were "floating" shelves, so no ugly brackets marred her display. She knew she should draw the curtains and hide the shelves when she wasn't there, thereby protecting the dolls from the soft light, but she couldn't bear to hide them so.

Each doll sat or stood to her best advantage. The collection was arranged by age, with the oldest dolls from 1912 to her left, then continuing to her right, with the resurgence of Rose O'Neill's drawings in the 1980s resulting in postcards and even stationary.

But no modern dolls, and in particular, none of those fake Japanese Kewpie dolls that had flooded the market in recent years.

Megan didn't have a lot of time that night, so she turned to her left and walked directly to the originals section. Here, she had over four dozen bisque dolls manufactured in Germany, even two signed by the creator, Rose O'Neill, herself. Most of them were the smaller dolls, between one to six inches tall.

None of the dolls were brightly painted—Megan didn't want a *restored* doll; she wanted them in their existing condition. She'd seen pictures of the more colorful museum dolls and thought it was a disgrace. The dolls should be allowed to age naturally, as she had.

When Megan had read about the auction taking place that night, she'd deliberately created a hole in her soldier section. The doll listed as part of the estate going up had a Kaiser helmet with a spike on the top of it and held a rifle in one hand.

Megan didn't have one of those. She had dolls lying down and pointing rifles, dolls in plain caps with guns and holsters, even the German "policeman" doll. But this was the only German doll that had that particular helmet, in that particular pose.

The doll going up for sale didn't have the heart-shaped sticker in the center of its chest, and it wasn't signed. However, it would complete her German army collection. Once she bought it, she would have one of each type of soldier-themed dolls manufactured between 1912 and 1915.

Well, except for the twelve-inch dolls. Maybe some year, if she won the lottery, she'd have a spare twenty-thousand dollars and could afford to buy one of those.

The estate going up for auction that night had a single Kewpie doll in it. The original owner of the estate had collected all things military. She wasn't interested in anything else on sale that night, especially not the antique guns and rifles. She had her own gun, one that Father had bought for her to protect herself, a small, ladylike, modern pistol that made a *tack-tack-tack* sound when she practiced shooting it.

Because there were so few dolls on sale tonight, she figured she wouldn't have much competition in bidding, except for a couple of collectors who felt the need to bid on everything. According to her books on doll collecting, this particular Kewpie doll should go for only two or three hundred dollars.

She had no hope that the auction house wouldn't have done their research. The bidding would start at a reasonable price, say, one fifty. Hopefully, she could keep the price low and still have money in her collection account when the bidding was over.

With a final wave to the rest of her collection (it would have been rude not to at least say goodbye), Megan turned and marched out the door, as if going to war herself.

She *had* to get that doll. She'd take it with her, up to Father's bed that night, where she'd pleasure herself while it watched. She always swore the Kewpie dolls winked at her as she lay there afterward in a pleasant stupor.

She wouldn't have to collect another doll for a while after that. But her need would grow, and nothing would make her happy until she'd found the next perfect doll for her collection. It was like Father's passions, which had only struck now and again. He always bought her dolls afterward. That had been the start of her collection.

Good thing one was going on sale tonight.

∞

Megan hurried down the empty street. The auction was taking place in the warehouse district south of downtown Seattle. No one really lived down here. The few restaurants only served breakfast and lunch and were already closed. Brisk March winds whisked around her bare legs. She clutched her purse closer to her, glad her little pistol was tucked inside. The air smelled of the heavy trucks that rumbled by.

The only thing that had gone right that night was that it wasn't raining.

Megan had missed her first bus. Though the bus had been early, she still blamed no one but herself, as Father had taught her. She'd spent too much time with her collection, indulging herself.

Missing the first bus had made her miss her connection. According to the timetable printed on the side of the bus stop sign, with the next connection, she should still make it to the auction before it started.

However, she hadn't counted on the second bus breaking down. It had lowered its front step for a passenger, then been unable to raise the step back up. Everyone had been told to get off the bus.

Another bus would come along eventually, but Megan would miss half the auction by the time it arrived. She didn't have a smartphone—Father had always said those things made you dumb—so she couldn't call one of those ride-share services (not that she'd trust any of them, or just blithely get into a stranger's car). The cab company she called couldn't get to her location for twenty minutes. It was faster to just walk.

So, Megan scurried along the sidewalk, tripping over the broken concrete. She wasn't a runner, had never done anything so undignified as go jogging, so she quickly got out of breath.

If only she had Kewpie doll wings!

The auction had already started by the time Megan arrived at the auction house. Luckily, the nice young man at the entrance processed her quickly, giving her a paddle with the number 338 on it in exchange for her credit card information.

The auction room itself had the feeling of a theatre. A three-foot-high stage took up the front of the room. It was brightly lit, with many chairs stretched across the length of it displaying items from the estate, each with numbers that matched the catalog of things being sold.

The room itself smelled of stale clothes and cigarette smoke. Had the estate owner been a smoker? Hopefully, that wouldn't affect the bisque doll. She'd just have to make sure that she cleaned it good when she got it home. Maybe even take a bath with it.

She shivered with excitement. A nice hot soak sounded lovely just then.

Megan quickly looked over the audience. Mostly men, as she had assumed, given the nature of the items available. No one sat in the chairs around the edges of the open space—everyone stood, holding their paddles.

Of course, the auctioneer wouldn't go through the catalog in order. He had to create excitement, so he cherry-picked the items, pulling out some of the rarer pieces for people to bid on, following that with a more mundane piece.

Had the Kewpie doll already been sold? She had no way of knowing, not without asking someone. And she'd never be so forward as that, to ask a strange man about a doll. Father had warned her too often about the dangers of talking with strangers.

As the evening drew on, Megan found herself growing more and more tense. When would they bring out the Kewpie doll? It had to be the next item. Or the one after that.

Maybe there *were* other doll collectors in the audience. Maybe the auctioneer was holding the doll until the very end, and there would be a frenzy of bidding.

When the auctioneer announced that the next item, a civil war rifle, was the last item of the night, Megan felt crushed. All the air flew out of the room. She struggled to breathe.

Someone else had bought the Kewpie doll. But who? How could she find out?

She was going to have to ask someone.

By the time the crazy bidding had finished on the civil war rifle, Megan had positioned herself close to the stage so she could talk with the auctioneer himself.

She assured herself that he wasn't really a stranger—she'd seen him before, working more than one auction. That didn't really help how the bottom of her belly twisted and knotted with anxiety.

The auctioneer was a round man, trying to hide his bloated belly behind a black wool vest. His nasal voice cut through the casual chatter of the audience. Though he used a microphone, Megan would bet that he'd be able to bellow loud enough to be heard even over a raucous crowd.

She waited patiently while the auctioneer thanked everyone for attending and told them about the next auctions coming up. Finally, he was done.

"Excuse me, excuse me!" Megan said as loudly as she could, waving her arm to get the man's attention.

"Well, howdy miss! What can I do you for?" the man asked. The nametag stuck to his breast pocket proclaimed him as Billy.

"I came in late," Megan confessed. "So I missed the Kewpie doll. Can you tell me who got it?" Maybe she could offer a little more money than the collector had paid for it.

"You missed quite a show!" Billy said. He squatted down so he could talk more comfortably with her. "Bid on that little doll went up to six hundred and fifty dollars."

"Really?" Megan said, surprised. "But how? Why?" That amount of money was completely unheard of for that figurine, particularly one that wasn't signed.

"It was him," Billy said quietly, nodding his head toward the man just behind Megan. "Announced a high amount first thing, so the bidding started at five hundred."

Megan turned to see a tall Asian man chatting with one of the regulars at the auction house. He was dressed in a dark suit with a white shirt, with long, straight hair that brushed his shoulders and big, square glasses.

She gasped in horror when she realized that he was a Japanese collector. He probably had an entire room full of those Japanese knockoffs of her beloved Kewpie dolls.

And he was going to stick *her* Kaiser helmet doll among them.

She had to get her doll away from him. She had so many plans for that doll! They were going to take a bath together. Go sleep on Father's bed.

She'd never gone so far as to pleasure herself using one of her dolls, but she'd thought about it more than once.

No. No pleasure for her. Not until she got that doll.

Father would be disappointed in her if she didn't.

∞

"Excuse me, excuse me!" Megan said as she hurried after the Japanese man. His long legs let him take long strides down the street. She'd been waiting for what felt like *forever* for him to finally leave the auction house after everyone else had gone.

"Yes?" he said, turning and stopping.

"Hi, my name is Rose," Megan said. It would be wrong for her to give a stranger her real name to anyone who wasn't family. Father had always insisted on that, so she frequently used the name Rose O'Neill, the creator of the Kewpies. "I came to the auction to bid on the Kewpie doll."

The man stared intently at her as if he didn't quite follow what she'd been saying.

"Doll? Kewpie doll?" Megan said.

"Ah! Yes. Kewpie," he said, the familiar name sounding so foreign as he said it. "My prize," he added proudly.

Megan nodded. Kewpie dolls had routinely been prizes at carnivals. All collectors called them, "My prize." Father had even called her that.

"Can I...can I see it?" she asked. "I really wanted to at least be able to bid on it." If she'd been there, she would have driven the bid even higher, up to one thousand dollars or more, and worried about how to pay for it later.

The Japanese man looked puzzled, but then he said, "Okay."

It surprised her when he reached inside his jacket and pulled out the small doll. Why wasn't he carrying it in a box? He could break the bisque so easily!

How dare he?

He didn't deserve such a prize. Certainly not *her* prize.

In the dim streetlight, Megan examined the doll. She didn't try to take it and hold it, not yet.

The original helmet would have been painted a bright blue. It had faded to a baby blue through age. The silver paint on the spike at the top of the helmet had chipped off. Only the rifle was still black and shiny. Though the Kewpie's eyes were bright, and the smile the doll gave Megan was encouraging.

"Give me the doll," Megan announced, her gun suddenly in her hand.

"You joking?" the man asked, looking startled. "For real? Like American gangster?"

"For real," Megan said, though she was no gangster. Just a *serious* doll collector. Unlike him. She took a tiny step closer. "Give me the doll."

The strangest expression crossed the man's face. Was it anger? Contempt? Disgust? She wasn't sure.

She was absolutely certain of his next word, though.

"No."

The man moved his arm to the side, then opened his hand and dropped the doll on the hard concrete.

"NO!" Megan screamed.

But it was too late. The delicate sound of breaking pottery echoed through the quiet street.

"You...you monster!" Megan said. She focused on the man and put three bullets through his heart. *Tack-tack-tack.*

The man dropped to his knees, then toppled over, like a falling leaf.

Megan stooped down beside the ruins of the poor doll. Through some weird stroke of fate, while the body had shattered, the head was still intact, though a crack now ran up the left cheek.

"Oh, you poor, poor darling," she said as she put down her gun and gently picked up the head of the Kewpie doll. "He was a bad man," she confided in the doll. She clutched the head close to her chest and rocked back and forth. "Poor thing. Poor thing."

No doll hospital in all the world would be able to put together the fragile bisque pieces scattered across the sidewalk. Too many of the shards had just turned to fine powder.

After what seemed like a timeless moment, Megan came back to herself. She found she was shivering with cold.

She had to get up. Get out of here. Go home.

But what was she going to do after that?

She looked over at the bad, bad man. He hadn't moved. She sniffed. At least she'd taken care of him. His collection would be free of him. Maybe his dolls would all find better homes.

A cold wave of reality hit.

Megan had just killed a man. Her stomach churned, and bile burned the back of her throat.

What had she done?

She started panting. Her palms grew clammy, and she felt sweat form under her arms.

The police would come looking for her. She couldn't deny that she'd been here. The auction house had recorded her information when she'd shown up. She'd talked with the auctioneer. The other regulars knew she was a doll collector.

What would happen to her Kewpies when the police came for her? They always got their man, or woman, at least on the TV shows.

They would take her collection away from her, then put her in a cheerless place with no dolls, no secret smiles to cheer her on, no stubby wings to fly away on.

No. She couldn't let that happen either.

Megan rose to her feet, swaying with the wind. She glanced at the other body lying on the sidewalk.

She'd leave *him* here. Let him be taken out with the trash.

Before she left, she deliberately placed the broken doll's head on the man's chest, a silent reminder of the real crime here.

∞

After Megan got home, despite how late it was, she spent the next two hours moving furniture into Father's bedroom: the kitchen table and chairs, the end tables from the living room, her own reading chair and lamp table. She arranged all the furniture around the bed, staging it just so.

Then she took a long hot shower, getting herself squeaky clean. She put on one of her long-sleeved, old-fashioned, white cotton nightgowns, the ones that Father had liked so much.

One by one, she brought her dolls out of the collection room and upstairs to the bedroom, loving them, talking to them, petting and caressing each one before she placed it on the furniture arranged like impromptu shelves around Father's bed.

She didn't keep the dolls grouped together by date of manufacture, however. Though she loved all her dolls, she loved some more than others. She kept the more beloved ones closest to the bed, in the front row, and let the others sit further back.

The very last doll she gathered up from her collection room was the very first doll she'd ever received, the plastic doll her grandmother had given to her when she'd been just a baby. She dressed the doll in a white cotton nightgown that matched hers, then cuddled the doll close against her chest as she walked back to the bathroom.

Several bottles of sleeping pills lined the first shelf of the medicine cabinet. Megan had gotten the prescription just after Father had died when she'd found she could no longer sleep. She rarely took the pills anymore, but she kept refilling the prescription anyway.

She knew she'd never be able to sleep now, not after what she'd done. So she took one pill.

One pill became two.

Then three.

Then, eventually, the whole bottle, followed by half of a second bottle.

By the time she was finished, her stomach was full, and the room was spinning. Megan held the doll's hands in her own and danced down the hallway, turning from side to side because she already felt dizzy.

Then she laid down on Father's bed, smelling his aftershave, feeling him close by. She could almost hear him calling her. "My prize."

All her dolls looked on her with kind eyes, giving her their best secret smiles, her angels watching over her as she dreamed her final dreams.

Ω

CURSE OF THE GHOULMASTER

Stephen Couch

I am sure you've heard about how you can boil a live frog to its death without having to even add a lid to the pot.

The premise is if you try to drop a frog into a pot of boiling water, it'll clearly sense the pain that indicates immediate danger, and it will try to escape. But suppose you place the frog in a pot of room temperature water and slowly raise the temperature to a boil. In that case, the frog won't realize what's happening – and thus won't leap out of the water. The slow and almost imperceptible change in temperature lures it to a complacency that can be deadly.

This brilliant tale by Stephen Couch illustrates how a deeply rooted passion can become such an obsession that recognizing the boiling water surrounding you is simply not possible.

Sometimes we can become so focused on something, on an end goal, on a desire for something to work that we leave no stone unturned in order to get there. And sometimes we don't realize how much we have given, how much we have invested, or how much we have lost until it is too late.

It happens to gamblers, who continually up their bids with the idea that they only need to win that one big hand to make back all of the previous losses. It happens in relationships, where minor affronts are overlooked to the long-term emotional detriment of a person constantly undermined or abused.

As Stephen explores in this story, and as I'm intimately familiar with in the book world, it happens to authors and to publishers. Particularly those who toil and invest an unending commitment of blood, sweat, and tears into making their publication happen or keeping that dream alive.

I remember the editor of a small press anthology explaining that his work on a World Fantasy Award-winning series was mostly "a labor of love." At the time, I understood it to be a comment on his passion but neglected to understand the subtle unsaid part of that statement. It was about love because it certainly wasn't about the money. Particularly not if you considered the time, the personal expenditures often invested in that project.

I didn't understand what he meant until I had my own experience heading up a small press quarterly magazine, and then, later, worked on editing different anthologies.

When asked about this story, the author says that it was born of three parents.

"My love of horror movie hosts," he says. "My brief involvement with the early-Nineties 'zine scene, and my

tendency to obsess over pop-culture minutiae no one else cares about."

The tale conjures up a wonderful nostalgia for those local cable-television shows that so many of us clung to and obsessed over. But it also illustrates the interesting way that, when one becomes consumed with a single passion, such as honoring a respected dead celebrity, they can ignore so many other important or poignant moments in their life.

Stephen Couch is a computer programmer, an occasional cover band vocalist, and a lifelong Texan. His fiction has appeared in such venues as 'Cemetery Dance,' 'Space & Time,' and 'The Best of Talebones.' You can visit him online and poke him with virtual sticks at www.stephencouch.wordpress.com.

But the ink on the aforementioned 'zine is now dry, so let's follow Stephen as he prompts us to turn the pages of this curious exploration of a man driven to give a local celebrity the acclaim and legacy that he feels his hero deserves.

My babysitter died yesterday.

I hadn't thought much about him over the last several years. Not about him, his deep voice and piercing eyes, his long black cape, his haunted castle, nor the vintage horror movies he broadcast.

But there in the paper yesterday was the obituary that brought it all rushing back:

*THURSTON 'GHOULMASTER' CROFT, LOCAL
CELEBRITY, DEAD AT 91.*

I cut the obit out of the paper, but I didn't know why. I carried it around my little efficiency apartment, reading it over and over, those three paltry paragraphs, pacing from living room to kitchenette to bathroom and back again.

I hung it on the refrigerator with a pizza-delivery magnet, reading it once more.

Three paragraphs didn't feel right. Local celeb. Retired fifteen years ago. No surviving family. Preceded in death by his wife, Bessie.

Ninety-nine words to sum up ninety-one years.

I folded up the clipping and put it in my wallet.

I didn't know why I did that, either.

∞

When I was a kid, my mother worked late hours, or she claimed to. I would catch the bus home from school, let myself into our apartment, fix an afternoon snack, and flip on the TV just in time to catch the Ghoulmaster every afternoon at four. Plopped down in front of the tube with my PB&J and a glass of chocolate milk, I would hum the show's theme song – *Toccata and Fugue in D Minor* – as animated lightning flashes burst around a photo-negative shot of a castle. Red, dripping letters appeared on-screen: *GHOULMASTER'S SPOOKY MOVIES!*

And then the man himself swept into the frame as the image dissolved to a shot of his laboratory. The place was tricked out exactly like you'd imagine: stone walls draped with cobwebs; smoking beakers and test tubes; electrical arcs eternally climbing a Jacob's ladder.

The Ghoulmaster held his cape over his nose and mouth, his greasepaint-rimmed eyes holding the camera and the viewers with a laser stare.

He winked, dropped his cape, and grinned. "Hello, Ghoulkids," he boomed, raising his arms to encompass everyone watching. "Who's ready for the shock of a lifetime?"

Sometimes my mother would be home by the time the Ghoulmaster signed off, but not often. I would do my homework without being told. I'd make myself supper as best I could, having been forbidden to use the stove.

I'd brush my teeth, get in my jammies, and tuck myself in. Those nights, when my mother came in after midnight, stinking of booze, I'd pretend to be asleep when she meandered into my room and kissed my forehead.

I'd keep pretending to sleep long after.

∞

I pulled that obituary out of my wallet and re-read it countless times. Folding and unfolding the newsprint so much creased and obliterated several lines of text. But I knew the whole thing by heart before then, all ninety-nine words.

Every read-through gave me a pang, and I wondered if anyone else in the city felt like I did about the Ghoulmaster passing beyond the veil into Bad Movie Purgatory.

No. Of course there wasn't such a thing as Bad Movie Purgatory. There wasn't anything; there wasn't even a veil to pass through. There was only suffering. You rotted away in a nursing home, dementia and cirrhosis eroding you down to nothing.

I shook my head and realized with a sick jolt that I'd crushed the obituary clipping in my fist, wadding it into a crumpled little ball.

I jumped to my feet, ran to the kitchenette, and spread the clipping out on the hard Formica counter, smoothing it as best I could, almost like I was doing CPR.

The paper tore neatly along one of those gauze-thin crease lines, and the feeling of sickening shock opened up into a chasm in my guts. Worse, the ink had begun to rub off on my fingers, leaving much of the text an illegible smear.

I panicked, hands frozen in claws over the ripped, ruined clipping, and began reciting the obituary from memory, over and over, fearful I'd forget it.

"No viewing or service will be held," I muttered, heart pounding. I reached the end and started again, looping back to 'no viewing or service will be held' in double time.

And how unfair was that? How many people would have liked to have seen him one last time, to pay their respects? I wrote him several times as a kid, but I couldn't imagine how many illiterate 'i liek your show mr goolmaster' messages he got in a week. Or a month, or a year? No, I wanted to tell him as an adult what he meant to me.

I wanted to tell him how he saved my life.

Even as I cycled back to saying 'local celebrity dead at 91,' I knew I'd forget it in time. It would fade with the next time I slept. I had to do something about it.

I left the tatters of the clipping where I'd killed it and switched on the computer. As soon as I got the word processor running, I transcribed the obituary, saving two copies in different locations.

As I stared at those three small paragraphs, blocky and formal in their Courier New, I thought again about all those people who wouldn't have a chance to say goodbye. Maybe they'd like to talk about the Ghoulmaster and what he meant to them. Maybe they were like me, Ghoulkids practically raised by the man. And maybe they thought this obituary, this last remnant of Thurston Croft's life, wasn't good enough.

I hit the RETURN key three times and started writing my own remembrance, one that *would* be good enough.

Its title? *CURSE OF THE GHOULMASTER.*

∞

I stopped hours later, hunger pangs gnawing at me. It was after midnight, and the only light in the apartment was the warm glow of the monitor.

What I wound up with wasn't simply a revised obit. It was multiple essays about what the Ghoulmaster and his show meant to me, plus tales of the rough times he'd gotten me through. I put together a glossary of his catchphrases. I compiled, with a memory better than I was expecting, a list of every Spooky Movie he showed. And as the centerpiece, a long reminiscence about the Halloween I'd dressed up as the Ghoulmaster, only to have every adult at every house I visited call me 'Dracula.'

No, it wasn't a new version of the obituary. It was a celebration. It was a loving, homemade encyclopedia.

It was a fanzine.

∞

I called in fake-sick the next day and went across town to the head shop near the junior college to load up on 'zines. I didn't know what I was doing, but if I wanted to do right by the Ghoulmaster, I needed to learn the art of desktop publishing. My good old Amiga 1000 could handle the computer side of things, but if I didn't get some kind of grounding in the process, it would be like buying a bunch of art supplies without knowing how to draw.

"Yeah, man," said the hippie girl at the register as she rang up my stack of amateur mags, "support local talent."

"I'm making one myself," I said.

"Sweet," she said and looked at me over her round-lensed glasses. "What about?"

"You know the Ghoulmaster?" I asked. "The horror-movie host? It's all about his show."

"Oh yeah!" she said, laughing. "We used to watch him in the common room in my dorm. What an old fruitcake! We had a great time making fun of all that stupid, cheesy crap."

Too late, I had given her my twenty, and she was already making change, or I would have stormed out. I didn't say another word, took my handful of coins and bag of 'zines and left, ignoring her wish that I have a nice day.

Cheesy? Crap? I fumed as I drove back home.

Issue One was filled with content, and I already knew what I'd write about for Issue Two, and possibly Three. People who didn't know brilliance when they saw it, that's what. People with silver spoons who never suffered, who never had to be raised by a TV show while their mothers...

The message light on the answering machine blinked at me as I walked in. As soon as I heard it was from the nursing home, I deleted it, the rest of it unheard.

∞

Dear God, was every fanzine on Earth about drugs?

Second question: was every fanzine on Earth produced on the world's oldest mimeograph?

I knew I could do better. I had *Deluxe Paint*; I had *PageStream*. I could format the text into symmetrical columns, like a real magazine. I could set things up in pleasing, professional fonts, rather than handwritten scrawls. I could adjust the contrast of images so they weren't blocks of unfathomable, photocopied black-and-nearly-black.

The only obstacles were time and money. The time I could eke out. The money...?

There were tons of people out there who loved the Ghoulmaster; I knew it for a fact. He couldn't have stayed on the air so long otherwise. All I needed to do was sell enough copies to break even. Easy! I could even get some kind of tax break for this, probably, and the twenty bucks I'd blown on 'zine research was my first business expense. Oh, and mileage to the head shop, however far that was.

I stayed up late again, working on the layout, whipping things into shape, and teaching myself as I went. I came up with the perfect cover: clip art of a gravestone reading THURSTON "GHOULMASTER"

CROFT. Below that, his date of birth. But for the date of death, I'd drawn an infinity symbol.

The debut issue would be forty-eight pages: a bargain at the price I'd need to charge. Two hundred copies to break even, then it would be time to prepare Issue Two.

Ghoulmaster fans across the city would be kicking themselves if they missed out.

∞

During lunch the next day, I wolfed down my employee-discounted burger while spending my whole hour on the payphone outside work.

A few quotes from print shops later, and I understood why 'zine creators opted for photocopiers.

The insomnia-addled math I did in my head left me with one option. Five hundred copies at double my planned cover price to break even? That seemed to be the only choice if I wanted this project to be of the quality it deserved.

If I was willing to pay the price of a hardcover for a tribute to my hero, so would five hundred other people. And if I was willing to cut back on food and heating and any other expense, I could slash to get the 'zine printed, they'd be willing to set aside a little extra money to afford a copy.

Could I afford to do it monthly, though?

The Ghoulmaster – Thurston – saved my life. He practically raised me.

Of course I could.

∞

The first box of *CURSE OF THE GHOULMASTER* was lighter than I expected, even with a printer's overrun of thirteen copies. I took that day off work, with much grumbling from my boss, and drove around town to comic shops, bookstores, New Age boutiques, and even that head shop where the cashier had the gall to mock my work. In a college town, most places were willing to stock amateur work on a commission basis, and I placed a quarter of my Issue One inventory by the time I got back home.

I hadn't figured commission costs into my break-even calculations, but what the hay. When this issue sold out, every store would be clamoring for more. I could negotiate a better commission percentage and be in the black with Issue Two.

Back home, I got on CompuServe, Genie, Prodigy, and every BBS I could find to place ads for the 'zine. I congratulated myself on being so forward-thinking. Selling over computer networks? Genius! Sure, my long-distance bill next month would be through the roof, but if everything worked out, I could be out of the red by Issue Three.

Possibly Issue Five.

∞

The next month came, and I began piecing together the second issue of *CURSE.* I had my salesman's route down to rote memory by then, zipping by all the stores in quick succession after (or before) work to see how the debut issue was selling.

As the weeks passed, I clearly hadn't done a good enough job of getting the word out. At the head shop, all I had to do was duck my head in the door. The girl at the counter would see me and shake her head with a sad little frown.

She could keep her pity, and those times she asked me if I 'wanted to, like, see a movie or something.' I had important things to do.

It wasn't like *CURSE* was going completely unsold. I got a few orders through the mail from people who'd seen my ads on a horror-movie BBS. The enthusiastic comments in their letters raised my spirits. There was a market for my 'zine, and there were readers willing to buy it. I just had to find some other way to let people know.

I sent review copies to *Cinefantastique*, *Video Watchdog*, *Fangoria*, and others. Against my better judgment, I even sent one to *Factsheet Five*. They panned it, but then, they panned everything.

During all this, my evenings were spent with Cup-O-Noodles and Issue Two prep. I had even more memories and content, and the layout ballooned to seventy-two pages. I worked out the cost with the rate card my print shop had given me and had to re-check my calculations, blinking as though chasing away a hallucination.

My online customers would pay this much, but would anyone else?

They had to. Even if someone picked up a copy out of curiosity, they'd see my passion. They'd feel the love and devotion dripping off the pages, and they'd come to care for the Ghoulmaster as much as I did. They'd be hooked!

∞

Issue Two was under-run by fifteen copies, so I had to re-figure my break-even point once more. I could save money by going the photocopy route – a ton of money – but I could also save money by writing the content longhand, not scanning and adjusting the contrast on photos, and a whole raft of cheapjack measures. But I'd wind up with a fanzine that said I didn't care about its subject matter.

You know, I needed an attitude adjustment about that. It wasn't a fanzine. I was making an actual *magazine*, by God. I might not have been able to afford color interiors or higher-tier production values, but by the time Year Two rolled around...?

I was planning out lucky Issue Thirteen, when I'd make that quantum leap in quality, before I'd even begun production on Issue Three.

Issue Two's sales were not good. None of my BBS customers ordered a copy, even when I sent them a friendly reminder postcard.

But maybe that was the way it had to be. Maybe I needed to build up an inventory of issues. A guy at one of the comic shops told me as much.

"Yeah," he said. "People come in, try the current issue of a comic, and then plow through the back issue bins, buying all the previous issues to get caught up," although he didn't look up from his copy of *Nexus* as he said it.

Before I knew it, I had four boxes stacked by my computer desk: Issues One and Two, and two boxes of Issue Three, since I'd have to sell that many more to get by.

∞

I lost my job at the burger place, but the good news about positions at the level of 'fry cook' was there were always plenty of them out there to be filled.

I got on at a convenience store. Night shift, so I could have my days free to do my sales route, even though that had shrunk from daily to weekly. The employees at different stores seemed less annoyed when I came in less often. Well, except for the girl at the head shop, who always smiled and said, "Man, I haven't seen you in forever!" I gave her a civil but noncommittal grunt.

She shouldn't have made fun of Thurston.

∞

I won't lie. Self-doubt crept into me by the time Issue Four rolled around. Mail orders from the computer were zero for Issue Three, so obviously cyberspace was a non-starter as far as commerce was concerned. While I still had plenty of thoughts of my own to fill the magazine, I wondered if I might be able to get some outside perspectives while still doing the writing myself.

All it took was some calls to the Ghoulmaster's former TV station, and then a trip through the phone book.

∞

UNPUBLISHED EXCERPTS FROM INTERVIEWS FROM ISSUES FIVE AND SIX:

Jimmy Powell, Director: Well, Thurston had seen or heard of other horror hosts. Ghoulardi, you know, or that Elvira lady. So he thought it would be a good thing to try. That was Thurston. Anything for a buck, especially after his kids' show, COWBOY JACK'S FUNTIME, got canceled.

Donovan 'Stick' Sturges, Set Designer: Make me a castle, he said, but all we had were backdrops from that old game show, KING'S POKER, which sort of looked like stone walls. Thurston was never happy with how those walls looked, but hell, he was half in the bag most of the time after his wife passed, and complained about everything.

Crystal Spradling, Co-host: He was old-fashioned, y'know? A gentleman, but almost cold about it. They brought me in for sex appeal when the ratings went in the toilet, but it was too little, too late. I wanted to take over the show when Croft retired, but who cared what the T&A girl thought, right?

Kiyoshi Sakamoto, co-producer: We were business partners for a long time, and this started back when people were leery about giving Japanese folks work. I'll always owe him for that. But we parted ways when he started having these hare-brained ideas. I'll tell you the big one: he wanted to syndicate...well, I suppose 'franchise' is a better word. He wanted a Ghoulmaster in every city, on every channel. Pay a franchise fee, wear the costume, and have your own horror-movie show. I knew it wouldn't work and, sure enough, no networks we contacted cared at all. It was a niche show for a niche audience. You can't expect something like that to have mass appeal.

∞

The tapes of those interviews sat in a box in my new storage unit, beside the boxes of unsold magazines. I couldn't afford the rent on the unit; I couldn't afford much of anything at that point.

There was a phone behind the counter at the convenience store where I could conduct business and interviews. It turned out there was also a security camera that recorded me gabbing with people all day instead of doing work, to the point of ignoring customers until they left without paying for their merchandise.

Another job gone. Another job, scrubbing toilets in an office building, found.

Issue Seven was looming, and I had a hell of a feature planned, with plenty of photos. I only hoped my switch to photocopying the magazine wouldn't ruin all those pictures.

I had another reason for that pricey storage unit, you see: memorabilia. Backdrops and props from Mr. Powell and Mr. Sturges. Costumes from Mr. Sakamoto in all sizes, left over from the franchising plan. All things they were going to throw out eventually, that any decent individual would want to rescue from the dump.

Every bit of it got shifted from their sheds and garages to its new home. I surveyed the riches: the laboratory equipment; the big prop shoe the Ghoulmaster planned to use to squash the big grasshoppers in *Beginning of the End*; and best of all, a tape of *Destroy All Monsters*, labeled with the show number in Thurston's own handwriting.

If this didn't turn the magazine into a hit...

I wanted to keep it all in the apartment, but there simply wasn't room, especially with the eight boxes of Issue Seven I'd need to produce. The price at the copy shop was right, and I could reduce the cost of the magazine by a massive margin.

I should have celebrated by going out to eat, but that was one more thing I couldn't afford.

∞

The stores started pressuring me to take back unsold stock. They couldn't sell it, and it took up shelf space. Even the comic-shop guy who'd been so hot on back issues was sick of seeing *CURSE* on his shelves. They all took Issue Eight, though, but made me promise I'd take back what hadn't sold when Issue Nine came out.

Turned out, that was almost all the copies. The clerk at the head shop (*HONEY*, as I finally read her name tag) was apologetic.

"I've been reading them," she said. "They're good. Really good. That old dude meant a lot to you, didn't he?"

Even with the magazine's reduced price, I still couldn't make a profit, and the storage unit was next to go. I got all the set dressing, props, and miscellany moved into the apartment, making it almost too cramped to move around in. I feared what would happen the next time the maintenance man came in to change the furnace filter. Would they throw me out for creating a fire hazard?

I arranged all the sets against the walls, transforming the apartment into a cramped replica of the Ghoulmaster's Castle of Spooky Cinema. Sleeping there, in that bent, shrunken copy of Thurston's lair, began to affect my dreams.

I started to write the editorial for Issue Ten and found myself shocked that Issue Nine had been made, printed, and distributed without my memory of its happening. The process was sheer autopilot now.

I'd find my writing dipping into the negative at times, but I'd always delete those passages and type something new. Something positive. Being downbeat now wouldn't help anyone, no matter how dark my dreams were.

∞

The call from the nursing home had come at two in the morning as I was getting home from another shift in Toilet Land.

I moved through my mother's room in a smeary daze, so disoriented to be doing something that didn't involve being a custodian or a biographer.

I collected my mother's belongings into a small box the smiling social worker gave me. There were pictures of me on the walls, more than I knew my mother had ever taken. School plays; junior college graduation; simple shots of me as a kid, sitting there doing nothing but looking serious. On the backs of each, dates and cheery descriptions.

I had them donate her clothes and books. I didn't have the room or use for any of that. It was part of my mother's life, not mine.

The closest I came to crying was when I tried to picture her face when she was young and happy, and I couldn't.

"Why couldn't you be someone people would want to make fanzines about?" I asked the empty room. Back to sterile blandness, it would house another dying person soon enough.

What about when it was my turn? Would my room at a care facility be filled with all my Ghoulmaster memorabilia, destined to go in a nondescript cardboard box? Or straight to the landfill?

∞

Issue Eleven was only eight pages long. Four pages of typing paper, folded double, and not even stapled. No colored paper for the cover, just stark white.

It was all about my mother.

∞

I started wearing one of the capes as I worked on Issue Twelve. It had taken a year to do the first dozen issues. A year since Thurston had died. A year of my life disintegrating as I gave everything to him, for the sole purpose of saying thank you.

He never knew I existed, did he?

The cape felt comfortable. It felt right, draped over my shoulders. I would wear it under my jumpsuit at work and wrapped around me like a second blanket as I slept. I didn't need greasepaint around my eyes; the dark circles from restlessness were better than anything the Ghoulmaster's makeup lady could invent.

I had it all. All of his life, crammed inside my apartment, every bit of knowledge and ephemera anyone could ever want about Thurston Croft.

But I was the only one who wanted it.

So much of my life gone. My mother's cremation wiped out the rest of my finances. My job covered my rent and utilities, and that was it. I would catch a city bus to the homeless shelter, where I would cadge free meals.

More than once, I wore my cape proudly to the shelter. The staff didn't blink an eye.

My life was in tatters, and only Thurston's life remained to fill the blank spots.

Bad Movie Purgatory was real, after all.

Finally, one night, when I dragged myself home from work, back aching and hands puckered with sweat, I was wracked with a headache from lack of food and sleep.

In delirium, I thought, *why not?*

His life is all the life I've got now.

I put on the full costume for the first time: tuxedo, shiny shoes, bat-shaped brooch. Pancake makeup, lipstick, and hair slicked back with mousse.

Water in the beakers and Erlenmeyer flasks, and electrical arcs zipping up the Jacob's ladder. I set up a mirror on the far wall so I could watch the Ghoulmaster perform.

I was eight again, and Momma wasn't coming home tonight.

I stalked into view, cape up over my face, and gave the audience a broad wink. The cape dropped, and I spoke, my voice neither mine nor Thurston's but something new, something in-between.

"Greetings, Ghoulkids," I said, and eight-year-old me clapped and cheered. I could taste the peanut butter and grape jelly. I could smell the rich, sugary chocolate milk.

And I could see the Ghoulmaster there in the mirror, in that vertical, stretched TV screen that used to be a full-length mirror. His first new episode in years and he looked so young, so ready to watch over me and all the other latchkey kids out there, to let us know we weren't alone.

It was so real I took a step back, bumping into one of the laboratory tables. The water in one of the beakers sloshed out and dripped on the carpet.

So real. My God, it was so very real.

That strange, hybrid voice again, whispering this time: "Ready for the shock of a lifetime?"

I knew, then. It was time for Issue Thirteen to be released. And per my plans from months ago, it would have a pronounced bump in its production value.

∞

"Hello, Mr. Sakamoto? Yes! Yes, it's me. It's good to speak to you again. Listen, I had some follow-up questions about something you mentioned in our interview..."

∞

The set dressing looked great; I had asked Mr. Sturges to come in and take a look, and he helped tweak things until they looked, as he put it, "indistinguishable from magic."

The studio here at the public access station was smaller than the old TV-station digs, but it'd be more than sufficient.

The crew hustled around, unpaid but eager to earn credit from the university film school. The director, ten years younger than me and full of energy, pointed her finger at me in the wings. "Five, four, three," she said, then finished the countdown with her fingers.

I strode onto the set, cape held up per protocol, winked and tipped my hat like I'd been doing it my whole life.

"Hello, Ghoulkids," I said. Offscreen, the crew applauded and whistled.

"Welcome to Ghoulmaster's Castle of Spooky Cinema. I'm so glad you could join us for an afternoon of chills, thrills, and good old-fashioned monster mania."

The director waved to the left, and I turned to the second camera. "I want you to know this is a safe place for you, Ghoulkids. Maybe you're a little down today. Maybe school was rough. Maybe Mommy and Daddy are working and won't be home until late. As long as I'm here, you don't have to worry about all that. We'll watch a movie, have fun, and forget the rest of the world for a while. Now, are you ready for today's cinematic shocker?"

The director called "cut" as the student in the control booth switched over to the public-domain Bela Lugosi movie we were showing today. I'd jump back in at the ten-minute mark, with a little off-the-cuff joking about the mysterious ape species known as the 'Brooklyn Gorilla.'

"Someone named Honey called in," said a crew member. "She said you're doing great!"

I hoped she'd like it. We had a dinner planned afterward to celebrate. It was back to the toilets after that, but that was showbiz.

As it turned out, all the legal paperwork for franchising the Ghoulmaster show was still legit, and the monthly fee was even cheaper than what it cost to produce the fanzine. Mr. Sakamoto was happy to get the money, if a little nonplussed. He even agreed to cover the public-access usage fees until we got up and running.

"I've been thinking about it ever since we talked," he said. "Maybe this town needs this goofy old show."

"Thirty seconds," called the director, and I walked over to a chalkboard containing a funny anatomical diagram of a gorilla and got my classroom pointer ready to tap on key parts of the drawing. I'd be improvising my dialogue, but that added to the fun of the show. I planned to improvise everything except that first monologue I'd given, welcoming the audience, and any kids watching, to the show. That, I had written out weeks ago and memorized until I knew it inside out.

All ninety-nine words of it.

Ω

THE LAST JULIAN

Annie Reed

"Letting go – saying a final goodbye," Annie Reed says when talking about this story, "is one of the hardest things I've ever had to learn how to do."

It's an inevitable thing since we know that nothing truly lasts forever. But that doesn't make it any easier when you are trying to say goodbye to a loved one.

We all have relationships that we wish hadn't ended, and we all miss loved ones we wish we could spend just one more minute with. Sometimes we find ourselves pining for those missed pieces of our lives and hearts. Sometimes we can become trapped by the overwhelming desire to have things back the way they were. Psychologist Elisabeth Kübler-Ross wrote about the predominant "five-stages of grief" model. But not everyone moves through the stages in the same order; not everyone deals in the exact same way.

And some can stay stuck in one particular stage for a significant amount of time.

"When I started this story," Annie says, "all I had was the image of an elderly man playing chess outside with his adult son on a stormy afternoon.

"It didn't take long before I realized the story was really about someone who is forced at long last to face a goodbye he's put off his entire life."

A frequent contributor to both Fiction River, *most recently in* Superstitious *and* Stolen, *and* Pulphouse Fiction Magazine, *Annie's longer work includes the near-future science fiction short novel* In Dreams, *the gritty urban fantasy novel* Iris & Ivy, *and the superhero novel* Faster. *Annie's short fiction appears regularly on Tangent Online's recommended reading lists, and "The Color of Guilt," originally published in* Fiction River: Hidden in Crime, *was selected as one of* The Best Crime and Mystery Stories 2016. *A founding member and contributor to the innovative* Uncollected Anthology, *Annie can be found on the web at* www.annie-reed.com.

But let's now hurry to witness the aforementioned father and son chess match Annie mentioned.

Because a storm is most certainly coming.

Dark gray clouds covered the sky, blotting out the sun and bringing the scent of rain and a distant rumble of thunder. So unusual, a storm like this in late October, but no one could count on the weather anymore.

Frank hunched his shoulders against a gust of wind that threatened to take his fedora on an unscheduled trip across the northern Nevada desert all the way to the Great Salt Lake in Utah. The day had started out warm—shirt-sleeve weather, his pops used to call it—but the wind brought the kind of damp chill that made his old bones glad he'd worn his jacket after all.

He snugged the hat down tighter on his head and stared across the chessboard at Julian. "You gonna make a move here anytime soon?" he asked.

Julian took forever to do anything these days. The two of them played chess every Tuesday and Thursday afternoon in a little park by the Truckee River. The city had installed concrete checkerboard tables near a stand of aspens back when Frank had been a young man. In the decades since, the city had grown and prosperity reigned before the inevitable crash and the slow rebuild. Through it all, no matter how tough times got, the park and the trees and the checkerboard tables remained. The aspens had grown tall and provided dappled shade from the summer sun, but with the storm blowing in, the few leaves still hanging on for dear life this late in the season rattled in the wind like tiny snare drums and ruined what little concentration Julian could muster.

Frank probably should have canceled the game, given the storm, but at least the board wouldn't blow away. Neither would the chess pieces. The set had been carved from granite by a local artisan, or so Julian—the first Julian—had said when he'd given Frank the chess set as a birthday present.

Julian's hand hovered over one of the white stone pawns. Frank tried to ignore the cracks in the skin covering Julian's knuckles.

"What, I need to install a timer?" Frank asked.

The timer was an old joke between the two of them, only when it had started, Julian had been the faster player.

"Hold your horses," Julian said.

Frank suppressed a grimace. Even Julian's voice sounded old and worn out.

Too soon. Far too soon.

He wasn't ready to lose another Julian. Time took its toll on everything, but Frank had devoted his entire life to the Julians, and he wasn't ready to let go. Nowhere near ready.

"Make a move before I catch my death out here," Frank said.

He pulled his jacket tighter around his shoulders as the first drop of rain splatted on the pitted top of the chessboard. The benches were in no better shape—too many years of scorching summer heat and winter ice and snow had taken their toll on the concrete—and the hard seat made his hips ache on the best of days. Today the incoming storm only made his aches worse.

Did Julian, this last Julian, feel the effects of time the way Frank did? He'd never asked, and he was afraid to ask now. Frank had built in subtle changes to the Julians to simulate aging. Yet in all the years he'd spent with this Julian and the ones before him, Frank had never bothered to consider anyone's feelings but his own.

Had he been like that with the first Julian, too? He didn't want to think that maybe he had.

The storm clouds had taken on a sickly yellow tinge. When Frank glanced up from the board, he caught sight of the tail end of a jagged bolt of lightning streaking toward the crest of a foothill only a few miles away.

Frank counted the beats between the flash and the rumble of thunder that followed. Old habits died hard.

Three beats. Three miles. Or was that just an old wives' tale his pops used to tell?

Frank had known the science, once. He'd known a lot of science, but his mind was failing him, too.

Julian's fingers closed over the pawn. He picked it up, but he paused longer than necessary before putting it back on the board.

"Your turn," Julian said, glancing up at Frank with eyes that weren't supposed to show emotion but did anyway.

More raindrops pelted Frank's back like hard little bullets made of water. Julian didn't blink as the rain hit him in the face. Julian didn't wear a hat. Frank's son, the original Julian, had never worn a hat either.

"I think we should call it," Frank said. "I don't like the look of this storm."

"Would you like to hear an updated forecast?" Julian asked.

"No." The word came out more sharply than Frank had intended.

That voice—that artificial tone—Frank had never been able to fully delete it from any of the Julians. It reminded him that this Julian, the one who was supposed to grow old with him, to sit in the park and play chess with him on Tuesday and Thursday afternoons, to watch movies with him every Sunday—to be the son that the original Julian couldn't—was nothing more than an artificial construct.

His son was gone.

No matter how many times Frank had been compelled to recreate him over and over and over again until he got it right (even though he never quite did), his son was gone.

"I would like to finish the game," this Julian said.

Another bolt of lightning shot from the clouds. Another rumble of thunder rolled across the sky. Two and a half beats this time.

"Your move," Julian said.

Frank stared at the expressive eyes in a face that could only mimic emotion. Julian's skin was slick with the rain. Tiny cracks had appeared at the corners of his mouth and in the thin skin of his eyelids. He sat waiting for Frank to respond, the picture of patience and understanding.

And acceptance. He knew what was coming.

Frank did, too.

He closed his eyes and nodded once. They would finish the game.

Their last game.

He looked down at the board and tried to concentrate.

His king wasn't in jeopardy yet, but it would be if he wasn't careful. Julian played chess as well as Frank did, if not better. Not that many years ago, their games had been rapid-fire events full of twists and turns. One small mistake or one small flash of inspiration was all that stood between defeat and victory.

These days Frank needed to study the board. He had to consciously map the moves in his head, and even then, he had trouble seeing more than a few moves ahead.

Today he couldn't concentrate on the game.

The wind whipped at the brim of his hat and whistled past his ears. He pulled the collar of his jacket up tighter around the back of his neck to keep the rain from soaking his shirt and glanced at Julian. Rainwater was running off the slight cleft in Julian's chin. His curly brown hair was plastered to his head, and Frank was surprised to see how much of Julian's scalp showed through hair that had grown as thin as his own.

He needed to make a move. Julian would wait for him until the end of time, and maybe that's what this day would bring. Frank wanted to make this day last forever, even though he knew he couldn't.

Would it be worse to lose this Julian than it had been to lose his son?

This Julian had been with him for nearly twenty years. The original Julian had died at eighteen.

Frank used a knight to capture one of Julian's pawns. A risky move, but risk defined the lasts in life. Hadn't the original Julian taught him that?

This Julian raised an eyebrow.

"Is that your move?" he asked.

Frank blinked.

That expression—the raised eyebrow, the quizzical tilt of the head—even the question itself so completely mimicked the first time the original Julian had beaten Frank at chess. And, for a moment, just a moment, Frank caught a glimpse of what his son would have looked like if he'd lived to be an old man, and it nearly broke him.

He blinked again, and the vision was gone.

The wind grabbed the fedora off Frank's head and blew it out across the choppy water flowing down the river. A dark, lonely bird in a stormy sky. The real birds had long since gone to roost to wait out the storm.

"Say hello to Utah for me," Frank called after his hat.

He turned back to Julian, who was still waiting patiently for Frank's answer.

"Damn right, that was my move," he said. "Your turn."

Another flash of lightning in the grayish-yellow afternoon, another crack of thunder, sharp and loud enough that Frank felt it in his bones.

One and a half beats this time.

The rain plastered his own thin, gray hair to his head and trickled down his back, sending shivers along his spine. His fingers had grown numb in the rain and the wind.

His jacket had been guaranteed to keep him warm on the coldest, wettest days, but the jacket had failed. He should complain to the manufacturer. Or he could just accept that everything failed over time. He'd had the jacket for years.

Julian moved his bishop across the board, capturing Frank's knight. "Check," he said.

Frank stared down at the board.

He hadn't seen that move coming. He should have. He'd programmed everything he knew—everything the original Julian had known—about chess into this Julian. But Frank hadn't seen that when he'd moved his knight, he'd put his king in jeopardy.

Any move he made now would result in checkmate. It was inevitable. The game was over.

"I resign," Frank said. "You win."

Julian tilted his head to one side, the move so slight that someone else might have missed it behind the thickening curtain of wind-blown rain.

"You've never given up, not in all the years we played," Julian said. "Why now?"

The wind shifted, and the rain now hit Frank on his left side. He shielded his face with one hand, which let him look directly at Julian without the rain getting in his eyes.

"In life, some things are inevitable," Frank said. "We learn to accept them."

"Like death and taxes?"

Frank nodded at the lie. He'd never learned to accept death. "Something like that," he said.

He pulled the old cloth bag he kept the chess pieces in from one of the pockets in his jacket. The wind tried to tear it away from his wet, numb, thick-knuckled fingers.

"Let me," Julian said.

Another flash of lightning went off like a strobe, and this time the crash of thunder was nearly instantaneous.

Frank flinched, and he lost his grip on the bag.

The wind carried the bag away before Julian could catch it.

Frank's wife had made that bag. After he'd lost Julian—after they'd lost Julian, their beautiful boy who'd had his whole bright future in front of him—she'd made him the bag as a special place to keep the chess set his son had given him. His wife was gone now too, time and grief and Frank's obsessive need to recreate their son doing to her what a stupid, stupid accident had done to their son.

Frank reached for the chess pieces, intending to put them in his pockets. He could replace his hat. His wife had left behind other things he could use to put the chess pieces in. But the pieces themselves were irreplaceable. They'd been his son's last gift.

Before he could grab his defeated king, the world around him exploded in a sudden burst of heat and light and the ear-splitting roar of thunder.

Something threw Frank off the concrete bench, a huge hand made of air that swatted him with the smell of ozone and burnt circuitry.

He landed awkwardly on his back, one leg bent beneath him, and he felt the bone snap.

The sudden, sharp pain consumed him. He screamed, but the wind ripped his screams away.

He existed for a time in a land called Pain, where the world was gray and cold and wet, and his body was electric with hurt so huge and deep he nearly lost himself.

When he came back to the real world, cold rain was slapping down on his face so ferociously, sheets of it now, that he thought he might drown.

The pain in his leg had faded to a dull fire that roared back to life when he tried to turn on his side. He bit back a scream and made himself move. He could feel the jagged edges of bone rubbing against each other.

Through the sheeting rain, he saw the aspen trees nearly bent in two by the wind. Most of their leaves had been blown away, but Frank couldn't hear the ones that remained. He couldn't hear the rain pelting the pavement beneath the checkerboard table. He couldn't hear anything except the ringing in his ears. He couldn't even hear himself crying out for Julian to help him.

But Julian couldn't help anyone. Not anymore.

What was left of Julian was still sitting at the checkerboard table.

The lightning strike must have been a direct hit. Julian's expressive eyes, artificial constructs that Frank had made with his own hands, were now two empty black pits. Julian sat forever frozen in mid-reach with Frank's black granite knight held in lifeless mechanical fingers. The skin on his hands had burned away, and the metal gears beneath the skin were charred black. His hair was gone, and so was the skin on his forehead and cheeks and nose. Only his mouth and his chin, that cleft chin the original Julian had thought was his worst feature, remained.

A pain far worse than a broken bone seized Frank. It stole his breath, choked his throat. Made his eyes water and made him beat a helpless fist on the rain-soaked earth beneath him.

Not like this.

It shouldn't have ended like this. *He* shouldn't have ended like this. Frank wasn't ready.

He hadn't been ready the first time, either.

The official notification from a grim-faced officer standing on his doorstep. The shriek from his wife from where she stood in the living room behind him when the officer's words sunk in.

No, it couldn't be possible. Julian, their bright, curly-headed boy, so full of life, so eager to learn new things, so ready to take on each new day like it was an adventure, killed in a stupid accident.

Frank couldn't bring Julian back, but he knew science. He had resources. He could afford the supplies he needed and hire out the work he couldn't do himself. He'd buried his grief with the work and buried his marriage along the way.

When the new Julian, the second Julian, was finally ready, his wife had sat stony-faced in their living room, her hands clenched in fists on her lap as her tea cooled in a china cup on the small table next to her. She'd refused to meet Frank's creation.

"That's not our son," she'd said.

The next Julian, the third one, was closer. The fourth one was nearly perfect. By the time Frank had created the fifth Julian — this Julian — his wife was gone.

Now, this Julian was gone, too.

The last Julian.

By the time the first responders found him, Frank had pulled himself over to the checkerboard table and levered himself onto the bench. He'd put all of the chess pieces in his pockets except the knight Julian held. The metal in his fingers had melted around the black granite chess piece, fusing the two together.

The storm had blown itself out. Only a few scattered rain showers fell as the first responders immobilized Frank's leg. The aspens stood tall and not quite straight; their branches bare now as faint sunlight peeked through cracks in the clouds.

The first responders brought out a black body bag.

"I'm sorry," one of them said. The woman looked only a little older than the first Julian had been when he'd died. "It's all we've got to put your property in."

His property? "Pardon?" Frank asked.

Her partner, the EMT who'd given Frank something for the pain before they'd immobilized his leg, shot her a look that clearly said the old guy wasn't playing with a full deck.

"Your construct," the man said. "We can't leave it here."

Frank understood. They were talking about Julian. But this Julian had been more than a simple construct to Frank. They all had.

71

"My son," he said. "He's my son, and the bag will do fine."

The medication had dulled the ache in his heart. Raw grief had turned into an ashy gray emptiness, but that emptiness gave Frank a clarity he hadn't realized he needed.

A man wasn't supposed to outlive his son. Frank had spent his life trying to right that grievous wrong, but in the end, he'd changed nothing. He'd outlived all his sons, even this one.

Had he wasted his life? If he had, did that even matter? He couldn't go back and do it all over again. What he could change right now was how he lived the rest of it.

He'd take Julian home. He'd bury him and grieve for him, and then he'd do for this Julian what he should have done from the start.

Frank would let him go.

He was finally ready to let them all go.

Ω

A RARE BIRD

Joe Cron

There are forces in the world that compel us to collect, accomplish, and experience things. Having a "bucket list" has become popular, and particularly among my own circle of friends, a "50 before 50" checklist.

But sometimes there's a more pressing deadline in front of us, less about an arbitrarily selected revolution around the sun, and having more to do with mortality.

Joe Cron tells me that his inspiring thought for this story was a classic what-if. And when he began to consider the world of birds and birders.

"What might happen," he imagined, "if the birds themselves took a more active role in birdwatching. From there, it was a matter of what sort of atmosphere felt best, and warmth moved to the front."

Joe Cron's novel **Alden Bridge** has been praised by readers as being a "wonderful tale of unconditional friendship and coming-of-age." I am certain that when you get to the end of this story, you'll see why readers react to his writing with all those "feels."

His diverse creative career comprises novels, short stories, essays, and theatrical productions, spanning some four decades of professional work. He is also an accomplished musician, and I'd been a fan of his fiction for years before I learned that. But the lyrical nature of his prose should have, long ago, been a tip-off for me.

I've had the pleasure of reading many of Joe's short stories, and the privilege of publishing one, "Henry and Beth at the Funeral Home" in Fiction River: Feel the Love as well as selecting his young adult mystery tale "The Untimely Death of Rachel Tamson" in Fiction River: Editor Saves. You can learn more about Joe's other writing at www.joecron.com.

One of the things I loved most about this obsession story is that while there are multiple forms of obsession in this story, displayed by the three main characters, none of them are dark or negative. They are obsessions born out of love, compassion, and commitment to pushing oneself to a higher cause. The drive, determination, and dedication are inspiring, and uplifting, and, as Joe mentioned, filled with an atmospheric warmth.

Pocker knew he was getting close. He had just made it over the sizeable and complex mouth of the Pascagoula River, and he was tired. Sick and tired of flying, in the strictest sense. An adventure, to be sure, but with an inescapable toll.

Flapping his wings as little as possible, he persevered to the northwest a few more miles. As one of the largest woodpeckers in the world, he made efficient use of the pleasantly aromatic saline air currents coming up off the Gulf of Mexico, which had provided for consistent stretches of gliding all along the coast from Florida. Now, though, he was headed a little bit inland, and those currents weren't quite as strong. He was encouraged by the pledges of assistance detectable within the cacophony of banter from the local seagulls but really hoped that wouldn't be necessary. Gulls could be a flaky lot.

Just a little farther.

At last, Pocker spotted a Mississippi sandhill crane with its plumage glowing in the orange of the low, December sunset, and glided down to land. A nearby tree stump, rotting away, provided both a perch and a potential snack. The crane didn't even wait for Pocker's talons to hit wood before launching into exclamations of hysteria.

"Oh my gosh, oh my gosh," said the crane. "I don't believe it. I can't believe it! Are you really…?"

Pocker had been getting a lot of that. He understood it, but he was nearly worn out—all the way out—and sometimes his patience for it ran thin. All the same, the crane was why he came through Mississippi, so he had little choice but to deal with it.

"An ivory-billed woodpecker?" said Pocker. "In the flesh."

The crane gave a little hop and an excited flutter of its large wings. "But that can't be! You guys are all gone."

"So I've heard," said Pocker. He looked around at a habitat that would have made for a grand life. Classic wet pine savanna. Tall grass in marshy areas blending into trees, some alive, some dead. It wasn't home, but he didn't need home. He needed something to calm his soul before he went, and this was doing beautifully. "But what can I say? Reports of my extinction have been greatly exaggerated."

"Oh, this is amazing. This is quite remarkable," said the crane, shifting weight from leg to leg. "I can't believe I haven't heard about this. I should have heard about this."

"And I'd be glad to tell you all about it," Pocker said, "but I need to eat something. I hope you don't mind."

"Oh, not at all," said the crane. "The gulls should have told me about this. My name is Rahni, by the way."

Pocker quickly dropped from the top of the stump down the side, darted his head around while examining the decaying surface, then picked a spot and hammered at it a few times. "I'm Pocker," he said.

"Well, pleased to meet you, Mr. Pocker," said Rahni. "Very pleased, indeed."

"Just Pocker. Hang on a sec." He hammered a few more times, and a chunk of old bark fell away. With a little prodding, Pocker's barbed tongue soon pulled a large beetle larva from the wood. He gobbled it down.

"So, tell me, Mr. Pocker, where did you come from?"

"Hold on," said Pocker, through some bits of crushed larva. He swallowed one more time and shook his head approvingly. "You know, you hear about these continental insects, but you really...well, you just have to taste them for yourself to understand. Know what I mean?"

"I'm not sure," said Rahni. "I've had insects, but not often. Is there something special about them?"

There was something special about everything that was happening. Pocker had never given a thought to the concept of a noble act, or a legacy to leave behind. Until he was driven to start this trip. Now, he felt he had unfinished business, but if he fell over dead at that moment, he would do so as a bird daring enough to act outside the box and behave as none had before him. And that alone would have made it worth the effort.

"Maybe it's just that they're different," said Pocker. "Sure is a treat, though. Glad I got to enjoy it first-hand."

"I don't understand. Different from what? Where are you from?"

"Oh, sorry," said Pocker. "Didn't mean to be cryptic. I'm from Cuba."

Rahni began more of the nervous weight-shifting. "Cuba! Oh my gosh, oh my gosh!"

"Yep, safe to say I've flown farther than any ivory-bill for a long, long time." As he said that, his mind raced through his travels to that point; first, the grueling trip over the ocean to Florida, then bit by bit up the Gulf Coast. It had all been truly exhilarating, and although it was also exhausting to the point of expiration, he was both proud and happy he'd undertaken the journey.

"That's so exciting!" said Rahni. "I never go anywhere."

"Most of us didn't, either," said Pocker. "But you know, way back when, my forebears went down to Cuba from the mainland, and I thought it would be appropriate to maybe come back and see where we were."

"Oooh—a vacation! I've heard of those."

"Yeah, you could call it that. A vacation to end all vacations."

Rahni paused for a moment. "And you're spending it in Mississippi?"

"Hang on," said Pocker. He hopped a few inches along the vertical side of the stump, looked around, and hammered a few times. "You have to understand—oh, wait." More hammering, with bark and wood bits spewing away. Then, out came another larva. Down the hatch. "Your insects would be worth it, but I also have ulterior motives."

"What are those?"

"Well, Rahni," he said, "it's like this. We aren't extinct...yet. But when I die, well—"

"Oh, no!"

"Oh, yes. It's been a hell of a run, but I'm it. I'm all that's left. I'm the very last ivory-billed woodpecker. And there's something I want to do."

∞

Janice Mowby sat in the padded vinyl chair in room 419 of Arkansas Children's hospital, an eBook device and an open bag of chip snacks on her lap, but staring absentmindedly at her son, Brett. He wasn't on a respirator yet, but plenty of other hardware clung to him, life-giving fluids or nerve signals or what-have-you going back and forth between his young body the beeping machines. Brett was eleven and small for his size, having spent way too much of his abbreviated life fighting for every moment and guessing when the end would come. *Unfair* was a word that had long since left their vocabulary for describing his situation.

She caught herself drifting in aimless thought and made her eyes look away, but without sharp movement of her head, so as not to startle Brett, who was calm at the moment and doing what he perpetually did: flipping through a book about birds. The room was appointed as most hospital rooms were. There was Brett's bed, the plethora of monitors on either side of it, a narrow nurse's desk with a computer, and the chair Janice was sitting in. Not much else. Lighting was dim and came mostly from what was directly above Brett; the walls could have been white or grey or beige, and no one would know the difference.

Her eyes having refreshed with other images for a few seconds, Janice moved them back to the only thing that mattered. Her son.

It was beyond grasping. Any day now, it would be over. They'd cried and talked so many times already about everything, but she knew full well the pain for her had only scratched the surface. She wondered if it would be worth it. She knew the answer as quickly as the question came up: it was unequivocally better to have loved and lost than to have never had Brett in her life to begin with. Silly as such questions were, though, they still popped up in her head. Couldn't stop that. Couldn't stop all the strange places your mind went when you are losing someone essential to your being.

That part of it seemed pointedly true. Brett had defined who she was. She was utterly immersed in parenting him and had been since well before he was born. Pregnancy launched her into an unrelenting mindset of all things motherly. Nurturing instincts took over in a big way, but so did conscious activities like research. She read libraries of data, opinions, papers, studies, anecdotes, social media posts, anything she could latch her eyeballs onto about being responsible for a new life.

Janice was completely that. The father had drifted after news of the impending birth. And Janice was really fine with it. It left her alone to do this how she wanted.

She hadn't felt much fear about it. She read a lot from new parents who were scared. Scared of what they didn't know, scared of mistakes, scared of those thousands of unpredictable moments, and how they would handle them. Janice never had that, and she was thankful for it. She always had a kind of peace from trusting that if she spent every waking moment figuring out how to be a good parent, it would work out. It would have to. There was no more to give than everything, so, by definition, it would have to turn out the best it could.

One of the places her mind went, then, was forward. Who would she be a few days from now? There's no word like *widow* or *orphan* to describe a parent who has lost a child. Perhaps because giving it a word makes it real, and this shouldn't be real. This time, at this moment, thinking of these things did not bring tears. Janice never knew when it would or wouldn't. She did know there were oceans of them to come.

The door to the room swung open, and two nurses entered. Janice only recognized one of them, Maggie, the overnight nurse from the past two nights. Maggie was fiftyish and tall, with greying red hair and a lot of homespun charm. She'd been around this block way too many times. Seeing the second one, slightly shorter and a lot younger, reminded Janice that it was around seven o'clock and time for shift change.

"Mornin'," said Maggie.

"Good morning," said Brett and Janice in unison. Brett closed his book.

"How are we today?" said Maggie.

"Fine," said Brett. He wasn't overly perky, but his relative pleasantness belied his condition, as it always did. Despite the many conversations about what was going on, Janice always thought that Brett somehow didn't get it. He couldn't be this resilient if he understood the situation. And they didn't talk directly about Brett's death—ever—but he wasn't stupid, and it was clear he could feel what his body was doing.

Maggie addressed Brett as she spoke but looked at Janice a lot in that common way that meant it was as much for her benefit. She stayed near the foot of his bed. "Brett, this is Leticia. She's your new nurse for today."

With very short, brown hair and a lovely smile, Leticia seemed energetic and personable as she moved around Maggie to stand near Brett's shoulder at the side of his bed. "Hi, Brett."

"Hello," said Brett. "Will we see Nancy today?" Nancy was the day nurse for weekdays. Brett liked Nancy.

"Not today," said Leticia. "It's Saturday, and I will be here with you today. And I will take very good care of you."

"All right," said Brett. He seemed open-minded about finding out if he'd like Leticia as much as Nancy.

"OK, Brett," said Maggie, "time to get a few things done here. You know the drill."

Leticia moved away from the bed, signaling to Janice to follow her out into the hallway. Janice stood and stretched a little. "Be right back, sweetheart," she said to Brett.

"Sure, Mom," he said.

Janice went with Leticia to the hallway, wondering if there was news about Brett's situation, but it turned out she just wanted to have an introductory conversation to hear straight from Janice how they came to be there.

"Is it true you were birdwatching?" said Leticia.

"Not me," said Janice. "Brett. He's completely consumed with birds. It's all he ever reads or does. He was the one birdwatching, and I was Brett-watching."

"But I see you're from Spokane," said Leticia.

"Yes. Yes, we are. It's a thing. We've been thinking about doing this for a while. It's called a big year. Birdwatchers do it sometimes, trying to count how many different birds they can see and identify in a year. They travel all over to do it."

"Even in Brett's condition?"

"Well," said Janice, "for us, it was especially because of his condition. It was now or never, and we were determined not to just let him sit and waste away. We decided to go for it."

"And then he took a turn here in Arkansas?"

Janice looked at the floor for a moment, pausing in thought. "Yes," she said. Then she took a deep breath, let it out, and looked at Leticia again. "But to be really honest, he probably shouldn't have even made it this far. Being on this trip and going out to find birds has invigorated him a lot."

"That's wonderful," said Leticia, then she cocked her head just a little. "If it's okay to ask, how many did he find?"

"Two hundred forty-nine," said Janice proudly. "That's nothing for serious birders, but trust me, for a terminally ill eleven-year-old who insists on getting his own pictures of every bird, it's pretty impressive."

"Oh, I believe you," said Leticia. "I haven't seen that many different birds in my whole life."

"And when we got to December and I started thinking we'd make it..."

It was one of those moments when the emotions instantly well up and paralyze you out of nowhere. Janice couldn't finish but was comforted by the warm look of compassion in Leticia's eyes.

Janice sniffled, then found her voice. "And I'll tell you," she said, "the look—." She had to stop again and gather herself to continue. "The look in his eyes when he sees one and figures out what some of these birds are." Another pause. "It's been worth so much more than every minute or every penny we've spent doing this."

Leticia lifted her hand and placed it on Janice's arm. "It sounds to me like you both had a very big year."

∞

Pocker swallowed down his third beetle larva. "Just outstanding," he said.

"What is it you want to do?" said Rahni.

"Well, Rahni, I came to see a Mississippi sandhill crane because I figured a couple of things."

"What's that?"

"First, you were all in one place. You weren't gonna travel on me."

"And second?"

Satisfied that three larvae would be plenty for a few hours, Pocker fluttered his wings and rose back up to the top of the stump. "Second, there's a watcher I've heard about who would also know you're all in one place and might have come through here."

"Oh, boy," said Rahni, "there sure are a lot of watchers that come through the refuge. How would I know the one you're talking about?"

"He's a kid. A sick kid."

"Oooh—I do know him!" said Rahni. The nervous tick of shifting weight back and forth on each leg was in full display. So much so that Rahni was even picking each foot up off the ground. "He was just here!"

"What do you mean, 'just' here?"

"Not like yesterday or anything," said Rahni, "but maybe ten days ago. Doesn't matter; we heard where he is now."

"Oh, yeah?" said Pocker. Jackpot. The strategy of visiting a crane on a wildlife refuge for information was working better than he ever imagined. He was a little concerned when he realized the gulls had been keeping Rahni out of the loop for some reason—a trivial social dynamic, no doubt—but apparently, she had other outlets for gossip.

"He's up in Arkansas," said Rahni.

"Arkansas?" said Pocker.

"Yup. Little Rock."

Bad news. That was still hundreds of miles away. Pocker was really hoping he was closer to the end of his flying journey, because for sure he was close to the end of his other one.

Rahni continued. "And if you want to see him, you'd better hurry. He's real sick."

Even worse news. Not only did he have a ton of flying to do, but he also had to push it. Pocker let out a sigh.

"Tell me, Mr. Pocker," said Rahni. "Why the boy?"

"Well, Rahni," he said, "it's like this. When I realized I was the last one, the very last ivory-billed woodpecker that would ever grab a branch on this planet, it just filled me with a sense of … I don't know, responsibility maybe. To do something bigger than just making holes in wood. Something that would mean something to somebody."

"Ah, I get it," said Rahni. "You want to make the kid's big year."

"Bingo."

"Well, Mr. Pocker, I have to say I admire that. That is a lofty goal."

"Thank you."

"But you had better get your feathers flapping. Word is they stopped traveling because he got worse and has to be in the hospital in Little Rock. You don't have long."

"All right, then," said Pocker. "No time to waste. Thanks very much, Rahni; you've been a tremendous help. Nice to meet you."

"Well, pleased to have made your acquaintance, Mr. Pocker," said Rahni. "Very pleased, indeed."

With that, Pocker flitted his head around a bit, checking on the sun and wind and directions, took a deep breath, and launched himself into the air, headed northwest.

∞

Brett closed his book and placed it on the table at his bedside. "Mom?"

"Yes, sweetheart," said Janice.

"I don't feel very good."

Janice began rising from her chair. "Let me call the nurse."

"No, Mom. I just want a wheelchair session. Leticia said I could."

"Yes, she did," said Janice as she moved to the door, "but we need her to get you set up."

"Okay."

Janice opened the door and asked Leticia to come inside. Leticia asked some questions and checked some monitors, but then, as promised, she unhooked some things, mounted others to the back of a wheelchair, and they got Brett mobile.

"Where to?" said Janice. She thought she knew, but wanted to let Brett tell her.

"The garden," said Brett.

"You got it."

That was exactly where Janice assumed he wanted to go. They were on the fourth floor, and part of the third floor was a rooftop garden. One of the fourth-floor hallways had one full wall of glass overlooking the greenery.

"I need my phone, though," said Brett. "You never know."

Brett had already taken several photos of birds in the garden, but they were all species he already had on his list. As ever, though, his hopes were high.

They reached the garden hallway, and Janice wheeled Brett slowly down the first third or so of it, then came to a stop. Neither of them spoke, choosing to just gaze out over the nature scene in silent reflection.

There were a few trees in the garden, including one just outside the windowpane where Brett sat. It was exactly two stories tall, such that the top branches were at Brett-level. Janice was startled by the sudden appearance of a large bird, seemingly plopping right out of the sky onto a branch, not fifteen feet from Brett. Brett was less startled than amazed.

"Mom!"

"What is it?"

"Mom! Do you know what that is?" His voice was practically trembling, and he fumbled a little with getting his phone up off his lap while keeping his eyes riveted on the bird.

Janice chuckled a bit at the obvious excitement as she replied, "No, son, I don't."

"That's an ivory-billed woodpecker!"

"A what?"

He was quickly pushing buttons on his phone. "Mom, that's an ivory-billed woodpecker!"

"Is that a new one for the list?"

"Yes, yes, yes!" said Brett. He held up the phone and took a picture.

Janice was deeply pleased and satisfied by this moment. "Oh, Brett, that's wonderful. Number two-fifty!"

"But that's not it. Mom, they're extinct!" He took another picture.

She chuckled again. "I don't think so."

"Well, not now, but Mom, nobody's seen one in forever. People say they do every now and then, but then they investigate, and they look at the evidence, and they decide it probably wasn't. Nobody's taken a picture like this of an ivory-billed woodpecker for the past eighty years!"

"Oh, my gosh, sweetheart. Are you serious? Are you sure?"

"Yes! Mom, this is huge!"

Janice was smiling a smile larger than she had mustered in a very, very long time. "Is he supposed to be standing like that?"

Brett was silent for a moment, taking note of the bird's posture, which was clearly anything but upright. He was moving his head a little, but leaning forward over his talons in a very odd way. Weak, almost. Then, he simply disappeared down off the branch and out of sight.

"Do you think he's hurt?" said Brett, leaning forward to try to see the bird below.

"Oh, I'm sure he's just moving on. You know how those extinct birds are," she said with another chuckle. Brett slumped even further forward. "Let's just stay here a little while and see if he comes back."

Brett kept looking toward the ground.

"Well, you got some good photos," said Janice. "If this is like you said, you are going to be big news, kiddo." He seemed suddenly less excited since the bird left the tree. She placed a consoling hand on his back.

"Brett?"

Ω

AT THE HEART OF IT ALL

Kari Kilgore

There are some people for whom almost any particular moment immediately conjures up quotes from television shows or movies or music lyrics.

These people can be a veritable human database of stored snippets of mini-clips that capture or reflect the moment so perfectly, so precisely.

I'll admit that I am guilty of that. For as long as I can remember, I have attended rather deeply to the lyrics of a song. Rarely does a conversation happen where a line or two from a song doesn't come to mind. And though I have learned to repress sharing those lyrics every time they come, a small trickle of those instances still make it to the surface.

Which is likely why people who know me associate me with earworms.

An earworm, sometimes referred to as Involuntary Musical Imagery (IMI), sticky music, stuck song syndrome, or a brainworm, is a catchy snippet of music that continues to repeat in a person's mind long after it is no longer actually playing.

Researchers have found, via controlled studies, that earworms are correlated to music exposure, but can easily be triggered, in the right individuals, by experiences that trigger the memory of a song, such as seeing a word that reminds them of the song, hearing a few notes from that song, or feeling an emotion that they associate with the song.

Like me, Kari has an earworm brain. She describes it as having a computer in her head that constantly serves up something relevant to what's going on around her. And, prior to crafting this tale, she says she had wanted to write a music-themed story for years.

Her first story in that realm, called "The Earworms" is about earworms attacking her hometown. It was one she had a lot of fun with, but she wanted the music itself to drive the story.

For "At the Heart of It All," she shares that the self-imposed rules she prescribed were that the song had to naturally come to her mind while writing.

"And," she says, "I had to either own a copy or think 'Oh, I need a copy of that!' The songs really did drive the story in that each one revealed a little more about the character's past. The songs told me the story and let me tell it in turn."

Kari started her first published novel Until Death, *which was included on the Preliminary Ballot for the Bram Stoker Award, in Transylvania, Romania. She finished it in Room 217 at the Stanley Hotel in Estes Park, Colorado, where a rather famous creepy tale about a hotel sparked to life.*

That's just one example of how real-world inspiration drives her fiction.

As you might already suspect, music is another frequent inspiration and constant companion for this writer. Several short stories and her novella In the Pines were inspired by specific songs, and she writes to a long and varied set of playlists depending on the characters or the mood and feel of the story.

Kari's fiction is regularly featured in 'Mystery, Crime, and Mayhem' magazine and holiday-themed anthology projects with Kristine Kathryn Rusch, and I have the honor of acquiring her first professional short fiction sale with "The Worry Trap" which appears in Fiction River: Superstitious.

When asked about her writing, she explains that she writes first and figures out genre later. That results in fantasy, science fiction, romance, contemporary fiction, and everything in between. She's happiest when she surprises herself, in writing and in life. She lives at the end of a long dirt road in the middle of the woods with her husband Jason A. Adams, various house critters, and wildlife they're better off not knowing more about.

For more information about Kari and her fiction, visit www.karikilgore.com.

In this story, the author introduces us to Sara, a woman for whom music plays a very important role, particularly when it comes to dealing with the tragic loss of her father.

Kilgore explains that her musically inclined brain helped her deal with the death of her own father as well as other difficult changes in her life. "The week before the funeral and on an overseas trip I'd planned and wisely decided to take a couple of weeks later, I had my earbuds in constantly." It was Nine Inch Nails in that particular case, she explains. "That music, and to this day all music in general, helps me calm down, get to sleep, deal with huge crowds of people, get through being sad and angry and even feeling better, and finally getting back to a routine of life."

But for now, let's pause and listen a moment, shall we?

Did you hear that?

Oh yes, if you're like me, or Kari, or Sara, this story's hero, that short snippet of conversation overheard in the next room, or on the bus, or in a crowded coffee shop is starting to stir up all of the right musical ghosts.

And sometimes the effect isn't as haunting as it can be comforting.

Even when, as that classic Kylie Minogue tune suggests, no matter how hard we try, we "Can't Get You Out of My Head."

Early evening was Sara's favorite time of day. Winter or summer. Home or work, or on vacation. No matter where she was or what she was doing, an elemental and vital part of her relaxed when the hour hand pointed straight down.

This six in the evening found Sara in her vast, nearly empty office building, almost at the end of her workday. The door to her small office open as usual, music playing through her computer's speakers as always. She could walk across the whole tiny room in five quick steps, but the pale wooden desktop had no need to accommodate anyone's coffee cups or elbows but her own.

Cream-colored walls held her own artwork, the shelves her own silly toys and mementos. No calendar, not this month, but one featuring classic electric and acoustic guitars would return in a few days.

The option to turn off the harsh overhead light in favor of a sweet lamp shaped like a tree branch – complete with a cardinal perched in the leaves – was one of the best parts of having her own space at work.

But not nearly as important as having the music.

The small cubicles and shared desks out on the main floor offered no such escape from glaring light overhead and cramped workspaces with barely enough room for a monitor and a mouse. A few other late-workers from the day shift in the huge medical records center lingered, huddled over transcriptions or translations. The low murmur of one-sided phone conversations so prevalent during the day had vanished, leaving only sporadic office chit-chat.

The night shift on the data entry side wouldn't arrive until eight or later, leaving Sara and a handful of others to enjoy the lull.

The one thing she did envy about the main floor that she didn't have in her office was a wall made of windows. Right now, the setting October sun transformed the bland walls and empty tan cubes into a red and orange and purple wonderland, glittering with islands of coffee mugs and monitors at just the right angle to return the light.

A scene Sara's father would have wanted to paint, to transform into one of the visions he saw in his head. *Visions in Blue* by Ultravox flitted through her mind, but only for a second. From 1983, the same year she was born.

Sara caught herself still staring into the strangely enchanted space when a low chime interrupted her computer playing Beck's *The New Pollution*. Her mind filled in the details as she turned back to her right-side monitor. From *Odelay*, his second proper album, released in 1997. She'd been waiting on that batch of new patient records to import so she could verify the integrity of the data, but that was no excuse to sit and let her mind wander.

She shook herself, clicked through the notifications of record mismatches, and focused on the left monitor while the import continued. Thousands of new records wouldn't be much good to anyone if Sara didn't finish designing the tables for them.

Beck giving way to Gordon Lightfoot made her smile at the little surprises of her own music playing on random. *If You Could Read My Mind*, album of the same name.

"Hey, Sara? Got a minute?"

She turned to see Jake, her supervisor for the last few months. Her belly flushed warm at his grin and his gorgeous eyes. Elton John's *Blue Eyes* fanned the flames in Sara's middle until she was afraid her chest and neck were turning red with the heat.

She hit pause on the Gordon Lightfoot, afraid that would only make her skin's overreaction even worse.

"Sure, Jake. What's up?"

He leaned against the open door, crossing his arms.

"I was trying to think of a song, but I can't remember enough of it for Google. My sister wants only music from the year I was born for my fortieth birthday." He rolled his eyes, but now he was blushing. Sara thought it was just about the sweetest thing she'd ever seen. "Smile while you can, Ms. Don't-t-Bother-Making-a-Fuss-about-Me-Turning-Thirty-five. Anyway, the song. A lot of saxophone and guitar, and something about a street, maybe?"

"*Baker Street*," Sara said with no hesitation. "That's Gerry Rafferty."

At Jake's raised eyebrows, she knew her cheeks were blazing. She should have pretended to think about it, at least. She usually knew better.

"Wow. You really do have a music computer in your head. That's amazing."

His smile seemed real, though, and he wasn't trying to back away.

"Yeah, it comes in handy from time to time."

"I hope you can make it to the party. Let Sis know if she makes a mistake?"

Men at Work sang out a warning in Sara's mind before she answered too quickly. *It's a Mistake*.

"I won't say a word if I notice, at least not to her. But I'd love to come."

He nodded, grinning again.

"About got that new batch of data sorted? Have to make sure the weekend crew has something to keep them busy."

Sara chewed her lip, determined not to quote Loverboy, of all things, to her boss, who she had a huge crush on. Even if *Working for the Weekend* seemed too perfect to ignore.

"Just cleared them to process through. They'll be ready before they get here at eight."

"Great, thank you. Night."

Sara waited until he was out of sight and hearing range before she closed her eyes and sighed. It was about time for her to pack up and head home herself, especially if she was going to act like a goofy schoolgirl. *Stupid Girl* by Garbage popped up in her mind to try to make her feel bad, shoving her too close the dangerous ground of the early 90s. She only shook her head.

She couldn't afford to react to such a weak opening attack, and certainly not so early in the day.

Worse would be along before this day turned into tomorrow.

Much worse.

Not wanting to risk even the quick walk out to her car without protection, Sara had her earbuds in and her mind on modern things before she closed her office door. Lady Gaga and *Poker Face* established the current century again and reminded her of a lofty goal to work for with Jake.

Just play it cool, is all. If she could manage to not act like a dork, they could keep building up a friendship. Sara hadn't had many friends over the years. So even if it never turned into more, it would be worth it.

She gave in to her mind's slightly dirty demands once she was in her sedan with the doors closed, queuing up Roxy Music's *More Than This* on her phone and through the speakers. Sara liked their 70s music better most of the time, but *For Your Pleasure* would likely set off Jake-centered daydreams too distracting for rush hour.

Sara's father had gotten her into all this music from before she was born. He'd pretty much installed the music computer in her mind that Jake and so many other people had been impressed by. Everywhere she'd ever worked the word somehow got around and people asked her about songs constantly, but Sara didn't mind. She liked the safe reminders of her dad.

She may have been born with the computer, really, but her father had at least installed the software and optimized it for music. The massive database she'd been filling as long as she could remember. Anything that changed after that hadn't been his fault.

She shook her head, muttering under her breath.

"Not now. Not while you're in this traffic."

She took advantage of a dead stop on the highway and called up Jimi Hendrix and *Crosstown Traffic* to distract herself.

Keeping the calendars out of her office helped some with this dreadful, painful month. Same with turning off the displays on her phone and her computers at work. Even if she'd followed her occasional impulse and spent all of October in some sort of technology and communication void, she'd know.

Part of Sara knew exactly what day it was. Every single year.

Smashing Pumpkins took over in her mind, insisting *Today* was what she needed to hear no matter what her phone was playing. No matter what she didn't want to be reminded of. Sara changed to the radio, deciding this was an ideal time for her regular expeditions into new music. Nothing like concentrating on learning new songs and lyrics to keep things under control.

That was one of the things that made her mother's suggestion of getting into computers, into IT, so appealing when Sarah was finishing up high school and at loose ends of what to do with her life. Always something more to learn. Safe ways to direct her concentration. Different tasks and technology to lose herself in.

New ways to try to direct and quiet her mind. Constant changes.

The clatter and jangle of commercials only opened new cracks in the layers of shields in her mind, so Sara switched away from the radio. Bowie's *Changes* replaced the noise, slipping her into a less frantic mental gear just as she accelerated out of the slow crawl of commuters and onto her exit.

She missed the days when she could volunteer for overtime to keep herself out of trouble. When she'd worked grunt level jobs with managers and co-workers who were always desperate to find someone to fill in, overnight if she was lucky. One problem with getting promoted was people depended on her for certain hours of the day. Her skills were too specific now to change her hours around so drastically.

And Jake would notice if she volunteered for a data entry shift. He'd be concerned about the workflow for her vital database administration work, sure. But he and Sara had gotten close enough that he'd ask questions she had no desire to answer.

She pushed the gearshift into Park in front of her cookie-cutter white house with black shutters, grabbing for her earbuds before music cut off. Keeping something playing at all times was her best defense today, the only way she'd found to minimize the pain. Silence gave that music database in her mind too much freedom to torment her at will.

George Michael's *Freedom 90* was uncomfortably close to the year Sara would spend the next several hours struggling to avoid. But it would work to keep her occupied on the walk from the curb to the sidewalk to the boring white front door.

The oddly shaped isolated cul-de-sac gave her privacy, but it kept her from the distraction of neighborhood greetings or gossip on a night like this.

When she could really use the small talk for a change. Her mind played along for a while, reminding her that the year was only in the song title because Wham! had a song with the same name only five years before.

A much happier time in Sara's life for certain, 1985. Not many memories lingered from her third year, but they were all good ones.

Watching her father practice his guitar and singing, learning song after song. Her mother home as much as she could be from her early law practice. Both of them delighted and laughing and applauding when Sara started mimicking her father, singing along as best she could.

Her own high-pitched voice and little girl lisp belting out *Take Me Home, Country Roads* burst out of her memories, drowning out the music in her ears as easily as she'd drowned out John Denver and her father on that night still so crystal-clear in her head.

She had to try three times to get the key into the lock with shaking hands, adding more scratches to an already scarred brass surface. She dashed inside and slammed the door, leaning against it and trying to catch her breath.

Not quite eight o'clock, and already it started. Sneaking through, slipping past, spilling over. Even with the earbuds, having its way with her before the night really got started.

Sara had a cold, hard certainty that even singing as loud as she could wouldn't help her this year.

Most of the time it did. She'd bought this relatively isolated house so she could do just that. Turn the music up as loud as it would go and sing herself hoarse, often until the sun rose on the morning of October 25th, and she had a whole year to recover.

That's what she'd expected to do tonight since tomorrow was Saturday. Get through the dreadful anniversary and move on. But if pumping songs almost directly into her brain with earbuds wasn't going to help tonight, neither would a sonic assault from speakers and a stereo that cost more than her car.

She tried anyway, connecting her phone and holding her breath until Chicago and *Saturday in the Park* filled her living room. She'd never heard her father playing this one, only singing along if it played on the radio. Not enough guitar to catch his true interest.

Of course, anything past 1991 should be fine. Safer. Less likely to trigger the cruel side of her mind, lingering underground all year long but fighting its way through to the surface to control her every October.

In her mind, Elvis broke through Chicago in her ears, offering up *Don't Be Cruel*. Sara laughed, but it was a desperate, choking sound.

1956. The same year her father was born.

She covered her eyes, not bothering to cover her ears. She'd never worked out how to cover the ones inside, so why worry about that?

"Look around," she whispered. "Find something here to focus on. At least for a little while."

Dire Straits whispered through her mind in return, echoing *Why Worry*.

Sara dropped her hands, taking in her neat and orderly and sadly bland living room. She'd barely focused on anything besides the stereo since she moved in five years ago. Shiny wooden floor, robin's egg blue walls, navy blue curtains. Unremarkable brown fabric sofa and loveseat and chairs. Cheap coffee table and end tables.

Then the only thing that truly mattered to her in the whole house. The wall of shelves that held that expensive stereo and everything that fed both it and the monster in Sara's mind.

A blinking light on one of the end tables drew her eyes back and sent her heart surging into her throat. Maybe someone had called from work, maybe *Jake* had called. Offering long, drawn-out apologies followed by a blessed request for her to come back in after all.

An emergency.

An escape.

A chance to recover before she sank too far down into the pit inside her head.

Sara staggered toward the house phone, stabbing her finger at the playback button before Nine Inch Nails and *Down In It* could get too comfortable in her skull.

"Hey hon, it's Mom. I know you like to keep to yourself today, but I'm worried about you. You're the same age he was now. That year. When…when he…" A soft sigh. "Just give me a call if you need to, no matter what time. Love you."

Sara took in a deep breath and held it.

That was it.

That was why.

She'd refused to celebrate her thirty-fifth birthday back in July without really thinking about it. Just another year passing, right? Why get excited about that one? It wasn't even a big deal, not like thirty or forty or fifty. She understood Jake letting his sister make a big deal about his fortieth, but she'd resisted even an office cake for herself this year.

Because her father had been thirty-five. He had *turned* thirty-five. The night he killed himself.

She let out her breath and gulped in another one, stopping the music streaming from her phone as she sank onto the loveseat. Maybe her internal jukebox wouldn't be quite so vicious if she stopped resisting. Another slow, deep breath brought The Police with it, and *Every Breath You Take*.

The three of them had gone out to dinner for his birthday that night, and her father seemed fine. Cheerful and happy, more so than he'd been for a long time. Even at eight years old, Sara had noticed the difference.

He'd been so sad and down. Barely speaking, never smiling.

And her mother so anxious and worried about him hadn't exactly eased Sara's mind.

That night Sara had gone to bed relaxed and fallen right asleep.

Everything was going to be okay. All of them were going to be safe now.

Until her mother woke her with a scream that still echoed in Sara's ears when she didn't force it away or drown it out with music.

That question echoed, too. The one she still asked sometimes when she drifted off to sleep, even the soft songs she played all night long, not quite keeping it at bay.

Why?

What had happened?

What had they done?

What had *she* done?

The Eagles drifted through her thoughts, singing the same thing Sara's mother told her over and over again. That night and the next, and the next week, and the next month and year.

I Can't Tell You Why.

Her mother said she didn't *know* why, over and over again. He hadn't told her anything or left a note. No clue, no hint what really happened. What drove him to leave them behind in such a horrible way.

Back then, when Sara was eight and ten and thirteen, and she never stopped asking, she decided her mother was just keeping it from her. Trying to protect her from some mysterious adult thing she wasn't old enough to understand yet. So, she waited.

She only asked once a year. On October 24th. And she got the same answer.

She stopped asking when she turned eighteen, not bringing it up again until she turned twenty-one. And twenty-five. And thirty.

That was another thing she'd refused to do this year, on her birthday or since. She hadn't even asked the question. Not to her mother, not to herself.

She wasn't sure if she'd given up or simply accepted. All she knew now was that she didn't want to ask anymore.

One more deep breath, in and out, a breath that finally relaxed her exhausted body and reeling mind.

Sara started her music streaming again, waiting for The Moody Blues to bring their own *Question* into her living room. Her father had learned this one to exact guitar and singing perfection, with the same passionate study he'd brought to every song he learned.

The same passion Sara continued to this day with her own never-ending pursuit and intake of music.

She played her mother's message again, letting her tears fall at how hard the voice on the recording was trying not to cry.

It had been her mother who taught her. Told her what to do. On one of the endless, agonizing nights when the two of them tried and failed to make sense out of the whole thing.

One too young to understand. The other too lost in her own shock and grief to pretend she understood. Too honest in her bones to make something up to comfort her sobbing daughter.

"Listen to music with him," she said, holding Sara close and rocking her to sleep. "On the stereo when you're here. In your mind when you're not. In your heart. That's where he lives now, for both of us. That's where it all lived for him, too. All that music. In his heart."

Sara wiped her tears, safe and calm within her mind for the first time since she'd left work. Maybe for the first time in years, since everything fell apart.

Maybe she could finally stop falling apart inside herself.

She tapped out a text message to her mother before bringing up one more song.

Tough night, but I'm okay. Give me a call if you want to talk. I finally found the perfect spot for one of Dad's guitars, too. Bring one over and spend the night if you're up for it.

We'll both feel better tomorrow. Love you.

Sara kicked off her shoes and curled up on the loveseat, smiling and closing her eyes as one of her father's most practiced and beloved Rush songs wrapped her up in a great, warm hug.

The closest she'd felt to her father–and to herself–since twenty-seven years ago on this same night.

Closer to the Heart.

Ω

NOT SICK ENOUGH IN THE HEAD

Robert Jeschonek

What is it about a person that makes a society declare them to be mentally unwell?

Who defines the norms?

Is it the masses who, ultimately, make that decision?

What about mass hysteria, then?

If everyone is hysterical, does that make the people who are calm the odd ones, the ones who need to be treated to fit in with the norm?

That's the type of dilemma Robert Jeschonek explores in this story.

Robert is an envelope-pushing, USA Today bestselling author whose fiction, comics, and non-fiction have been published around the world. His stories have appeared in Galaxy's Edge, Fiction River, Pulphouse, *and many other publications. His young adult novel,* My Favorite Band Does Not Exist, *won the* Forward National Literature Award *and was named one of Booklist's Top Ten First Novels for*

Youth. He also won an International Book Award, a Scribe Award for Best Original Novel, and the grand prize in Pocket Books' Strange New Worlds *contest. Visit him online at www.bobscribe.com. You can also find him on Facebook and follow him as @TheFictioneer on Twitter.*

But right now, you'll find Robert introducing you to a most peculiar situation, and peculiar situations are a recurring theme in Bob's fiction that I have come to appreciate about his stories; and which I have had the privilege of presenting to readers in the Fiction River *anthologies* Feel the Love *and* Feel the Fear.

When I asked him about the inspiration for the story, he responded with a question.

"Can there ever be too much obsession?"

Not according to the world of advertising, he goes on to explain. The barrage of messages encouraging us to always want more and to go out and get it.

"Consumer culture is," he continues, "well, obsessed with this theme, even as we're also advised that addictive behavior is a bad thing."

The result is a society with a split personality, perpetually in conflict with itself. It's an unhealthy paradigm and the key inspiration for "Not Sick Enough in the Head."

How far are we from a world in which the line between obsession and addiction is erased? A world in which extreme obsessiveness is considered necessary not only to economic growth but mental fitness as well?

"I think," Robert says in reply to these questions he poses, "we might be closer than we know to Irene's future of unbridled consumerism boosted by mental health professionals co-opted by corporate interests."

Ten pairs of eyes stare hard at me through the musty church basement air, exerting pressure that is almost a physical force. Heart pounding, I glance around at them, then turn my gaze to the glossy gray cement floor in the middle of the circle of folding chairs.

"No, I'm sorry," I say at last, answering the question that was asked a moment ago. "I didn't blow my paycheck on *shoes* this week."

Everyone in the room except Doctor Ava Brandt slumps and sighs in disappointment. They all sympathize, not that it makes me feel any better.

"Tell us about that, Irene." Dr. Brandt, sitting directly across the circle from me, brushes her long, blonde hair behind her ears. She's in her twenties, at least ten years younger than I am, but still seems so much smarter and more mature. "Tell us about your week."

I want to get up and leave, but therapy's mandatory these days for *everybody*. Walk away now, and I'll be sitting in another group session tomorrow, in *prison*. Welcome to the 22nd century.

Who knew universal mental healthcare could suck so bad?

"Not much to tell." I adjust my biowire-framed glasses and wish the spotlight would move elsewhere. Why doesn't anyone interrupt and go off on a long-winded tangent when you *need* them to? "The E.R. was crazy. There was a bus crash."

"What about the *shoes?*" asks Brandt. "You said last week you were going *shopping.*"

"I did." I can't help sounding apologetic. "But then I...I just didn't..."

"Didn't what?" Brandt's eyes narrow, and she leans forward.

I scrub my fingers restlessly through my black half-shag/half-crewcut. Instinctively, I find the lump above my left temple, the one that's been there for the past few months. It's important, though it's also a secret, at least for now. "I didn't *want* them! I didn't *need* them!"

A few people shake their heads, which makes me angry. Like they're so much *better* than I am, just because they're making more *progress?*

The fingers of Brandt's hands twitch as she makes a note on the midair augmented reality (AR) screen that only she can see through her ocular implants. "But you said you *love* shoes. You *picked* them as your new *vice of choice.*"

"Then, maybe I picked wrong." I check the clock on the wall behind Brandt and my stomach clenches. We still have fifteen minutes to go in this session.

"Don't feel bad, Irene. Ups and downs are part of the process." Clara, a fellow patient in her early 20s with short brown hair in a pageboy bob, smiles supportively from her seat beside Brandt. "I *still* have days when I hardly gamble *at all.*"

A few chairs from Clara, old Roy Jackson chuckles. "You ain't gonna *believe* this, but there was a day last week when I didn't *think* about *porn* for almost *five solid minutes.*"

"There's no shame in backsliding," says Paula Ott, a heavyset woman in her 40s at the opposite pole of the circle from Roy. "What matters is where you go from here."

As well-intentioned as they seem to be, I don't want to hear it. Today's session is like last week's all over again...and the one before that, and the one before that. I'm still the biggest underperformer in the group.

"Are you hearing what they're saying?" asks Brandt.

"I guess so." I've been sitting on my right leg, and it's fallen asleep. I curl it out from under me and try to rub some life back into it. "But I'm just not *feeling* it like the rest of you."

"Tell us more," says Brandt. "When you say you're not *feeling* it..."

"I guess it makes me a freak, but..." A tear burns in my eye, and I dab it away. "I don't feel the *longing* like I should. The all-consuming *desire.*"

Brandt frowns. "I wonder if I should've encouraged you to try a different vice."

"It doesn't *matter,*" I tell her. "I'm just not *wired* that way. God knows, I wish I *was.* Of all *people,* I *should* be. But I'm *not.*" Tears flow freely, and I let them come. "I can't be the good citizen I'm *supposed* to be."

Thoughtfully, Brandt watches and taps her lower lip with the tip of an index finger. For a long moment, she and everyone else remain silent.

Then she nods firmly as if she's come to a conclusion. "I think I see where this is going." Her fingers twitch over the AR screen. "I know what we need to do."

I stare at her through the tears. Has she *understood* a single word I've said?

"Time to change things up." Brandt continues to work the screen. "Forget the shoes."

"You mean *another* vice?" I ask. "But I've already tried wine, marijuana, nostalgia, romance novels…"

"Stop." Brandt waves me off. "It's out of my hands now. Your new personal therapist will make that call."

I frown. "But I don't *have* a personal—"

She cuts me right off. "You do now, and she makes *house calls*. In fact…" Her fingers twitch some more, and her eyes flick over her AR screen, reading whatever text is visible to her. "…she will arrive at your apartment in two days at 7:45 a.m." Brandt smiles.

The group goes dead quiet. Eyes widen and fix on me as the implications settle in.

I'm not cutting it, and the doc is upping the ante.

"Perhaps you've heard of her." Brandt winks for my benefit. "Dr. Evelyn Godfrey of the Impetus Foundation?"

My heart races, but I don't say a word.

Of course I've heard of her, and we all damn well know it.

"What about our shopping trip that day, Irene?" Clara, God love her, takes a shot at helping me out. "We're supposed to leave for the mall at 8 a.m., right?"

"You'll have to reschedule." Brandt rises from her chair, wiping away the AR screen with a wave of her hand. "On the bright side, you'll really be able to *max out* that shopping spree after your new doc gets done with you."

"We're so happy for you, Irene!" Paula clasps her hands and smiles warmly. "Next thing you know, you'll be a *stalker* and a *substance abuser* like the *rest* of us. Maybe *better* than us, even."

"Let her know how we all feel about her, group." Everyone claps as Dr. Brandt crosses the circle and puts her hands on my shoulders. "*Rehab's* going to work out for you *after all.*" Smiling, she folds her arms around me as the applause rises around us, filling the room in a charged, dramatic moment.

But all I can feel in my heart and gut and mind is my *secret*, twisting like an animal in the dark, baring its teeth. Because the truth is, I'm a success story and a good citizen, after all.

I've got my own hidden obsession, and Dr. Brandt would shit herself if she knew what it was.

∞

Riding home that evening aboard a self-driving bus, I gaze out at the dilapidated city under a gray and drizzling sky. It's like watching civilization collapse in slow motion—buildings slumping, streets pitting and cracking, streetlights flickering or dark, garbage blooming. Chicago's circling the drain, just like every other city, town, and village in the U.S. of A.

All because of a lack of focus and innovation, the psychocrats tell us. All because, when we drugged and shocked and bred the obsessive, addictive tendencies out of our species over the past century, tamping down the volatility of humanity, we inadvertently got rid of what made us great. What helped us not only *survive* but *thrive*.

It turns out the biggest breakthroughs, greatest inventions, and boldest gambles come from people who are driven. Not so much from people in a flattened-out stupor.

Which brings us to the Want-Want project, designed to make humanity crave again. Five years after it launched, people are more of a hot mess than ever, tangled in conflicting impulses—but the boss-lady who dreamed up Want-Want keeps telling us all to hang in there. American ambition is making a comeback in a big way.

Or is it? From way down here in the weeds, it looks worse than before.

I'd love to ask her about it, the know-it-all bitch. And maybe I *will*.

After all, she's coming to see me. All hail my new personal therapist, Dr. Evelyn Godfrey, founder of Want-Want.

And founder of me, as well.

∞

Two days later, when I answer the door at Dr. Godfrey's knock, she stares back at me with clinical dispassion as if I'm some new species of giant insect. I haven't seen her in person in close to a decade, but she doesn't look the slightest bit energized about it.

"Hello, Mother." I step aside, opening the door wider to admit the only family I have left in the world.

She just stands there at the threshold in her smart black pantsuit, shriveled and tiny as a gherkin, her face pinched and waxen. "Would you like me to come in?"

Like is a strong word. "Please, come in." My gesture is formal, as if we're strangers, which is fitting. The two of us have *never* been close.

With the slightest nod of her dark-haired head with the bun bound tightly at the back, she walks stiffly into the apartment. As many times as I've seen her in streaming videos over the years, she looks much older in person. Time has *not* been kind.

"Thanks for stopping by," I tell her. "I cleaned up the place and everything."

Evelyn clears her throat and doesn't look around. "Tell me." So much for niceties. "When did you last feel obsessively about something?"

Leave it to Mom to cut to the chase. "Does it really matter?" I push the door shut. "In the grand scheme of Want-Want, nobody *cares* about little old *me*, do they?"

"The restoration of true mental health is vital to *everyone*." Evelyn sounds like she's quoting a speech. "We must leave no mind untroubled."

It's *my* turn to stare like she's some kind of giant bug. "Gee, thanks for the pep talk, Mom."

Evelyn blinks slowly and purses her lips, looking annoyed. I wonder if she'll just walk out on me at some point; it's what she does best, after all.

"Has it occurred to you," she says, "that you're actively resisting treatment in the hope of hurting *me?*"

"Not *everything* is about *you*, Mother."

"What better way of lashing out at someone you perceive as having caused you pain?" Evelyn gazes up at me, watching for a reaction. "It's a theory, wouldn't you say?"

"I knew it." I lean down so our faces are close. "That *is* the only reason you're here, isn't it? Because I'm making you *look* bad. The daughter of the founder of Want-Want doesn't *want* anything."

It's true, we both know it, but she'll never admit it. It's no coincidence she showed up here today for the first time in a decade.

Any more than it's an accident I got her to *come* here. Pretending to be incurably non-obsessive through all those group therapy sessions took patience, but I always believed the docs would eventually call in my mother, given her prominence in the field. I always believed, with her reputation at stake, that she would leap at the chance to accept the invitation.

"I assure you," she says coldly. "It will take far more than an obstinate, estranged offspring to darken *my* good name." This time, *she's* the one leaning closer to *me*. "Not that I have *any* concern other than *curing* a poor unfortunate who doesn't seem to have an obsessive bone in her *body*."

We stand there for a moment like that, gazes locked, neither of us willing to step away first. Then, finally, we both lean back at once.

"Can I get you anything?" I bob my head toward the kitchen. "Coffee? Tea?" I don't remember what she prefers.

"Get your coat," says Evelyn. "I think some fresh air will do us both good."

Shit. I've planned this out to the letter, made arrangements to escort her to a certain place at a certain time—but not yet. She's already at the door, though, so I need to juggle my timetable.

"Sure, okay." When I go to the closet for my coat, I crank out a quick text message to the person I've arranged for her to meet. He fires back an answer, perfectly fine with meeting earlier, but not *too* early.

That works for me. Letting Mom think she's taking charge ought to help her drop her defenses for later.

"Excellent." Evelyn pulls on her black leather gloves. "I'm a firm believer in the power of a good constitutional."

"No kidding." I smile as I pull on my red wool coat and striped scarf. "I guess we have something in common, after all. Other than DNA, that is."

∞

Evelyn has a self-driving limo waiting outside, and the car takes us straight to the shopping mall on Michigan

Avenue. We end up going for a walk, all right—an indoor stroll past one high-end store after another.

Didn't she read my chart? Does she really think shopping therapy will work for me now after failing so many times in the past?

"I think those would look nice on you." She stops at a store window and points out a pair of glittery pink stilettos with sequined hearts on the toes. "Why not try them on?"

"No, thanks. Those things cost a fortune."

"Is *money* holding you back?" Evelyn dips a gloved hand into her black pocketbook and fishes out a featureless black plastic card. "Take this."

"I don't want your card, Mom." I fold my arms over my chest and keep walking. "I don't need it."

"I've seen your apartment." She slips the card back in the bag. "It's no wonder you're afraid to impulse-buy."

"Hey, what do you think of this?" I stroll over to another display window and point out a navy-blue dress with white trim on a brown-haired holo-mannequin.

"You like it?" She sounds hopeful and digs out the card again.

"Uh-huh." I nod slowly, stroking my chin. "Let's go see how it looks on you."

This time, it's Evelyn's turn to walk away. "You used to *like* shopping when you were a child."

There are *so* many things I could say to that, but I don't. Better, now that I'm so close to what I want, to keep my eyes firmly on the prize.

Just then, Evelyn stops in her tracks. "Irene, look." Her voice is hushed. "Look at *that.*"

Up ahead, looking at something in the window of a jewelry store, is the handsomest man I've seen in forever.

"Wow," says Evelyn. "Those *muscles.*"

She's right. His tight black t-shirt accentuates the perfect bulges of his arms, chest, and shoulders. His midsection is lean, his six-pack clearly defined to the waist of his jeans.

"He's got such a strong jawline, doesn't he?" Evelyn tips her head to one side. "And can't you just imagine running your fingers through that dark hair?"

I can, actually, but that's none of her business. "Give it up, Mom."

"Why don't you go talk to him?" She gives my sleeve an encouraging tug. "What can it hurt?"

"I'm not going over there."

"But you're a grown woman. Nobody's going to *judge* you."

I shake my head, disgusted. With any normal mother, this would be typical pushy meddling, trying to set me up for a love match. With Evelyn, who has zero maternal feelings, this is just about curing me, saving her reputation, and improving the success rate of Want-Want.

Enough.

Just as she sticks two fingers in her mouth to whistle at him, I grab her shoulder.

"Do you want to know what I'm obsessed with?" I ask. "*Really* obsessed with?"

Evelyn frowns. "Not him?"

"*None* of this. None of what you *think* or *want* to think."

"But there *is* something? Or someone? An obsession?"

"I promise." It isn't a lie.

"So, tell me."

"I'll do better than that." Turning, I head for the exit. "Let's go."

∞

She hesitates when I insist we take a bus instead of the limo, but she gives in. Whatever worries she might have are outweighed by the possibility that a daughter-sized headache might finally be about to go away.

She clearly isn't comfortable on the crowded bus, though. Maybe that's why she keeps talking as we lumber across town to our destination.

"I can't help noticing," she says over the noise from the engine and passengers. "You never ask me what *my* craving is."

I shrug and rub the lump above my left temple, staring out the window at the slowly collapsing city. "It's not polite to pry."

"Yet it's a common deflection strategy used by patients. When treatment becomes uncomfortable, they attempt to turn the tables on the therapist."

"I'm not that insecure," I tell her. "I don't need to deflect."

I feel her eyes on me as I watch the scenery pass. Does she know the real reason I don't ask about her personal obsession? Does she suspect it's because I already know what it is?

And it sure as hell isn't me or my well-being, or my little brother Rafe, or the shit show she left in her wake when she got the fuck out.

If I were a gambler, I'd bet the whole Want-Want project on that.

∞

It's a busy day in the E.R. at Mediplex One, as most days are. When I give Evelyn the ten-cent tour, I have to be careful I don't get drafted into service.

"This is it," I tell her. "If there's one thing I'm obsessed with, it's my job."

We both jump back as a gurney crashes through bearing a patient, surrounded by nurses and a doctor barking out orders. One of the nurses catches my eye on the way past, and I think for an instant she's going to tell me to get to work.

Then she does, shouting for me to bring over the crash cart *stat*.

I do just that, leaving Evelyn alone against the wall. Of course, things get complicated, and it's more than a few minutes before I manage to get back to her.

"So this is your day off?" asks Evelyn.

"Yes." I'm a little out of breath.

"Yet here you are."

I nod. "Here I am."

"Classic workaholic." Evelyn grins. "Pretty tame as obsessions go, but it's still on the spectrum."

"You're telling me I'm sick in the head like everyone else?"

"Let's just say there's hope for you yet." Evelyn looks relieved. Her face isn't nearly as pinched as it's been since she turned up at my door this morning.

That means the time is perfect for what's coming next.

"Let's celebrate." Nodding and smiling, I start toward the exit, gesturing for her to follow. "This way."

"Celebrate? In a hospital?"

"C'mon!" I gesture again and keep walking, trying to *will* her to come with me. Everything I've wanted, my longtime true secret obsession, depends on her joining me now.

As I slip through the door into the hallway, I'm almost afraid to look back. She abandoned me before; what if she does it again?

But this time, she stays with me. Apparently, curiosity has gotten the better of suspicion, at least for now.

Heart pounding, I lead her down the hall toward our next destination, trying not to look too excited though I've got every reason to be.

∞

Like most hospitals, Mediplex One is a maze. Does Evelyn keep track of every turn in our route as I lead her down to the basement and through its corridors? I doubt it.

Our destination is a room at the far end of the complex, one that's hardly used anymore. There isn't even an identifying sign on the wall other than a placard bearing the room number.

"What is this place?" asks Evelyn as I open the door. "A morgue?"

I switch on the lights and hold the door open for her. "Mostly storage these days."

She hesitates, peering through the doorway. "It doesn't look like much of a celebration to me."

"It will be. This is where we sneak off when we need a break. We always keep some—*refreshments*—down here."

"Why, 'Reney." Evelyn beams proudly. "Are you an *alcoholic*, too?"

"What can I say?" I smile back at her. "I'm full of surprises, Mom."

She decides to enter the room, and I close the door behind us. As she looks around at the stacks of old boxes, I walk to a metal wall cabinet and pull a key out of my pocket.

"This used to be part of the old psych ward." I unlock the cabinet and pull out an object, concealing it against my forearm. "Back in the days when they thought they were *curing* everyone by taking away their motivation."

Evelyn walks over to a big cardboard box and fishes through the paperwork inside. "We didn't know any better back then," she says. "We didn't realize the damage we were doing."

"No, you didn't." I stride quickly up behind her and stick her in the arm with the object I pulled from the cabinet—a loaded hypodermic. "Or was it just that you didn't give a fuck?"

As I press the plunger, injecting her with amber fluid, she twists around, looking horrified. "What…what did you just…?"

I yank out the needle, grab the phone from my pocket, and send a prearranged signal via text to the person we're here to see. "Don't worry, that's good shit," I tell Evelyn. "Just relax and enjoy the ride."

She shakes her head slowly and slumps down onto some boxes. "Why would you…what are you…?"

Moments later, the door swings open. A middle-aged man with a big gut in blue scrubs sweeps into the room, looking excited.

"Is this her?" He paws at his curly salt-and-pepper hair. "Is this the patient?"

Evelyn is almost out but still manages to open her eyes for a look. "Who?" Her voice is faint.

"This is Doctor Joe," I tell her. "He's here to help you."

"Hey there." Joe gives her a wave. "It's a real honor to work on the founder of Want-Want."

"You'll like Doctor Joe," I say. "He's got an *awesome* obsession."

"I really do," says Joe.

"He gets off on performing unauthorized surgeries," I explain. "Just like the one he's about to perform on *you*."

Evelyn's too loopy to react. Her head lolls on her chest, drool dripping from her wrinkled red lips.

"It's a minor procedure, really." Joe rolls in a gurney, and we lift Evelyn up onto it. "Just the subcutaneous insertion of an implant near the left temple of your cranium."

"That's right, Mom. Easy-peasy." Leaning over her, I point to the lump above my own left temple. "When you're done, we'll both have lumps in the same spot. For different reasons, though."

Evelyn burbles something from the depths of her stupor. Joe pulls out a white wand with a glowing yellow bead the size of a pea on the tip.

"What's the worst that could happen?" He chuckles as he lowers the bead toward her head. "Other than the three of us exploding, I mean."

∞

For a moment, as Evelyn's eyes flutter open, she is docile. Then, when she tries to move her limbs, full awareness crashes upon her like a breaking wave.

"Let me up!" She thrashes as much as she can with her wrists and ankles restrained on the gurney. "Let me *go!*"

I watch from my perch, a nearby stack of boxes, with grim amusement. "You're such a drama queen, Mom."

"Help! Somebody help me!"

"You might as well save your voice. This place has been a secret love nest for hospital staff for ages. Trust me, no one who matters hears the screams from down here."

"Oh, my God!" She thrashes some more. "Help! Please, help!"

"Yell all you like if it makes you feel better." I shake an index finger at her. "But the sooner you calm down, the sooner I'll undo your restraints."

"What *is* this? What did you *do* to me?" She scowls as memories trickle back to her. "That so-called *doctor.* He was going to *operate.*"

"Relax. It was a very minor procedure."

Her scowl deepens. "Something about a *subcutaneous implant?*" She sounds like she's teetering on the brink of towering rage or utter panic, which is music to my ears.

"It's nothing. Just a little bump. I mean *bomb.*"

Evelyn stops fighting her bonds. "Did you say *bomb?*"

"You heard correctly."

She falls silent as the bad news sinks in…but the silence doesn't last. "You're telling me I have a *bomb* in my head? Why?"

I hop off the boxes and show her the round black device in the palm of my left hand. A bright red button glows in the middle of its face.

"This remote controls your implant," I say matter-of-factly. "Now tell me about *your* obsession, or I'll blow you to kingdom come."

"My *obsession?*" She repeats the word as if it's in some foreign language. "*Chocolate*, you mean? Classic *hip hop*?"

I walk to the side of the gurney, holding up the remote with my left thumb hovering over the button. "The obsession that made you abandon our family," I say coldly. "The reason you ran away and left your own *son* to *die.*

"*That's* the obsession I'm talking about."

∞

I remember the last dinner Mom made us was spaghetti and meatballs out of a can. It's been a long time since I was ten, but I've hated spaghetti and meatballs ever since.

I remember how she packed her suitcase that night, telling us she was going to an out-of-town conference the next day. My brother Rafe, who was six at the time, was the only one who was upset...but he *always* got upset when she went away. He was *such* a mama's boy.

I remember how noisy the house was the next morning, instead of the usual quiet Mom demanded (for her work, always her work). It was like Dad had been replaced by an alien, one who broke things and cursed at random and shouted over the phone.

Rafe and I cowered in the corners, piecing things together like terrified detectives. We overheard there was a cryptic farewell note, and valuables were missing, and Mom's phone was shut off. Someone named "Bill" was involved, and Mom loved him, and Dad had his gun out of the safe.

We were shell-shocked. It was as if we'd been plunked down by a twister in the Land of Oz, where the rules were all different from the ones we'd always known. One wrong move, and the flying monkeys or wicked witch would scoop us up and take us away forever.

Little did we know, we were already gone for good.

∞

"I hurt you," Evelyn says calmly. "I'm sorry."

Her composure is back. She sounds like she's conducting a therapy session instead of strapped to a gurney with a bomb in her head.

Apology not accepted. "How could you just *leave* us like that? How could you be that *obsessed* with someone?"

"I can't explain it to you," she says. "You wouldn't understand."

"I'm not a *child* anymore."

"But you've never been head-over-heels in *love*, have you? Completely *obsessed* with another *person*."

Leaning down, I bark my next words in her face. "And *you* weren't obsessed with your own *family*."

Her steely blue eyes lock tight on my own. "Is that what's *really* wrong, 'Reney? You *want* so badly to fall in love, but you just can't *do* it?"

I stay where I am, inches from her face, seething. I want to slap her, hard as I can, but I hold myself back.

"I think the *better* question is, how could a woman become the *poster child* for *wanting* when she didn't even want her own *children*?"

Evelyn's composure slips. "Don't you *dare* try to tell me—"

"And how could a woman think she could save the *world* if she couldn't even save her own son's *life*?"

∞

I was the one who found him.

Rafe never got over Mom's leaving. He was just too damn young and attached to her. Dad raged, I withdrew, but Rafe…

Rafe blamed himself.

And one day, a month after Mom ran off, I heard a single loud blast from the garage. We were on our own, Dad wasn't home, and I knew I shouldn't go see what had made that loud noise.

But I went anyway. I called Rafe's name, and he didn't answer, and part of me *knew* or at least *feared* what I'd find. Dad had stopped locking his gun in the safe, after all.

And even as I opened the side door and looked in, I remembered one sunny afternoon that Rafe and I had spent in the yard, playing good guys and bad guys. He'd played dead so perfectly, I'd worried he might *be* dead until I tickled him and he jumped up running.

This time was just the same except he never jumped up and ran, and parts of him were blown away for real.

∞

"You didn't even go to his *funeral*." The words are a snarl from my lips.

"I wasn't *welcome*," says Evelyn. "Your father blamed me for Rafe's death as if I was the one who left the gun where he could find it."

"You *were* to blame!" Decades of anger boil out of me like lava from a volcano. "Didn't it ever *occur* to you that you might ruin your *kids* when you left?"

She lifts her head, then lets it fall back on the thin pillow on the gurney.

"And what about Dad? He was *never* the same after that. He died young, and you didn't come to *his* funeral, either. Didn't you *consider* what you were doing to *him?*"

"No," she says simply. "It never occurred to me."

"*Seriously?*" I want to shake some sense into her, shake the truth out of her, just *shake* her.

"All I could think about was *Bill.*" She releases a long sigh. "Our love was…all-consuming. Our obsession blotted out everything and everyone else."

"But there *was* no obsession anymore, was there? Humanity had *lost* it by then."

Evelyn looks away. "Not all of us." She meets my gaze again. "I was a throwback. So was he. People like us had a way of finding each other."

"Thank God for that," I say sarcastically.

"I like to think it was the spark of the whole Want-Want movement." Evelyn sounds wistful. "The inspiration for the project to reinvigorate humanity's obsessiveness."

"But you still couldn't want *us* that much, could you? It wasn't that you weren't passionate about *anyone.* You just saved all your passion for *someone else.*"

Evelyn winces, looking pathetic. "Stop this, 'Reney. You've made your point."

"Is that what you think this *is?* Me making a *point?*" I laugh out loud at her. "You think I'd go to all this *trouble* just for that?"

She frowns, confused. "Then why…?"

"Because I'm going to make something happen." I waggle the remote in my hand, thumb perilously close to the trigger button. "Something that should've happened *long* ago."

"What *kind* of something?" snaps Evelyn.

I lean down over her, smiling coldly. "I'm going to *fix* you whether you like it or not." I kiss her forehead softly and without the slightest trace of affection. "Meet your new therapist, Dr. Godfrey. Let's call your first session 'How Not to Blow Up.'"

∞

I'm back in my apartment, weeks later, when there's a knock at the door. It happens a lot these days, ever since that fateful encounter in the basement of Mediplex One.

"Hello, honey," Evelyn says sweetly when I open the door. "So good to see you again."

I smile and lean close for a peck on the cheek. Mom is positively *fanatical* about never missing one of our get-togethers.

Who would've thought that would ever be the case? Who would've thought my unapproachable mother would come bearing fresh lattes and scones on a Saturday afternoon? Who would've thought she'd sit at my kitchen table for hours and chat with me as if we'd been doing it all our lives?

It's funny what a subcutaneous bomb in someone's head can do for their disposition.

"How are you feeling today?" she asks, sounding concerned. "How was the latest round of chemo?"

I pat the lump on my left temple through the colorful scarf on my head and shrug. "It's going as well as can be expected."

"The side effects aren't too bad, I hope?" asks Mom.

"I've had worse."

Having family come around is especially nice when you've got the big C, and it's terminal. It's great taking your mind off *that* preoccupation—and make no mistake, it's an obsession with a capital "O." Dying from brain cancer is enough to drive you crazy for real.

Why else do you think I went to such extremes to force the bitch to act like she cares? To force her to be part of my life again after so many years?

When you're on the way out, even a mother who shit all over your life and triggered your little brother's suicide can be better than no mother at all.

"I might be late for next week's visit," she tells me, watching eagle-eyed over her coffee cup for my reaction. "I have a meeting at the White House that day."

Fuck her if she thinks I'll let her off the hook. "Just get here when you get here." I stroke the bomb remote control on its chain around my neck, running my fingertip over the glowing red button.

As long as she doesn't forget Lesson #1, we'll get along fine: *Show up or blow up.*

There's no other option, as I've made clear. The bomb in her head is booby-trapped, guaranteed to blow by Dr. Joe if anyone tampers with it. If anyone tries to take the remote from me, it's another guaranteed big bang. As soon as the remote loses contact with my skin for more than a few seconds, the bomb will go *boom*.

"Let's have some wine." Mom pours from a bottle she brought on her last visit, and we take it out on the balcony for some fresh air.

The sun is setting, and the sky's a swirl of gold and red, scorching the slowly collapsing buildings of the city. Everything's falling apart in slow motion, including us, and God, isn't it glorious?

She stands alongside me, glass in hand, as if I never had a bomb planted in her skull. As if I didn't have to threaten her life to get her to come here.

It doesn't bother me a bit. I think I deserve a little decency after what she did all those years ago. I'm pretty sure Rafe would agree it's the least she can do.

The sun melts like ice cream or butter, flaring yellow as it sinks below the horizon. Evelyn puts an arm around me and gives me a squeeze, her hand resting below the remote control at my breast. I don't push it away.

We stand there aglow, impermanent as the sunset, perfectly happy to let ourselves be consumed by the darkness or the light as long as we get what we want in the end.

Ω

BRINGING LIGHT INTO DARKNESS

Dayle A. Dermatis

Dayle A. Dermatis uses the following catchphrase for her writing: "My voices will get stuck in your head." That is, of course, quite fitting for a tale for this anthology's theme.

She did not, however, write this story for Obsessions, *she tells me. She actually wrote it with another anthology in mind, but she missed the deadline.*

"Still, the idea would not let me go," Dayle says.

That, to me, is a good start for any story. And, in particular, a tale to be used in an anthology about things that people just can't let go of.

"I'd been thinking about the horrific murder of Emmett Till, and how someone can destroy another person's life just to maintain face or protect their own, comparatively minor,

secret," she says. "If we had the opportunity to go back in time to right a wrong, would we do it? If so, can we also look at the world of today and find ways to prevent the wrongs that are committed every day?"

Dayle, who has been hailed as "one of the best writers working today" by Dean Wesley Smith, is the author or coauthor of many novels (including urban fantasy Ghosted and Gothic romance What Beck'ning Ghost) and more than a hundred short stories in multiple genres appearing in such venues as Fiction River, Alfred Hitchcock's Mystery Magazine, and DAW Books.

She is the mastermind behind the Uncollected Anthology project, and her short fiction has been lauded in year's best anthologies in erotica, mystery, and horror.

To find out where she's wandered off to (and to get free fiction!), check out DayleDermatis.com.

But in the meantime, let's join Dayle as she introduces us to Janelle, a woman obsessing about righting a wrong and hoping to alter the course of a loved one's broken life.

My grandfather is a broken man.

I don't mean to say he's angry or mean; in fact, most of the time he's warm, funny, and caring. The love he and my grandmother share is heartwarming. They still hold hands everywhere they go, and he always kisses her before he leaves the room.

But there's a sadness in him, one that doesn't go away. Neither will the permanent limp from an injury he refuses to discuss.

He refuses to discuss any of it, really, so when I was in my teens and old enough to understand there was a dark place in him, I asked my grandmother. She looked me up and down, her brown eyes searching mine, and then nodded as if agreeing that now was the right time.

She was sitting in her favorite club chair, the one covered with orange and black African kente-print fabric. She ran a hand over her tight curls, which had long gone from black to grey, then picked up a bottle of her favorite hand lotion. She had them stashed all over the house. I'd say she used it obsessively except that she had the softest hands of anyone I'd ever met.

Plus, I'd picked up the habit. At any given time, one or both of us smelled like rosewater.

"All right, Janelle, baby. Your grandfather was a young man in the South in the Sixties," she began.

Oh, shit. Suddenly I knew what was coming. Not the details, but the hideousness of it.

"Let me guess: Jim Crow laws," I said.

She closed her eyes for a moment, and I could tell she was holding back tears. I was, too. She took a deep breath through her nose, opened her eyes, and continued.

"In a way, yes. Although he didn't do anything wrong, even by those laws. He was falsely accused."

With that stated so firmly, no jury could disagree with her, she plowed ahead with the awful truth.

My grandfather, I knew, had been a reporter from an early age, working his way up to editor-in-chief of a black-run newspaper in Washington. Now, I learned, this almost hadn't happened.

On the basis of his writing samples from his small-town newspaper, he was invited to Washington, DC, to interview for a position at *The Washington Chronicle*. He didn't own a car, so he had to take the bus—and he didn't have the money to stay overnight, so he had to take the earliest bus possible.

So, it was at the barest hint of dawn when he was walking briskly down the street, and a woman came out of an apartment building and down the steps to the sidewalk.

A white woman.

It barely cools down in the summertime in Virginia, even at night. Still, the woman was wearing black and had a scarf over her face.

My grandfather, focused on not missing his bus, didn't see her. It was highly unlikely the woman saw him.

They bumped into each other.

My grandfather leaped back as soon as he realized what had happened. He touched his hat and said, "My apologies, ma'am."

That should have been enough. Perhaps she might have given him a dressing-down to add to her feelings of superiority.

But apparently, that wasn't enough for her. She summoned the police and claimed my grandfather had laid hands on her.

Even though it had happened decades ago, my blood boiled.

He was arrested, tried, found guilty (with no witnesses, it was his word against hers, and who would believe a Negro over a respectable white woman?), and jailed. It was sometime during that process that he retained the injury that left him with a permanent limp and a cane. (Although he'd taken to collecting interesting canes, and had stories about each one.)

He wouldn't tell anyone, my grandmother said, her voice tight in a way I knew she was again holding back tears, not even her, what had happened. He swore it didn't matter anymore.

But even I knew it did. The experience changed him, caused the dark place within him.

∞

That might have been the end of it, my knowing the truth and living with it as the rest of my family had been. But I was too stubborn to leave it be.

I needed to know more.

I dug up newspaper articles about the event, the trial, the sentencing. The reporting—the language—made me sick, but I pressed on.

The woman's name was Carol Pierce. I stared at her picture in the grainy photocopy until I saw her in my sleep. She was slender, pretty if you like blond coifs and self-satisfied smiles. She was also the wife of Ronald Pierce III, whose family practically built the town. They were the closest thing to royalty in small-town South.

I was able to pick out quite a few details about Carol Pierce. She'd organized charity events, smiled and sparkled on her husband's arm when he ran for the state senate. (He lost.)

Reading between the lines, I guessed that for all her outer beauty, she wasn't someone well-liked, just someone people stayed close to because of her influence. Didn't surprise me one bit.

Unfortunately, I also found obituaries. Carol Pierce was dead. Cancer. Her husband, heart attack. I couldn't get revenge on her, any kind of closure from them for my grandfather, even if I'd wanted to. (But what would that have served? A young black woman getting in the face of an old white woman, demanding she recant a story from decades ago?)

Sometimes old cases can be reopened, and those found guilty in the past can be exonerated. But everyone involved was dead or old, and anyway, it was still only my grandfather's word.

So, I tucked all the information away and let it lurk in a dark corner of my brain, like a spider deep in its web, waiting for the opportunity to come to her. Patient.

I didn't forget, though. Like my grandfather, I could never forget.

∞

That would have been the end of it—a horrible story lost to the past, except where it lived on in our family's memory, and eating in my memory like a worm in an ancient book—had a random encounter in graduate school not given me a chance.

A chance, just maybe, to make a difference.

A crazy, stupid, near-impossible chance.

To make ends meet, I tended bar at a local dive frequented by university students. Mostly from the science and engineering departments, for some reason.

One of the regulars, a quiet white guy who usually orders a Blue Moon, chats with his friends, and then leaves, showed up one night in an ebullient mood. He'd clearly had a drink or two already, and that night he ordered champagne. He and the two friends with him (also white guys; I could tell them apart by their hair color) were clearly celebrating something, and he stayed longer than he ever had—even after they'd left.

He'd switched to beer—again, more than usual, even after the champagne—and was sitting quietly at one end of the bar, which was otherwise empty. Finally, I headed over to him.

"Getting late," I said. "Last call."

He looked up as if he'd forgotten where he was. Blinked.

"You're really pretty," he said, almost focusing on me. "And you smell good."

"Thank you," I said politely. He wasn't being offensive, and I was pretty sure he was bad enough at social situations that he wouldn't go any further.

He didn't indicate that he wanted more, and he still had half a glass left, the orange slice floating on the amber surface.

I grabbed a rag and wiped up some nearby moisture rings. "You and your friends looked like you were celebrating tonight," I said, just to make conversation.

"Oh, yeaaahh," he said. "I can't believe we really did it."

"Did what?" I asked.

He looked around the room. "It's a secret."

"Okay."

He leaned toward me. "I bet you can keep a secret."

"That's a bartender's second job, after serving you drinks," I said.

He glanced right, left, right again. Leaned closer. I leaned towards him.

"We did it," he said in a stage whisper. "Time travel."

And then he threw up on the bar.

∞

I cleaned up, cleaned him up, cashed out, and got him home. His name was Mike, and he lived in a decent apartment building, and by the time I got him there, he was able to get himself inside. I still went in and made sure he drank some water, took some ibuprofen, and had an empty trash can next to his bed.

That wasn't, obviously, the end of it.

I'm not proud of the fact that I used Mike. I showed up the next day to check on him, gave him my cell number, invited him out for coffee. I didn't stalk him, although if he'd resisted my advances, I can't say what I would have done.

But everything I said and did was to make him trust me enough to show me how time travel worked.

I flirted, I dated, and if I'm going to be honest, yes, I slept with him. I know it makes me horrible and manipulative, but I made that choice with a clear mind. If time travel was indeed possible, it was the answer to everything. I could go back, make things right. Change my grandfather's life.

Fix my grandfather.

To be honest (again), I liked Mike. A lot. He was smart and kind and geeky in an adorable way. If he was someone I could hold hands with when we were in our eighties...I refused to think about that. I did tuck away the thought that if I succeeded, and he never found out about my deception, we might have a chance at something more, something true.

But right now, that wasn't going to stop me.

I can't say how time travel works (honestly, I really don't know), and I'll never tell where the device is or anything about it. Like Mike and his colleagues, I don't want it to get into the hands of the government.

But when I understood *how* to do it, I made my plans.

∞

I tamed down my natural as best I could and crammed on a short, respectable-for-the-1960s wig. I wore a vintage suit: butter-yellow wool gabardine with three copper buttons down the front and one on each faux-pocket flap near the waist. Underneath, a white blouse with a Peter Pan collar, Black cat's-eye glasses. Sensible, low-heeled black pumps.

I snuck into the lab. Mike never covered his hand when he punched in the code, and it was easy enough by then to get his fingerprint.

Hands shaking, I attached two small silver dots, about the size and shape of watch batteries, to my temples. I entered the date, time, and place into the black handheld thingie, about the size of a small smartphone.

I took a step forward.

Everything went black, and then white, and then into colors again.

∞

I'd obsessively studied 1960s maps of the town and knew the very corner on which to ambush the young man who would end up being my grandfather.

"Excuse me, are you headed to the bus station?" I asked in a breathless voice, as if I'd been hurrying. In fact, I was overwhelmed by what had just happened and was barely keeping myself together.

My grandfather was a handsome young man—I'd known that from photographs, but it struck me even harder in person—smartly dressed in a brown suit. The cuffs of his jacket were worn, and the pants were a little too short. I couldn't tell in the dim light, but I suspected his brown shoes were polished as much as possible to make any scuffs unnoticeable.

"Yes ma'am, I am," he said, clearly startled, but politely touching his brown fedora anyway.

"Would you mind escortin' me? I hadn't realized it would be so dark, and I'm not comfortable bein' alone."

"Why, of course," he said, and I tucked my hand into the crook of his arm and smiled at him.

We walked briskly down the street. The air smelled fresh: not as many cars choked the roads, I guessed. I was used to humidity, but the pace we kept made me a little sweaty. Or maybe that was nerves.

I might fail.

I might make things far worse.

I might change the course of history and wink out of existence and never know the outcome.

I was here now, though, and I would see this through to the best of my abilities. I *would* change my grandfather's future.

"Where are you headed off to?" he asked.

I named a town in Georgia, the opposite direction, adding that I'd been visiting a cousin here.

"What about you?" I managed through a dry mouth, keeping a nervous eye on where we were on the street. How close we were to the apartment building Carol Pierce would emerge from. My stomach churned.

"Headed to the city for a job interview," he said. He paused, then added, "I confess I'm nervous."

"I'm sure you'll do fine," I said.

He started to say something else, but we were at the apartment building, and I had stationed myself between him and Carol Pierce, and I knew to watch for her. I stepped sideways, trying to avoid colliding with Carol, but my grandfather wasn't expecting this, and didn't move as far as I'd hoped.

My left elbow grazed Carol Pierce's arm.

We all stopped dead in our tracks. I saw firsthand Carol's icy beauty, the sharp cut of her cheekbones, the intensity of her eyes, although in the dim light, I couldn't make out their color.

"I'm so sorry," I stammered. "Please forgive me…Miz Pierce."

Her eyes widened. "I'm sorry, do I know you, girl?"

Although every modern part of me bristled at her tone, I knew not to act on that.

"No, Miz Pierce, I'm sorry. I was one of the help at your last fundraiser, the one for your husband's campaign. I don't expect you'd recognize me."

Her nostrils flared. I was impressed with how she kept herself together, even being caught out like this.

I'd studied Carol Pierce's life, and I'd studied the maps of this town, and I knew damn well the apartment building she was exiting at the crack of dawn was not where she or her husband lived. It was where her alleged lover lived, a younger colleague of Ronald's, and the whiff of this affair was rumored to have tanked her husband's political aspirations.

It was possible, I'd conjectured, that her motivation in accusing my grandfather of assault was a way to prevent him from gossiping about where he'd seen her.

Now she had two witnesses. And she would have a harder time claiming she was assaulted by a dirty Negro man when there was a witness.

"No, I expect I wouldn't," she said with a sniff. "Be more careful where you walk, girl."

"Yes ma'am," I said, bobbing my head, and then I tugged on my grandfather's arm, and we continued on our way.

He wanted to see me off on my bus—a gentleman indeed—but I said that I had to use the facilities, and I didn't want him missing his own ride.

At this time of day, the black women's bathroom was empty. I breathed through my mouth against the stench—clearly, it wasn't a priority to be cleaned—and pulled the small dots and the handheld thingie from my pocketbook.

I entered the coordinates with shaking hands—a moment after I'd left—stuck the dots to my temples, gulped a breath, and took a step.

∞

I could have opted for revenge. I could have found a way to take down Carol Pierce before she ruined my grandfather's life. Believe me, I fantasized about that.

In the end, though, I chose not to replace one evil deed with another.

It's possible I ended up making Carol's life better. Letting her know someone guessed her affair might have caused her to break it off, avoided the whiff of scandal that had, in the end, ruined her husband's political dreams.

I don't know because I've never looked back. My days of poring through microfiches and dusty archives were over.

As for my grandfather, I sat with him and teased out stories from his life, claiming it was a project for a history class I was taking at university.

I eased him around to that morning, to the day he made it to the city and got the job he dreamed of.

He still visited his home regularly, and a good thing, because it meant he still met my grandmother at the appointed time.

"She smelled of rosewater, and she had the softest hands," he said of the woman he met that fateful (to me, but not to him) dawn. "Even in the darkness, I could tell she was beautiful. When I met your grandmother, I thought that woman was her, but she swears that never happened." He shrugged. "Maybe that woman pointed me in the right direction."

He meant that she'd pointed him towards his future wife.

I knew differently. My heart twinged in my chest. A twisting pain, but a good one. It meant only I knew the truth, knew the past that could have been, that broke a part of my grandfather, deep inside.

∞

My grandfather is a happy man.

Ω

A MATTER FOR GOD

Kristine Kathryn Rusch

Kristine Kathryn Rusch, a New York Times *and* USA Today *bestselling author, writes in almost every genre. Her novels have made bestseller lists around the world.*

As an editor, Kris has worked at Pulphouse, 'The Magazine of Fantasy & Science Fiction,' *and the original anthology series* Fiction River, *published by WMG Publishing. She edited the highly acclaimed* Women of Futures Past *for Baen Books and co-edited* The Best Mystery and Crime Stories *for Kobo Publishing.*

Kris's short fiction has appeared in more than twenty best of the year collections, and she has won more than twenty-five awards for her fiction, including the Hugo, Le Prix Imaginales, *the* Asimov's Readers' Choice award, *and the* Ellery Queen Mystery Magazine Readers Choice Award.

I have had the good fortune to work with and learn from Kris over the years, and also had the honor of publishing her story

"*Puckish Behavior*" in Fiction River: Superstitious. *I am thrilled to again have the privilege of bringing another one of her fabulous stories to readers.*

Kris tells me that she got the idea for this story years ago at her mother's funeral.

"My mother was an extremely difficult woman who became more difficult in the last part of her life," Kris says. "As a result, only her family showed up...and my dad's friends." (Her father had been gone for seven years at that point.)

Kris relayed that her nephew had only been at the funeral for the sake of his mother, and not because he actually wanted to be there. "Mother had pretty much alienated everyone else.

"I knew, but hadn't realized, how many funerals occur without attendees at all, for a variety of reasons." She has mixed feelings about that, and has written a companion story called "Flower Fairies" that is one of her personal favorites, which is a similar situation – a woman without obvious mourners – but it comes to a different conclusion.

"A Matter for God" is also one of the few stories that directly uses Kris's upbringing as a PGK (Pastor's Grandkid).

"It's not a part of my writing that I haul out very often," she says.

I am most certainly glad that she allowed us a peek behind that curtain, and I'm most certain, dear reader, that you will be too.

Come now, do you hear that faint chords of the organ?

Can you begin to smell those freshly cut flowers as we walk up the church stairs to this most somber service?

It was my third funeral of the week. The first was a large, gaudy affair, as perfectly timed as a wedding, flowers draping the aisles, the pews, even the choir loft in the back. Pastor Valera even had us put extra chairs at the end of aisles and at the back. It interrupted the flow of the service — the boys and I, we have a routine — but it turned out to be necessary. A handful of people even had to stand.

I'd seen few funerals like that one. Some out-of-town choir came in — famous, Pastor Valera said — and sang Mozart's "Requiem," or at least parts of it. The *Lachrymosa*, a few other sections. Pastor Valera didn't want much more. He said a requiem was Catholic and the only time we uttered that word in this holy place was when we recited the Apostle's Creed, and the church fathers have been arguing for some time about accepting the reformed version where we substitute "holy Christian church" for "holy catholic."

The words we use usually don't matter to me. I've been coming here for seventy-five years — was born down the block, baptized at the very font up front, and will probably lie in state before the altar, just like the folks we put to rest week after week, year after year.

Strange thing about those folks: not all of them are ours. The second funeral belonged to a young kid who hadn't set foot in a church, but he died slow and messy, some wasting disease, and his grandparents insisted on a good Christian send-off as if the lack of church in his life was the reason his body had turned on him and gave him eight years when the rest of us get decades.

The boys and I, we preside over these things — or so Pastor Valera says. We're the ones who decorate the sanctuary, carry the coffin if the funeral home director lets us, make sure the family gets the front pews, and help everyone process in. We wear the suits we used to wear when we worked nine-to-five, or if we never worked a dress-up job, the suits our wives used to make us wear every Sunday of our lives.

Harold, his wife likes it that he spends his days at church now that the bank no longer wants his time. And she's not the only one. The two other wives feel the same way. Only Stan and I are without, me because Agnes died five years ago, and him because he never married.

Agnes's funeral was strange: me sitting alone in that front pew — our son James and his family weren't able to come — and the boys, my friends, helping me out of the church like I was a stranger. I think on that funeral at every one I attend, and I try to offer my arm as comfort, my silent presence as reassurance to anyone who needs it. Once I found a little boy sobbing on the floor of the men's room, and I held him for a good five minutes, his tiny fingernails poking a hole in my sleeves, his tears making dark circles on the wool. When the storm subsided, I sent him out on his own — I hate these days when even offering simple comfort arouses suspicion — and by the time I emerged, he was in his mother's arms, thumb in his mouth, head on her shoulder, and eyes closed.

If only grief were that simple for me.

Agnes used to work the funerals too. Downstairs, in the basement of the church, she made finger sandwiches without the crusts, sheet cakes, and soft sweet butter cookies. The other ladies, they made coffee and sweet Kool-Aide and Presbyterian punch. They put the sugar cubes in tiny bowls and milk in the pretty creamers, but Agnes organized the feast.

After she died, the sandwiches were sometimes stale, the sheet cakes were store-bought, and the cookies were Mrs. Field's.

I don't go downstairs anymore, except before the service. The smell of coffee makes me think I'll see Agnes as I round the corner past the daycare, see her standing in the big old-fashioned kitchen, an apron she embroidered around her ample waist, and hands strong and sure wrapped in mitts as she pulled her creations out of an oven built to house two roasts.

James never told me why he didn't come to his mother's funeral. He didn't have to. Later his wife mumbled something about deadlines and work and the difficulty in getting plane flights, but we both knew she was lying to make me feel better.

James never lied. He never mentioned it at all.

And because I didn't either, the deadlines went away, the work became less important, and somehow my son's family found the time to fly. Maybe he feels the need to see me, the one still alive, or maybe he regretted missing the opportunity to stare at his mother's dead face, and to know, once and for all, she was gone.

You see, nights alone in front of my television set, these things rattle through my brain. I cook myself a healthy dinner, just as Agnes would have wanted, and while I eat, I read. But there's only so much reading a man can do, and after a while, the television becomes company: human faces, human voices. They matter in ways I'd once taken for granted, back when I had deadlines and work and not enough time to see the family. I think about such matters even more after a funeral like that third one that week.

Several things were different about that funeral. It was an early afternoon service, and for some reason, the family had an hour of visitation before the service. Most folks have visitation at the funeral home the night before, but not these people. Maybe they knew that no one would show up. Pastor Valera did. When he'd been asked to do the service, he'd looked at me and said softly, "The Lord works in mysterious ways," and closed his office door.

He wasn't mourning. None of us mourned the death of Edith Kahill. She had been the bane of our existence since she returned to the church about ten years before. She'd served on Ladies Auxiliary until Agnes found a way to ease her off — the other women were refusing to come as long as Edith was there. Edith, who insisted on deciding which funeral got the silver tea service and which one "would ruin it." Edith, who believed that sheet cakes were tacky and coffee should be made from fresh beans. Edith, who once sent Sophie Stanglass home because she wasn't dressed well enough to work in the kitchen during old Mayor Frasier's funeral.

I later found out that Pastor Valera was upset because Edith's family had asked for the full-service funeral, complete with homily. That afternoon, I found him at his desk, texts open around him, yellow legal paper crumpled and lying on the floor, hand under his chin and eyes staring at the weeping cherry tree outside his window.

"Want to hear a confession, George?" he asked.

I stood in the door, hands hanging at my side. Pastor Valera and I had never been close, through no fault of his. He was a young man, younger than my son, and I'd always seen him as a part of the new school. His sermons were about life now, how to reconcile God with the pandemic and governmental scandal and too much debt. I liked fire and brimstone, what Pastor Robbins preached long about fifty years ago when I was a teenager and needed to hear it. Pastor Valera didn't really speak to me, but I thought maybe God had moved on, or I had already learned my lesson, or maybe I had stopped listening in just the right way.

"All right, Reverend," I had said.

"Come on in." He beckoned me with an ink-stained hand.

I'd never realized he'd written out his homilies. I thought that he used the fancy computer that sat on his credenza and, God forgive me, I thought he had an entire series of sermons listed by topic, and simply opened a file and printed out the sermon the night before.

I came in and, after glancing at him for permission, closed the door. Slowly I sank into the plush chair across from his desk. He didn't seem to notice my hesitation. I hadn't sat across from a minister since the day I planned Agnes's funeral.

"George, how did you do it, year in and year out?" he asked. "How were you so polite to her?"

That was when I realized we were talking about Edith.

Some in the church thought she had singled me out because they saw me, every Sunday, nod and disappear down the stairs after Edith yelled at me. She thought the church too cold for the elderly, and she blamed me since I was the one who had headed the committee that hired the janitor.

Every Sunday, I went down the stairs halfway, pretending to talk to the janitor about the heat. I waited until Edith was in her pew, sweater wrapped ostentatiously around her, leather gloves on her tiny fingers. Then I came up, flashed her a high sign, and she would frown at me as if I were making a promise she knew I would break.

Every Sunday after service, she would come over to me and say, "You know, George, if the church were this warm when the service started, we wouldn't have so many out ill during the winter." I, of course, refrained from telling her that the church was warmer at the end of the service because of the number of people in it, not because anyone had touched the boiler.

How did I do it? How was I so polite to her?

"I never figured it was worth being anything else," I said.

Pastor Valera nodded, half smiled and said, "You know she tried to get me fired."

I had not known that, and I was a deacon. "You're kidding."

He stared at me. His eyes were as dark as my son's and lined with the webbing that marked the first stage of middle age.

"She did," he said. "She went above the Elders, and to Presbytery. They wrote to me and asked me why one of my flock was so unhappy. It's hard to explain that she was always unhappy. I tried, and they said it was my duty to make her feel at ease. I said nothing, of course, but I wasn't even sure God could do that."

Probably not, I thought.

"But I sit here and try to write her funeral sermon, and I can think of nothing kind to say."

"Don't you have a sermon for folks you don't know?"

"You mean Sermon 187?"

I flushed. He wasn't supposed to know about the nickname. The boys and I, we called his standard "Going Home to the Lord" sermon, the one he gave when he had no other choice, Sermon 187. I confess that the name was mine because I had assumed all his other sermons were by the number as well.

"Yes," I said softly.

He shook his head.

"It's not right, George. I knew her." He templed his fingers, rested their tips on his chin, and sighed. "What a sad commentary on me, isn't it? That I lack enough Christian charity to find something good in one old woman."

"She did make it difficult," I said, thinking of the squabbles after Agnes died, the way Edith had nearly killed the Auxiliary with her rules and her pettiness and her sharp, biting words. "But who said you have to be kind?"

He let his hands slide down to the desktop. "I can't speak ill of the dead."

"But you can speak the truth," I said. "You can talk about how women like Edith made it a challenge for those of us who believe in God."

"She did test our faith, didn't she?" he asked.

I nodded, thinking that to call it a test was to be polite.

"Thanks, George," he said, pulling his legal pad close. "I think you might have saved me from sermon 187 yet again."

∞

The day of Edith's funeral dawned sunny and beautiful. It was one of those warm spring days that reminded you summer was just around the corner. I went to the church early, and in a silent tribute to my old nemesis, I did talk to the janitor and made sure the church would be the right temperature. There wouldn't be much body heat to fill the sanctuary that day.

I went up the stairs and found Howard sitting in the front pew, staring at all the floral arrangements. I recognized them; they were the ones that were left from the two previous funerals that week. I saw no new flowers.

"Where're the deliveries?" I asked.

He pointed to a spray of yellow roses that were on the communion table, marked *In Memorium,* and signed *The Kahills.* Beside the yellow roses were four small vases, all signed with the name of institutions. I recognized one: it was the one where Edith's daughter worked.

"Well," I said. "Let's arrange them."

He caught my arm and looked at me. "Don't you remember?" he asked.

"What?"

"What she used to say?"

Then I stopped. I could hear her stentorian voice as clear as an organ chord in the center of the sanctuary. *Really, gentlemen, if they weren't well-liked enough in life to merit flowers, do you think we should share those of the people who were well-liked in death? It's almost as if you're lying before God, saying that these wonderful bouquets are a tribute to someone who didn't deserve it.*

I swallowed. "It's custom, Howard."

"It's a custom she didn't agree with."

What a pitiful arrangement it would be if we simply had her flowers there. A spray of yellow roses across the bottom of the open casket, and four smallish bouquets on the table above her.

"She deserves the respect," I said.

"Really?" Howard asked. "She didn't think anybody else did." And then he got up and left.

In the end, I moved three card tables across the back and sides of the sanctuary, and with Stan's help, moved the older bouquets. The cards had been removed long before, and so we simply arranged things as best we could: roses and spring flowers up front, Easter lilies in the back. It didn't look like a tribute, but it didn't look like a slap, either.

Funerals, I so well knew, weren't for the dead. They were for the living. But, as Agnes used to say, they weren't for the living to perpetuate a lie. Maybe Howard had been right. I didn't know. All I did know was that I couldn't stomach the thought. None of us knew how we'd be at the end of our lives, and if Edith Kahill had known she was making that pronouncement about her own funeral, she might not have made it.

The boys and I spent the next hour with the funeral director, moving the coffin into its position at the front of the church. That wooden box was surprisingly light. We put the spray of roses against the bottom half as the director opened the top half.

And there she was: Edith Kahill in all her splendor.

I hadn't realized what a tiny woman she had been. Her voice, her personality, had loomed so large that I hadn't realized they were housed in such a fragile frame. She wore a blue dress that I had never seen before, made of silk and woven with small silver threads that accented her hair. Her rings were gone — apparently, the family was keeping them — but her signature silver posts glimmered in her ears.

She did not look as if she would wake and tear into us. She did not look as she had in life at all. Without her chin-jutting bravado, she seemed like a tortoise without its shell, or a nearly blind man without his glasses, weak and vulnerable and about to shatter.

I hadn't even known she was ill. No one had. She had been rushed to the hospital, and by the time someone thought to call Pastor Valera, she was dead. Her obituary had said she was eighty.

The family started to arrive shortly after the funeral director. I had only seen the daughter, and then only once. I hadn't realized until that day how much she resembled Edith. I had always thought the daughter frail and so small that I often wondered how she had stood up to her mother. She probably didn't have to stand up at all.

The daughter wore a black pantsuit that molded to her tiny frame. A single diamond stickpin glinted from the collar. She examined the flowers before looking at her mother. Then, as the mourning often do, she stood with her head bowed, just staring at the body until something seemed to jerk her from a waking dream. Then she moved on.

The son and his family arrived shortly thereafter, and then the second daughter and hers. A granddaughter, the first daughter's daughter, the one who had accompanied Edith to the hospital, arrived last.

She was young enough to wear her hair long and her skirts short and to have both look good. She had a narrow face, drawn as if she had gotten no sleep. Unlike her grandmother, she was tall and solidly built, with the muscles of a training athlete. In my day, girls didn't have muscles like that, but now it's considered attractive, even desirable.

I was lighting the last of the candles as she approached the body. She stood over the casket for a long, long time. Other family members, cousins, aunts, the handful of spouses, walked past. I tidied the pulpit and kept an eye on her.

Sometimes, I confess, I go to funerals to watch the other mourners. Somewhere I had gotten it in my head that there is a normal way to mourn, a right and proper way to behave when a beloved dies. What I have seen runs a gamut from the rigid to the incredible. Many people grimace, hold in whatever they feel. Usually, the sermon or a hymn, or sometimes the sight of the body itself brings tears. Sometimes it's as simple as a kind word. Some folks sniffle and dab. Others weep and wail and carry on. Once, the boys and I had to break up a fight between the beneficiaries of an estate, and once a family had to haul some of its shouting members outside — a group that hadn't seen each other since 1959 and had hated each other that entire time.

But I had never seen anyone like this granddaughter. She didn't have the glazed semi-shocked look of a person stunned by death. There was malevolence in her gaze, a hatred so profound that I felt as if it violated this sacred place.

She waited until all the others had gone by her, then she placed her hands on the side of the coffin. They gripped the side so hard that I half expected the wood to buckle.

She leaned over and said, "I'm not sorry, Gram. I'd make you die all over again if I could."

And then she walked away.

A shiver ran through me that had nothing to do with the temperature of the sanctuary. That look, those hands, that tone. The suddenness of Edith's death. It all added up to me. I don't know how I knew, exactly, but I knew.

Somehow, her granddaughter had caused her death.

I staggered out the preacher's door, searching for Pastor Valera. He was in his office, the door closed. The boys were scattered, finishing their work. None of them would be a moral compass anyway.

What could I do? I was an old man who overheard a good-bye that, on the face of it all, seemed ambiguous at best. I couldn't interrupt the service. I had to wait until the mourning was over.

Then I'd decide what to do.

∞

Somehow, we got through the ceremony. Twenty-five family members, the boys, the organist, and Pastor Valera. The daughter, the one who had arrived first, cried. Everyone else sat stony-faced. They seemed relieved by the sermon, which was about the ways that God tests us and often tests us most through death, and I heard the son thank Pastor Valera for finding something good in his mother's life.

What an epitaph.

There was more laughter than I had ever heard at a funeral reception. The sheet cake and the coffee disappeared. The cookies and finger sandwiches remained.

And within an hour, it was over.

Pastor Valera went to the graveside service, and I, my stomach churning, went back into that sanctuary. But I didn't talk to God. I talked to Agnes.

She had been the one in charge of difficult emotions. She had been my moral center, which hadn't always worked. When our son married that little Jewish girl — well, let's just say our moral center failed. But usually, Agnes knew what to do, and I didn't.

So I asked her in that place where she had spent so much of her life what she would do. I could almost see her, not as she had been when she died, all skinny and cancer-wasted, nor as she had been when she headed the Ladies Auxiliary, her frame matronly and round, but as she had been the night I met her, her dark hair swinging, her eyes sparkling.

George, she had said in that chiding flirtatious tone I had loved so much, *you already know what to do. You always do.*

And I guess I did.

∞

Pastor Valera returned from the graveside service shortly after that, his hair windblown and the hem of his coat covered bits of newly mown grass. The boys had cleaned up, and downstairs I could still hear the bang of dishes as the ladies were finishing their tasks.

"You still here, George?" he asked. He shook his head. "What a sad day. I don't think anyone mourned. What kind of life have you lived if no one is sorry that you died?"

I couldn't answer him. There were no words. I couldn't ask him about my dilemma, either. He was younger than my son. For all his training, this man had no more wisdom than I did.

"George?" he asked. "Are you all right?"

I clearly wasn't. I glanced around the vestibule, and then said, "If I overheard something in that sanctuary, someone talking to the dead, is that considered sacred communication?"

"You mean like confession?" he asked.

I nodded.

"We're not Catholic," he said. "And even if we were…" He paused, frowned at me, and asked, "What did you overhear?"

So I told him. I told him all of it, right down to my suspicions. As I spoke, he led me into his office and closed the door behind us. The office was neat this time, like it usually was, and it smelled vaguely of pipe smoke.

"She had a bad heart, George," he said when I was through. "She had a heart attack and died in the emergency room, screaming at the nurses."

I hadn't expected that. I started to leave, embarrassed. Then a thought hit me. I stopped, and said, "Heart attacks can be triggered."

"Her granddaughter brought her into the emergency room."

"Still," I said.

He studied me for a moment. "Why?" he asked. "Why would her granddaughter do that? She wasn't going to inherit. The money isn't going to the family at all. Or the church. It's going to some arts organization back east."

There was some disappointment in his tone, some acknowledgment of a plan gone wrong. We had all thought a portion of Edith's money would come to the church. She had said so often enough. But then I remembered the attempted firing and wondered if she had changed her will after that.

Probably.

I'm not sorry, Gram. I'd make you die all over again if I could. Such hatred. Such repressed violence. So very much emotion packed in those words.

And absolutely no one mourned.

"George?"

I thought of standing on those stairs every Sunday, waiting for Edith to go to her pew, and wishing that she was gone, wishing that she would leave me alone once and for all, wishing that I would never ever see her again, and knowing I would do almost anything to prevent it.

"George?" Pastor Valera was looking at me.

I shrugged. "Guess in my old age, my imagination is acting up."

"Maybe," Pastor Valera said. "Maybe not."

My gaze met his. He shrugged. "The Lord works in mysterious ways."

"You believe me?" I asked.

"I don't disbelieve you," he said. "Her granddaughter might have triggered the heart attack."

"But that's murder," I whispered.

"Is it?" he asked. "Edith pushed everyone else to the limits of their tolerance. It sounds as if her granddaughter might have done the same with her."

Then he went behind his desk, pushed the yellow legal pad to the center, and said, "Have you ever thought, George, that Edith's granddaughter might have been trying not to apologize?"

"*Not* to apologize?"

He nodded. "When Agnes died, remember what you said to me?"

I closed my eyes. That day was as clear as this morning. "I said, 'I should have done —'"

"More," he said, finishing for me. "They all say, 'I should have done more.' Maybe Edith's granddaughter felt as if she should have, but didn't want to. Maybe she had apologized one too many times in her life for something she didn't do and wasn't going to apologize again."

I opened my eyes. He looked like a young man. A wise young man. Jesus had died a wise young man.

"That's a very Christian way to interpret it," I said. "But if I'm right and you're wrong —"

"It becomes a matter for God."

His words hung between us. Finally, I asked, "You can live with that?"

He looked down and pushed the pad. "I live with things like that every single day."

∞

I guess we all live with things like that. The granddaughter, if indeed she purposely provoked Edith's heart attack, must live with her action until the day she dies. Edith lived with the consequences of each action, each sentence, each word.

Agnes lived with it too. James and I never discuss her, never mention her. He has not forgiven her for turning away from his wife, and he probably never will.

And me, I continue to step toward the abyss and watch as others cross over. I go to church every Sunday, I watch the mourners during the week, and I watch to see if they know something I do not, if they find comfort in it, if they find hope.

Some of them do.

I simply find more questions, questions I do not like. And they are not the obvious questions either, the ones that I asked Pastor Valera, or even the ones I brought to Agnes. No, they are the small questions, the ones that, in the end, may matter more than others.

No one cried at the big gaudy funeral either, not even the widow who dabbed at her dry eyes beneath a thin black veil. The tears all belonged to the second funeral of the week, the one for the little boy who hadn't been raised in the church. Such wailing, such moaning, such sadness.

There was no sadness for Edith, except Pastor Valera's sadness at the lack. What had she done to deserve an emotionless send-off? And had she known that was how her funeral would be?

Had Agnes known that James wouldn't be able to say good-bye?

Do we ever know?

I ask and get no answers. I sit in funeral after funeral and think about the lives that have passed, the choices made, the actions not taken. I think about what lies ahead for me and wonder who'll tend to my flowers, who'll sit in these familiar pews, staring straight ahead.

It shouldn't matter, but it does.

Naked we are born and naked we return, and what we leave is all we've ever had.

I keep thinking if the granddaughter caused Edith Kahill's death, then that's Edith Kahill's legacy—her bequest to the following generations.

Just like the gaping silence between James and me is my bequest to mine.

I'm not going to change the bequest. Changing it feels like a betrayal of Agnes, something I'll never be able to do.

But I worry about it like I worry about all the other things I can't change. And I wait for my time, hoping God'll grant me an extra few moments on this green Earth to see the funeral someone plans for me.

I can almost imagine my ghostly self standing beside the pews, Agnes beside me. She'll slip her arm through mine and remind me in that gentle chiding voice I miss so much: *Funerals are for the living, George.*

And I'll do my best to remember that most of the time, she was right.

Ω

SILVER LININGS

Leigh Saunders

Leigh Saunders uses a phrase in this story that brilliantly describes the role of actuary: a 'professional worrywart.'

An actuary is a business professional who analyses and deals with the measurement and calculations of risk and uncertainty, often essential to the insurance, health, pension, banking, and technology industries.

In the 18th and 19th centuries, computational complexity was limited to manual calculations. More modern development within that realm involved the convergence of modern financial theory with actuarial science. Toward the early 1990s, actuaries made a distinct effort to combine financial theory and stochastic methods into their previously established models.

This stochastic element seems to play a significant role in both a fateful event and how Mattie Halliday and the other members of Howard Oglethorpe's Garamundi Actuarial Services *deal with an unexpected intrusion into their corporate environment.*

Leigh knows plenty about the corporate world she explores in this story because when she is not writing speculative fiction, she writes computer software manuals.

But within fiction, she enjoys writing "social science fiction," stories that focus on people — or "things" that are also people — and how magic, futuristic events, or advances in technology impact their lives. She has won awards from the League of Utah Writers *for both long and short fiction, and her short story, "Tendrils," was listed on the* 2018 Tangent Recommended Reading List.

You can learn more about Leigh and sign up for her occasional newsletter at www.leighsaunders.com.

As for this story's inspiration, Saunders employs that passion for social science fiction with what sounds like the brainstorming that might happen in a corporate board room.

"When you start tossing ideas around," she says, "you never really know which ones are going to stick together in ways to make you tilt your head sideways, start to smile, and know you have to see where it takes you."

She explains that the words "workaholic" and "ghost" were just two of the words that stuck to her whiteboard when she was tossing around ideas for this story.

Like Mattie's unfortunate workaholic colleague, I'm sure this tale you are about to read will linger in the air long after you finish it.

Moments before his death, Harold Oglethorpe was on an airplane, halfway between Chicago and Denver, staring out the tiny window at the lights winking on the wing and calculating the odds of *whether* versus *when* the plane's engines would explode. In point of fact, Harold's interest in a diversionary explosion was usually in direct proportion to the length of the flight and the lack of legroom – he being nearly six feet, seven inches tall, and seldom finding the "comfort" seating options worth paying twice the price for an additional three inches.

On this particular trip, where he was wedged in between the tiny window on one side and a sweating, suited, rotund gentleman who was overflowing his own seat on the other, Harold was hating life more fervently than usual, which was actually saying quite a lot.

"Excuse me, sir," said the flight attendant, rousing Harold from his visions of a fiery demise lighting up the night sky. "Would you like a snack? I have packets of peanuts or cookies."

Harold dismissed the peanuts without even a first thought, much less a second, his demeanor brightening ever so slightly when he glimpsed the packet of Biscoff cookies in the flight attendant's hand. The Biscoffs were one of the few things that made airplane travel even marginally tolerable, in his opinion.

Unfortunately for Harold, it was at that moment, as he raised his hand and the words "Cookies, please," began to form on his lips, that he died. And while the cause of death would later be listed as a blood clot, the result of deep vein thrombosis brought on by wedging his long limbs into tiny airplane seats, and not by his heart simply giving in to the general sense of ennui Harold always carried around with him and simply choosing that moment to say, "Oh, what the hell," the net result was the same: Harold's heart stopped.

His arm dropped into the portly gentleman's lap, and his head lolled to one side. The flight attendant turned slightly pale, but simply said, "Nothing for you, then, sir?" before tucking the Biscoff and peanuts back onto the serving cart and hurrying off to confer with the other attendants about what should be done with the dead man in seat 17A.

It took Harold a moment to realize what had happened, and he simply stared at the Biscoff longingly before it occurred to him that he was looking at the cart from *above*. As it turned out, his spirit had drifted up out of his body and was now wedged between the top of his sagging head and the overhead luggage compartment.

Unsure what to do about this, Harold froze in place. As a result, while his ghost remained exactly where it was, the airplane continued to move around him, seemingly in slow motion. As the plane slid by, he startled an elderly woman in seat 37B, closed his eyes as he passed through the rear washroom – or it passed through him, he really wasn't sure – and soon found himself hanging in the open air, the airplane, the elderly woman, and his Biscoff disappearing in the distance on their way toward Denver.

Slowly, cautiously, Harold stretched out his long limbs – it was glorious! – and then, because he had no idea what he was actually supposed to do next, he dropped through the darkness into the roiling air currents in the airplane's wake and followed it.

∞

Mattie Halliday stepped onto the elevator, pressing the button for the seventeenth floor. She perused her reflection in the mirrored elevator wall. Not that she was vain or anything, but she did have an image to maintain that did not include looking like she'd been up half the night (*she had*) or knocked back a Bloody Mary for breakfast (*which she also had*). As the car was empty, she pulled a travel-sized aerosol can of hairspray from her purse, smoothed down a few loose strands of hair, and generously sprayed them into place.

Harold Oglethorpe was dead. She was still having trouble wrapping her head around the idea. But as one of five senior partners at Garamundi Actuarial Services, Mattie had gotten the call in the middle of the night – Harold having no next-of-kin, and only her name and number in his wallet as his emergency contact.

It was so like him.

Mattie was not alone among her co-workers in thinking that Harold had always been an unpleasant sort of person to be around for any length of time. He'd been a natural, perhaps even brilliant, actuary – his pessimistic demeanor well-suited to analyzing the potential for undesirable events to occur so their clients could plan for or avoid them – but he lacked more than the most rudimentary of social skills and never seemed to enjoy life in any meaningful way. It was as though he preferred going around with his own personal cloud of gloom hovering above his head at all times.

Still, his death had come as something of a shock. Mattie was sure he hadn't anticipated it and found the oversight somehow ironic.

"Shouldn't think ill of the dead," she muttered.

"No, you shouldn't," a dry voice said behind her.

Mattie whirled, hair spray raised like a can of Mace, finger pressing down and spraying before she even realized what she was doing.

There, in the *(empty?)* elevator with her, was Harold Oglethorpe. "You shouldn't use that in an enclosed space," he scolded, waving at the cloud of hairspray that simultaneously enveloped and passed through him.

"You're dead," Mattie said. "I identified your body…" She looked up at Harold, trying to ignore her writhing stomach. Death hadn't improved him. His lean frame would now be better described as gaunt, and his sallow complexion had paled to near-transparency; there was no reflection of him – *his ghost*, she corrected herself – in the mirrored walls. Mattie gulped, tucking the hairspray back into her bag as she edged toward the elevator doors. "You seem...taller."

Harold shrugged, coils of the hairspray-cloud shifting around his shoulder, shadows sticking to the swirling mist. "What was that spray?"

"Long-lasting Super-Hold."

"Seems aptly named."

Mattie didn't know how to respond – this was already a longer conversation than she'd ever had with Harold in the three years she'd known him. When the doors opened behind her, she whirled and fled across the small, seventeenth-floor lobby and through the heavy glass doors of Garamundi Actuarial Services.

The receptionist, Christine, looked up. "Is everything all right, Miss Halliday?"

"Yes," Mattie said, slightly breathless. Of course, since Christine wasn't going pale at the sight of a ghost over her shoulder, she assumed – she didn't want to turn around to verify – that Harold hadn't followed her out of the elevator.

She took a deep, calming breath, ignoring the lingering scent of hairspray, and schooled her features into a more professional demeanor, hoping she sounded more composed than she felt. "Actually, no. Would you ask the senior partners to meet me in my office immediately, and have everyone else join us in the conference room in ten minutes? It's important."

Three minutes later, behind the closed doors of her mahogany-paneled office, Mattie told the partners of Harold's untimely demise. The news was met with silence and somber nods, even as the room brightened slightly, shadows being pulled from under the edges of the bookshelves and window ledges into a swirling cloud that hovered innocuously in one corner of the room. As none of the partners seemed to notice, Mattie thought it unwise to point it out to them.

Seven minutes after that, Mattie shared the news with the rest of Garamundi Actuarial's staff of actuaries, their assistants, and other employees. There were a few gasps of surprise, but as Harold had not gone out of his way to make friends, no one burst into tears or reacted strongly to his unexpected passing. Mattie did note, however, that a hairspray-scented shadow rolled through the conference room at the moment she made the announcement, causing several people to sneeze and then look around in embarrassment.

After another five minutes, mostly spent in a brief discussion of dividing up Harold's client list, together with the tasks of notifying said clients of the circumstances, Mattie left the conference room.

Just outside the conference room, running the length of a full wall of southern-facing windows with a spectacular view of downtown Denver and glimpses of the mountains beyond, was the row of offices shared by the firm's dozen remaining junior actuaries and their assistants. Though the offices had no doors, all opening onto a wide corridor, peppered with occasional seating arrangements for receiving visiting clients or holding impromptu meetings, the offices were separated from each other by floor-to-ceiling, glass-topped partitions that left them feeling spacious, while at the same time providing a semblance of privacy for conversations with clients as well as letting the light from the windows shine into the interior of the office.

This particular morning, as it typically did, the sun shone brightly through the glass partitions all along the row.

Except for Harold's office.

Located directly in the center of the row of glass-walled cubicles, with six offices to the left and six to the right, Mattie had initially thought they might repurpose Harold's office as a smaller meeting area for a few months, to let the air clear from his passing, rather than attempt to replace him too quickly or leave the space sitting awkwardly empty.

But the office appeared to be awkwardly *occupied*.

A faint, gray haze hovered in the space immediately surrounding his chair, and as Mattie drew closer, she saw Harold – the gaunt, too-tall, ghostly version – sitting in the chair, translucent hands resting on his computer keyboard, eyes staring at his blank monitor. He glanced over as she passed, his expression no more or less grim than it had been in life. The misty cloud of Long-lasting Super-Hold swirled around him, attracting more shadows toward it as he moved.

Mattie shuddered and hurried on, slipping into her office at the end of the row and closing the heavy wooden door behind her, intensely aware of the comforting smell of books and furniture polish that surrounded her – and the distinct lack of any scent of hairspray. She relaxed, but only slightly, leaning back against the door, her heart hammering like it was auditioning for a hard rock band.

As an actuary, it was her job to calculate the various risks a company might face and help them prepare for them.

But as far as she knew, there were no calculations for determining either the risk or likelihood of being haunted, and no boilerplate list of mitigating steps to take when it occurred.

∞

By the third day after Harold's death, his ghost had become visible to almost everyone in the office, and even those who hadn't yet seen him could feel – and smell – his presence. After a week had passed, it was clear he had no intention of going anywhere.

During this same period, Mattie had gotten past her initial shock at Harold's return, calculated the likelihood of everyone in the office potentially experiencing a mass hallucination, and finally come to grips with the idea of Garamundi Actuarial actually having an office ghost-in-residence.

Once she'd sorted out her own thinking, she began to watch both the ghost and how the members of her staff reacted to him, noting her own preference for approaching the situation from a purely analytical point of view. After all, she observed, locking herself in her office until the ghost went away would have seriously undermined her cool, calm, professional image.

Since speaking to Mattie in the elevator, Harold hadn't spoken to anyone, not even her. Not that he had ever really talked much at all when he was alive. It was as though he'd used up his reserves of social interaction ability. So, after a few half-hearted attempts on the part of his co-workers to engage his ghost in conversation, most of them studiously tried to ignore or avoid him.

They mostly failed.

While his physical features had all but faded away, Harold's perpetually pessimistic attitude had intensified, the figurative cloud of gloom that had always surrounded him becoming an almost tangible cloud of hairspray-scented apprehension. The cloud announced his arrival at 7:59 each morning with a wave of uneasiness bordering on anxiety. It lingered until long after his shade had drifted through the large glass doors at precisely 5:01 p.m.

With the exception of a brief respite during the lunch hour, when he would vanish to spiritual planes unknown to the rest of them, Harold would sit at his desk all day, staring blankly at the darkened computer screen for hours on end. And as he sat there, his dark cloud slowly expanded around him, pressing against the window and the glass walls that separated him from the offices on either side of his until it completely filled Harold's office and overflowed from the open fourth wall and into the corridor, small tendrils of scented dread drifting gently across the floor and curling around the furniture like the fake smoke from a dismal Halloween party.

By odd contrast, Mattie noticed that as the cloud grew, it sucked away the shadows from the rest of the office. It was pleasant, at first – a kind of silver lining to the whole "being haunted by a workaholic ghost" thing. The glass walls separating the actuaries' desks glittered in the sunlight, metal lamps and fixtures shone as though lit from within, and even the mahogany desks and paneling of the partners' offices glowed like they had been recently polished.

And in a way no one could quite explain, all of the actuaries' calculations grew sharper, their risk assessments more on-target in the harsh, shadow-free light of Harold's cloud.

That's not to say that it wasn't also taking a toll on everyone.

With each passing day, the shadow-less light grew increasingly harsh, drawing stark, glaring lines that were painful to the eye. Sunglasses quickly became standard office-wear.

The actuaries who worked to either side of Harold, initially intrigued by the specter and oddly energized by the swirling mists on the other side of the glass, grew increasingly tense, jumping at the slightest interruption, until Sam, one of the other partners, suggested they work from home for a few days. They fled, barely pausing to snatch up their laptops.

Harold's former assistant, Barbara, had tried to ignore the bleakness that now filled the formerly sunny space, remaining steadfastly at her post; but when Mattie found the woman weeping at her desk, overwhelmed by the pervasive sense of anxiety, she recruited several of the other assistants to help relocate her to one of the empty intern cubicles.

Something was going to have to be done about Harold.

∞

Christine, the receptionist, had done her best to keep morale up, in spite of the growing clouds of doom and hairspray permeating the office. She used funds from petty cash and purchased packages of mints and eye drops, together with several spare pairs of cheap sunglasses, which she put in large bowls on one of the tables in the breakroom.

More importantly, she had become obsessed with finding a way to combat the chemical smell of hairspray that surrounded the office ghost.

She ordered vases of fresh flowers. They wilted immediately.

She set out bowls of potpourri. They crumbled into dishes of desiccated flower dust in a matter of minutes.

She even tried making multiple bags of microwave popcorn. But every bag burned, making the office smell even worse.

And each day, the odor of Long-lasting Super Hold just grew stronger, leaving a sharp, acid taste on the tongue and burning everyone's eyes.

That morning, nearly two weeks since Harold's ghost had arrived, Christine decided to fight fragrance with fragrance, following along after the ghost and spritzing "happy" floral air fresheners into his cloud of gloom. But rather than nullify the Long-lasting Super-Hold, the combination had sent most of the staff into coughing fits. Many of them had gone home for the day, and Christine had had to brace Garamundi Actuarial's glass doors open for several hours until the fumes faded.

As five o'clock approached, the office was empty but for Mattie, Christine, and Harold.

"We've got to do something about Harold," Christine said as she and Mattie were putting on their coats and preparing to close up the office for the day.

"Got any ideas?" Mattie asked.

"We could try banishing him," Christine said. "Isn't that what you're supposed to do when you're being haunted?"

"I'd feel awful banishing Harold. He was always a good worker. He's just trying to do his job."

"What?" Christine said, her voice almost squeaking in disbelief. "The way he sits at his desk, staring at the computer? He's creeping me out, that's what he's doing." She didn't even bother to suppress the shudder that ran through her. "And why smell like hairspray, of all things?"

"The hairspray was an accident," Mattie said, dismissing that part of the argument with a wave of her hand. "But I was serious about him trying to do his job. Think about it – if you had to name the emotions coming off the cloud, how would you describe them? First impression, off the top of your head?"

"Depression?" Christine guessed. "Or fear?"

"Close. I think he's *worrying*."

"About what?"

Across the office, the cloud shifted as Harold rose from his desk.

Christine and Mattie exchanged a glance. 5:01. Right on schedule.

The two women watched in silence as the ghost drifted toward them, feet not quite touching the floor. He nodded slightly in their direction, then floated out of the office, across the lobby and through the closed elevator doors, the cloud wafting past them with the aforementioned hairspray-fragranced funk.

Mattie turned back to Christine. "You've heard of adrenaline junkies?"

Christine nodded, shaking off the residual dread from the cloud's passage.

"Well, Harold's an actuary. A professional worrywart. And unless my calculations are way off the mark, he's worrying about *everything*."

"On a cosmic level," Christine agreed.

Mattie paused, looking after the now-vanished specter, "If you ask me, I think we've got a workaholic ghost who's obsessing over everything that can possibly go wrong in this world or the great beyond. And the only way we're going to survive this haunting is if we can find something else for him to think about."

∞

And so began the most bizarre office challenge Mattie had ever envisioned.

The moment Harold disappeared down the elevator shaft for his lunch break the next day, Mattie and Christine summoned the rest of the staff into the breakroom. A few of the actuaries were working from home that day, but they still managed to pack twenty-some people in there at once.

Mattie slipped off her shoes and stepped up onto a chair so everyone could see her.

"Thanks for coming so quickly," she began. "We don't have long – Harold will be back in," she checked her watch, "forty-seven minutes, and I know you all have busy schedules of your own. And before you ask, we're meeting in here because this is one room I've never seen the ghost enter."

Briefly, she summarized her observations and analysis of the cloud and Harold's obsessive worrying.

"So, you're suggesting an intervention?" asked Barbara.

"Of sorts," Mattie replied. "At the very least, a distraction. You worked directly with him, Barbara. I'd like you to make a list of the things he was interested in—"

"He never talked about anything other than work," interrupted Barbara.

"And he's not talking about anything at all now, which would be helpful. So think of it as a research project," said Mattie. "See if his apartment has been cleared out yet – if not, go over. Look for indications of any hobbies. Talk to his neighbors; maybe they noticed something helpful. We need to re-focus Harold on something less disruptive than worrying about…everything."

"Less disruptive?" asked one of the actuaries.

"Yes. That's a critical criterion," Mattie said, writing the words *less-disruptive distractions* at the top of the whiteboard in large, purple letters and underlining them twice. "For example, besides the legal implications – or the difficulty of implementing it – can you imagine a ghost hooked on drugs?"

"His cloud of gloom would go all sorts of trippy colors," said one of the assistants from somewhere near the refrigerator. "And probably us along with it."

"Exactly," said Mattie. "And that's only if he responded positively to it. So, trying to medicate him isn't worth the risk. Harold's been rather passive so far, and he hasn't demonstrated any ability to manipulate objects, but do we really want to take the risk of completely destabilizing him?" she paused to let the image sink in.

"Pot's legal here, and it's calming," piped up someone, Mattie wasn't sure who, though the voice seemed to have come from the cluster of younger assistants near the vending machines.

"Right," said Sam. "And I suppose you'd like to keep some burning on his desk round the clock, like incense. *That* wouldn't be the least bit disruptive."

"Hey, at least nobody would be worried anymore."

A ripple of laughter filled the room.

"How do you plan to distract him?" asked one of the other actuaries. "It's not exactly like he pays much attention to us – not that he ever really did when he was alive, either."

"I'll admit, I have no idea," Mattie said. "That's why we're brainstorming. To be perfectly honest, I don't even know if it can be done. But we've got to try. So if you can think of anything – no matter how outlandish – please post it here," she tapped on the whiteboard with the marker, "and coordinate directly with me before you attempt to implement it."

"Welcome to the nuthouse," muttered one of the assistants.

"I'm thinking of it as more of a controlled experiment," Mattie said, looking down at him. He squirmed, but didn't say anything else.

"Why don't we just move?" asked Barbara.

"We've discussed that," said one of the partners, from somewhere near the center of the crowd. "And we're not discounting it as a last-resort option. But not only would getting out of our lease present problems of its own – as would finding a comparable space at a reasonable price in this market – there's no guarantee that Harold wouldn't just relocate with us."

Mattie chuckled. "He is a workaholic. And knowing him, he'd probably do just that." Several people nodded in agreement.

"In the meantime," added another of the partners, from the far corner of the room, "we also need to be sure to support each other, and find healthy ways to cope." Everyone shifted to face him as he spoke. "This is a… *weird* situation, for lack of a better word. We understand that. And if you need to work from home occasionally while we sort things out, please do so. But check in with your supervisor first – don't just go dark, okay?"

Over the next several days, members of the staff added a variety of possible distractions to the growing list on the whiteboard. Since many of the ideas shared a common delivery medium – a television – the first thing they tried was replacing Harold's blank computer monitor with a large, flat-screen TV.

On Monday morning, nearly a month after Harold's ghost had first drifted into the office, they rotated through all of the sports channels. Harold ignored the television and stood facing the window. An afternoon of music videos didn't appear to interest him either, and though the cloud pulsed slightly to the beat of the music, it remained otherwise unchanged.

On Tuesday, they played a series of action movies. Harold watched them and seemed entertained, but so did half of the staff. Mattie circled the words *"less-disruptive"* in red on the breakroom whiteboard and crossed *"movies"* off the list of options.

They tuned in to news channels and talk shows on Wednesday morning. The cloud grew progressively darker, and by lunchtime, had overflowed Harold's office in deep gray waves that swirled around Mattie's knees as she walked down the corridor. The light in the rest of the office grew as sharp and bright as if stadium lights had been installed overhead. Actuaries and their assistants argued over trivialities.

Desperate, they switched the afternoon programming to the shopping networks. The cloud faded to its usual shades of pale gray, and the general feeling of anxiety filling the office subsided along with it.

Later, analyzing the weekly progress reports, Mattie noticed that the productivity that morning had been as high as the tension. When she presented the findings to the other partners, they all agreed that it was an interesting but unsustainable correlation.

Harold ignored most of the cartoon programming on Thursday morning, though the actuaries seated to either side of his cubicle noted that occasional swirls of color touched the cloud from time to time.

When the programming changed to soap operas that afternoon, Harold stood near the entrance to his office, staring balefully at anyone who passed by as though pleading for someone to change the channel. The cloud, usually swirling around him in shades of colorless gray, took on a slight blue tinge. No one in the office viewed this as a positive sign, and they quickly switched away from the soaps and over to a lineup of sitcoms and stand-up comedy.

"Well, you were right about him being a workaholic," said Barbara that afternoon, coming into Mattie's office with a stack of news magazines. "He was a total news junkie. I think he was subscribed to every current events magazine that's still in paper—" she dropped the magazines on Mattie's desk "—and probably had news feeds to all of the digital services. I couldn't get into his computer to check, but he had sticky notes all over his desk about trends he was watching for different clients and his projections for where he thought they would go."

"I think the man was born an actuary," Mattie observed. "No wonder he was so good at it. And now he's replaced his core obsession – staying on top of the news and analyzing the outcomes – with its emotional component of worrying about things."

"So why don't we just turn on the news for him?" Barbara asked.

"No good," said Mattie, shaking her head. "You weren't here yesterday morning. Watching the news made his tension level skyrocket, and everyone else's along with it. We've got to find some other way to distract him. Something calming."

"Well, he watched quite a few documentaries," suggested Barbara, handing Mattie her inventory of what she'd found in his apartment. She'd spent most of the week researching Harold, with little to show for it. His home had been Spartan in its décor – minimalist, modern-style furnishings, maybe Swedish? Ikea? He had no videos or music albums, suggesting that any entertainment was likely digital, consumed through streaming services. Probably the same with books, though he had a few classics in hardcover. He had no pets, and there had been no signs of any hobbies – or any particular vices, so far as she could tell. His neighbors had described him as "quiet," which Mattie found unsurprising, and not that helpful.

"No wonder he chose to haunt the office," said Mattie after listening to Barbara's summary. "It doesn't sound like he had much of a life outside of work." She skimmed the list of his recent Netflix selections and drummed her fingers on her desk. "We'll try documentaries tomorrow. If that doesn't work, I don't think television is the answer."

Documentaries weren't the answer. Though, to their credit, they did appear to capture enough of Harold's attention that the cloud didn't overflow his office space for the first time since he'd arrived.

∞

The second week of the "distract Harold" campaign was no more successful than the first – and possibly even less so. One of the assistants brought in a humidifier and subjected the entire office to a variety of essential oils, blended especially for their calming properties. Except for a slight greenish tinge, the cloud remained unchanged, and most of the staff opted to work from home.

Mattie outlined the individual letters of *"less-disruptive"* in two shades of blue and crossed *"essential oils"* off the list of options.

Moving Harold's belongings to one of the enclosed "guest" offices and giving his space to another actuary was a dismal failure. The tall, pale ghost loomed gloomily over the actuary seated in his usual spot for nearly an hour, waiting for him to vacate his chair. When the actuary finally caved, he left the office at a dead run and didn't return to work for three days.

The rest of the staff switched the offices back to their usual places while Harold was taking his cosmic lunch break.

Meditative music and harmonic crystals placed all over Harold's desk and at the entry to his office had absolutely no effect, and he completely ignored the medium who spent most of her $150/hour visit marveling at the cloud, only to come out of Harold's office making dramatic, dire predictions of doom and gloom and the imminent end of the world.

Even the incense burner on which one of the associates carefully lit a small – and, he insisted, perfectly legal – pile of medicinal marijuana had no effect on either Harold or the cloud.

Mattie turned to Sam. "You approved that?" she asked. They were well away from Harold's office, watching the cluster of somewhat relaxed employees lounging in the easy chairs near Harold's fragrant – and still cloud-filled – office.

Sam grinned. "Desperate times, and all that. Had to at least give it a try."

Mattie looked at Sam curiously, but with his eyes hidden behind the dark lenses of his sunglasses, she couldn't tell if he'd lingered around Harold's desk a little too long himself. He did seem more relaxed than she'd seen him in weeks.

"I'm almost sorry it didn't work," she said.

They stood there in silence for an awkward moment before Sam spoke again. "I've been thinking," he said, "and I wonder if we're taking the wrong approach here."

"How so?"

"We're trying to wean him from being a workaholic."

"Yes."

"What if we just let him be himself – and figure out a way to work around it?"

"It's an interesting idea," Mattie said. "But I don't know how we'd manage it."

"Look around. Not today – with the weed – but generally. We've already started adapting." He tapped his sunglasses. "Letting people work from home occasionally has been a long time coming, but it's already proving to be productive. Our projections for the past month have been sharper, more focused than ever."

"And we can't allow any of our clients to visit us," Mattie countered. "We'd lose all credibility."

"Because we let an obsessive, workaholic ghost handle our worrying?"

"You've been sitting too close to Harold's desk," Mattie said, shaking her head. "If word ever got out…"

"So, what if we enclosed his office?" Sam said. "Put up a wall to keep the cloud in, expose him to limited doses of current events to keep him happy and us sharp, and treated him as our own proprietary secret?"

"A cosmic think-tank," Mattie murmured, looking past Sam at the mesmerizing swirls of gray mist filling Harold's office. She had to admit, she'd become accustomed to it. And she was pretty sure the hairspray smell was beginning to fade. Or maybe she'd just gotten used to it.

"Well…it wouldn't be the worst idea we've tried," she said slowly. "And if it works, it would be a silver lining to his cloud."

"My thought as well," said Sam.

"I'm never quite sure how much of what's going on around here Harold's actually aware of. We'd have to do it in such a way that it didn't upset him."

"A glass wall, with a door."

"And blinds all around, just in case," Mattie mused, thoughtful. "You know, it *could* work."

∞

(Three years later)

"Welcome to Garamundi Actuarial Services," Christine said, handing the visitor a pair of shrink-wrapped sunglasses from the bowl on the reception counter. She was wearing a pair of designer shades with blue plaid frames that complemented her outfit. "We keep it bright around here. You'll want these."

The visitor stared quizzically at the sunglasses, then pulled his own from his suit jacket's inner pocket and put them on. "Thanks. I've got my own," he said. "I'm Eric Carlson. I have an appointment with Mattie Halliday."

"Yes. She's expecting you."

Mattie came out from the inner office just then and greeted Eric. "So good of you to come. Let me show you around."

"I've heard good things about Garamundi," Eric said, following her. "One of the best actuary firms in the country, if reports are to be believed."

"We do our best," Mattie said. "In addition to our senior partners, we've been fortunate in retaining a dozen top-flight actuaries, and—"

"What's that?" said Eric. About halfway down the row of glass-walled actuary offices, sat a tall glass cube, swirling gray mist pressing against its heavy, double-paned, semi-transparent walls.

Mattie laughed. "Trade secret, I'm afraid."

"Some sort of supercomputer?" Eric ventured.

"Something like that," Mattie agreed. "You've heard our slogan – *'we do the worrying for you.'*" She gestured at the glass-walled cube. "Well, you could say the think-tank does the worrying for *us*."

She looked at it fondly.

"We call it Harold."

$$\Omega$$

BLOOD OF HEROES

Ezekiel James Boston

Sometimes all that an author will need is a title to inspire a story. On some occasions, the tale comes to them immediately. And on others, the title might stick with them for years before the right story finally gestates.

Such is the case with this particular title.

Ezekiel says that this story's title first came to him during a discussion about underrated science fiction flicks of the past.

"What I imagined from the title," he says, "was very different from the film renamed and re-released after a throwaway line in the movie."

For years he wanted to write a story using that title.

But each attempt he'd made either didn't capture the essence of what he was after or was too cartoony. It wasn't until he saw a special about solo first responders in smaller vehicles that the idea took a form that felt right to him.

"A first responder could foster an obsession for a grim collection seeded in admiration of heroes," Boston shares. *"Unsupervised, they could spirit away pieces of greatness.*

"Then I thought about the toll that this would take on a person torn between their drive to assist and their macabre obsession."

"Blood of Heroes" takes place in Ezekiel's Ultrahumans universe in which he has also written two novels: A Boy Named Evil *and* A Hero Named Pearl. *Boston enjoys reading and games of all sorts. He chose to give up active sports after jamming his fingers and discovering that an author cannot slam their forehead onto a keyboard and have the story appear on the screen. If you want to check out more of the words that come off of his keyboard, you can visit him at* www.ezekieljamesboston.com.

In the meantime, it's a cool Dallas night. There is the echo of sirens in the distance as Ezekial introduces us to the conflicted and obsessed Deidrick Jackson, a man who not only has collecting in his blood, but blood in his collection.

Deidrick Jackson's pulse remained in high gear. Even though it was after two a.m., the emergency entrance at Dallas General was far from inconspicuous. Anyone coming up could easily see him in the back of the paramedic truck. This wasn't his rig, and he shouldn't be in the box. Yet he was.

The cold Dallas night pressed on Deidrick's face, neck, and latex-gloved hands. It bit at his ears, nose, and fingers. His long johns, paramedic coat, Dickies, and Suregrip steel toe boots kept the rest of him comfortable enough. The trickle of sweat that ran down the center of his muscled back to his thermals was due to nerves.

He shouldn't be here. He shouldn't have taken the gloves from the rack.

Yet he was and he had.

Deidrick had tried to get help several times before but had always chickened out at the last minute. As much as he wanted to stop this, he feared seeing a shrink would jeopardize his job. Again, the sinking feeling that the only way he was going to get help was if he were caught.

Wanting to avoid that, Deidrick put researching discreet psychologists on his to-do list.

Several distant police sirens wailed. They'd been going near constantly throughout Dallas since midnight.

A yet-to-be publicly identified group of super-powered villains had coordinated hits on two targets: The Federal Reserve building and Alcazar Enterprise before going after Joy's Long-Term Garage.

It was thought that they were after the Federal Reserve for money and Alcazar Enterprise for the bleeding-edge tech, but no. Current word had it that there was a secret prison under Joy's Garage, and the first two attacks were to pull the heroes of the Power League away from the third.

The bio bin clunked open when Deidrick depressed the pedal. It was near capacity with wrappers and bloody gauze. None of the gauzes on top had the bright red gel-ish blood typical of those with powers.

It didn't make sense.

Deidrick had seen Bob and Ken load up the hero Melody into their rig. As the only little person who wore Power League black, it couldn't have been any other hero. Sure, guards and cops were injured and treated, but there should've been something from the deep cuts all over Melody's body.

Melody was known to be one of the Power League's best fighters and almost never got hurt enough to need transporting. But the little guy did get that hurt. And there was nothing to show for it.

Since there was already blood on his coat, regular human blood, Deidrick wasn't shy about carefully digging down into the bin.

Amongst the bandages were several swatches of bloodied police uniforms that had to be cut away to treat wounds. There were also bloodied three-inch-long bone tines that one of the yet-to-be-named villains shot from her knuckles. Deidrick had removed a few of them from people at the Federal Reserve. Neither those tines nor these had gel-blood on them.

While on scene, he had removed them and dropped them on the street so he could work. Now though...

Not thinking, Deidrick pulled one of the tines and slipped it into his left pocket. He didn't care for keepsakes from villains, but they were always worth good trade.

Trade. Just like a junkie.

His obsession had caused the rift between him and Diana, his ex-fiancée. She hadn't found out about his morbid collection, but he'd missed one too many date nights acquiring blood samples. Because he and Diana were still on good terms, Deidrick had gotten the feeling that she had her own secrets. Stuff he would've noticed if he had committed to their relationship with half the energy that he sunk into cataloging blood of heroes.

Realizing what he had just done, Deidrick's self-loathing climbed onto his shoulders as he picked out four more and put them into the same pocket.

Elbow deep in the bin, a set of headlights lit him in the box.

An ambulance had pulled up behind the rig.

Deidrick didn't mean to freeze up, but he did. Nothing looked more guilty or suspicious than someone who—upon being discovered—stopped doing what they were doing.

He continued as though nothing was out of the ordinary about what he was doing. They were ambulance jockeys. They probably had no idea what real medics did in the back of their rig.

The ambulance door fast-creaked opened. A guy yelled, "D!"

Shuddering at the sound of his nickname, Deidrick shielded his eyes as he turned.

The guy said, "We could use a hand." The headlights cut off. It was Gilberto Jimenez of Temperance Ambulance Service. The dude was a regular at the field training sessions that Deidrick gave at the station.

"'Sup?" Deidrick withdrew his arms from the bin and was ducking as he headed out of the box.

Gil hopped from the driver's side and headed to his box. "We're double-haulin'."

Deidrick was hoofing it right behind him. "Stable?"

"No." Gil opened his box. "Got one bagged." It was a cop. "And a CBRN." The chemically burnt second person was so bandaged—dressing done right—that it was hard to tell gender, no less occupation. They were belted into the plus-one seat.

Deidrick didn't know Gil's partner for the night, but upon seeing the dressings, he instantly respected her.

She said, "We'll roll the cop." They were already bringing the gurney down.

Deidrick nodded. Gil's partner didn't finish and didn't have to.

Deidrick sprinted from the ambulance to the emergency entrance. He grabbed an empty wheelchair. The wheels had a steady squeak. He was halfway back to the ambulance when he passed Gil and partner taking the cop in.

At the back of the ambulance, Deidrick put the brakes on the chair and said, "You're at Dallas General." He hopped into the back and started removing the seatbelts. "They do good work here."

He wasn't sure if the burn victim was conscious or not, but a soothing voice explaining what was going on never hurt.

Deidrick said, "I'm going to move you to a wheelch—"

Some blood showed at the head bandages.

It was bright red. The high crimson of a powered person.

Thinking fast, he grabbed a small gauze pack from the rack and stuffed it in his pocket.

Deidrick said, "Scooping you up."

The person didn't yell, grumble, or gripe. Unconscious. While it was always better when folks were conscious, this person being out cold, instead of in agony, was a blessing.

Scanning the driveway, he saw nothing but a streetlight at the end, signaling non-existent traffic to keep on moving.

Deidrick slid his arms under and cradled the person. With a grunt, he scooped them up and used the step to ease down to the ground. He slid them into the chair.

He glanced back over his shoulder. Still no cars. No one on the side of the building taking a smoke or vape break.

All was clear.

Deidrick ripped open the package, stuffed the wrapping in his right pocket, and set the gauze on the dressing. He then undid the breaks and wheeled the burn victim toward the doors.

He had planned to take the extra gauze just before the breezeway, but two nurses—a skinny sister and a stocky male islander—came out of the hospital, heading his way.

When they got to him, he was supposed to surrender the chair and the patient to them. But the gauze was still in place, and they'd see if he took it. And then rightfully question why.

The nurses were nearly to him.

Deidrick tried to think as fast as his heart was beating.

∞

Having been raised Roman Catholic, Deidrick's family had gone to mass every Sunday, and his mother typically bundled up him and his siblings for Wednesday evening mass. While he still struggled with his faith, he made it a point to visit his parents twice a month—when work allowed—to attend Sunday mass with them.

While it's impossible to know where he stood with the Lord, Deidrick was fairly certain that he was near the path God intended for him. But there's a world of difference between *near* and *on*. He wanted to be on the path, but this damn compulsion that always got the better of him was proof that he wasn't.

Closing the rear ambulance door, the male nursed asked, "What we got?"

Deidrick found his hands tightening on the wheelchair handles. "CBRN." A bitter taste—guilt? Fear?—lit in his mouth. Disgust. He wanted to spit.

The sister asked, "Name? Source?"

Deidrick shook his head, "Don't know." He jutted a thumb over his shoulder. "Temperance brought 'em."

The male took hold of the handle that Diedrich had released.

Usually, Deidrick would've jumped out of the way, but he hadn't moved fast enough.

The nurse hip-checked him like he was a rookie because being in the way was something only rookies did.

Deidrick let go. "Sorry."

The nurse nodded. "No prob."

And, like that, the squeaky wheelchair was no longer in his control. Thinking how he could still get that gauze, hoping that he would, and praying for the strength not to, Deidrick sped walked next to them.

The sister said, "What a night."

"Yeah." Deidrick snaked out a hand to the gauze on the burn victim's head. "Lord, please watch over this servant." Thumbing the gauze in half, Deidrick pinched the edge between his thumb and index. He pulled it away and brought his hands together. "Amen."

His heart thumped like the Lord was punching him.

Deidrick stopped.

They continued.

He had expected them to call him on it. To call him in to explain himself. To curse him out.

They didn't. They had a hospital filling up of injured first responders. If they had noticed, the oddity probably slipped their attention under the greater burden.

Alone at the entrance, Deidrick tucked the gauze into his right pocket. He turned to look down the driveway. Still no cars. Usually when a police officer was injured, the driveway would quickly be filling up with squad cars. Brothers in blue ready to give blood and moral support.

But not on this cold night. There'd been too much damage. Too much chaos.

And then there was Deidrick. A supposed soldier for Christ, and a complete asshole.

The compulsion to get back to the bio bin in Bob's rig came slinking back. However, Deidrick was too disgusted and ashamed of himself. His impulse to have a memento from Melody was nothing compared to his guilt.

Feeling like shit—like he always did after scavenging scraps—Deidrick wanted to take the gauze out of his pocket and walk away. You know, just leave it there.

He put his hand in his right pocket and balled his fist around the soft contents.

If he could pull his hand out and throw the gauze down, he might be able to finally throw down the sick habit with it.

His want was strong, and he tried to will it away. But his hand stayed in his pocket.

Sighing, he unballed his fist. He took his hand out of his pocket and took off his gloves.

What was wrong with him?

That thought stayed with him—plagued him—to his car, all the way home, and into his brownstone apartment.

It took Smokey, his green-eyed Russian Blue cat, rubbing against his calf at his entry to break the bleak cycle. She always snapped whatever funk he happened to be in.

It had taken him and Diana several years to find a place that they both liked. For her, it was all about the kitchen having an island and the bedroom having wide eastward facing windows. For him, the place needed a niche in the wall just inside the front door for the small painting he made of St. Christopher.

Though Diana no longer called the apartment home, on nights like these, she'd come by and feed Smokey. And, from the smell of pot roast or stew in the air, feed Deidrick, too.

He set his keys in the corner of the niche and looked down at Smokey. Since she wasn't leading him to the kitchen, Deidrick asked, "Want up?"

Smokey stilled and meowed at him.

Deidrick smiled. "Silly question, I know." He scooped Smokey from the floor, cradled her purring body to his chest and scratched under her jaw.

Following his nose around what Diana called *the Christopher wall* into the kitchen, Deidrick found a note from Diana on the counter asking him to go to her place and fix the guest toilet.

Deidrick nodded at the note. "Consider it done." He then checked the slow cooker. It was on low, and there was stew with big chunks of carrots and potatoes, just the way he liked it.

Before Diana, he was more a steak and potatoes guy. She had expanded his palate.

He gave half a thought to eating before the strain of the night started to weigh on him. His shift was supposed to only be twenty-four hours. The emergency had him putting in two extra, and his compulsion had him put in an extra one.

Ready to drop, he unplugged the slow cooker and went to set Smokey down.

She dug her claws into his coat.

Deidrick pulled her back to his chest and walked her to his L-shaped computer desk in the corner of the small living room. Even sitting in his chair, Smokey didn't want to give up his chest. He pulled her away and set her on the desk. She instantly laid across his open MacBook Air.

Deidrick smiled. "Nice try, but I'm not logging on."

He opened the lower desk drawer and took out the thinnest of the three photo albums there. Deidrick had just started Volume Three at the start of the year and already had four samples inside.

Each blood-soaked gauze or blood-splattered scrap of clothing had its own page on the right. On the left was a column that he typed up and printed about the situation surrounding how he had attained the memento. The hero's name was always at the top. The next page or two were devoted to newspaper clippings or website printouts from sources that had the story close to correct.

Since his books were chronological, Deidrick peeled open the next available page. He pulled the CBRN's gauze from his pocket, fetched his scissors from the lower drawer, and trimmed away the excess. Then, carefully, he pressed it into the upper right corner.

Why was he putting this one in there? He didn't know who it was. Hell, for all he knew, it could've been a villain.

Up until now, there were no unknowns in his book. He shouldn't have added it until he knew who the blood belonged to. Shit. He wasn't thinking straight. Too tired.

Tomorrow, he'd have to find a way to casually bump into Gil to see if he knew who the CBRN was. Well, it didn't have to be casual. They had just bumped into each other. It'd be a good reason to have coffee, see how Gil was doing with his EMT-B training, and catch up.

Or maybe it'd be on the news.

Deidrick found his eyes closing as he slowly lowered to the desk. He snapped to sitting up again.

Maybe he should just take his ass to bed.

Deidrick set Volume Three down, fetched his phone from his pocket, and stood.

Heading back to the entry to go down the hall to his bedroom, Deidrick spoke to Smokey. "Come on."

Smokey just looked at him.

"Fine." Shrugging, Deidrick scroll through his contacts as he went to his room. He found Gil and started composing a message about meeting up at Starbucks tomorrow.

While he had only wanted to compose the message, Deidrick was dimly aware of the send sound as he faded out.

∞

Someone was pounding on his front door.

Shit, he'd fallen asleep in his uniform. Again. Luckily, he had only treated regular humans, so the blood had dried before he got home, but still: *shit*. Why'd his mouth taste like whiskey? Had he taken a shot before bed? Hell, had he woken up, taken a shot, and gone back to sleep?

The bottle of Jack and tipped-over shot glass by his bed said yes.

Bone-weary, it felt like he'd just gone to sleep.

Against the side of his head, Smokey stretched and rolled over.

Deidrick said, "Yeah, I don't want to get up, either." But he could use a nice hot shower.

Another round of pounding on his front door.

Since he kept the black-out shades pulled over Diana's glorious morning view, Deidrick consulted the clock. How could it be three? He'd gotten home at —

Must be p.m.

Deidrick sat up to a slump and rubbed his face. Whoever was at his door would just have to leave disappointed.

His cell rang.

Since he always kept his *do not disturb* on, it was either work or family, and family rarely called. As much as he always wanted to let it ring at times like these, it might be an emergency. Not caring to wake his voice up, Deidrick grabbed his phone and swiped to answer.

More of a groan, he asked, "Yeah?"

A gravelly voice asked, "D?"

Deidrick's breath caught in his throat. Adrenaline pumped. It was Mike Stanton, the station chief. Whenever he was called into action on his days off, it was usually the station lieutenant. Never the chief.

Deidrick cleared his throat and sat up straight. "Yes, Chief?"

"Son," Mike said, "Gonna need you to come to the door."

Stuck between asking *what* and *why*, Deidrick's lips pursed in confusion. A rhetorical question popped out. "Are you here?"

Mike said, "Come to the door."

Shit. With the previous day flashing through his head, Deidrick got to his feet.

The booze still in his system rocked him. Rumbling for release, it rolled in his stomach.

He held it down.

Still a little out of it, Deidrick scanned around for a robe before remembering that he was still in uniform. Stumbling from his bedroom, he caught his stride halfway down the hall. He didn't think to check the peephole, and he hadn't locked the door last night.

Deidrick opened the door. The cold and bright afternoon sunlight made him wince.

Sure enough, also looking tired, Mike was there inside the railing on his narrow landing in a brown leather coat, a black knitted cap, and jeans. Next to him was Samantha Kaminski, the woman in charge of the Power League Oversite Committee. She was shorter and wore a black trench coat over a power blue pants suit. Their breaths were puffs of clouds.

They looked him over, too.

Instinctively, Deidrick scanned the street.

No cop cars. No news outlets. Next to his red and white striped First Responder Ford Explorer, there were just the usual few mid-day cars parked at the bottom of their stairs in front of their brownstones.

About to invite them in, Deidrick remembered that Volume Three was open on his computer desk. Christ!

His heart thumped.

He was so screwed.

Before they could ask to come in, Deidrick stepped out onto the narrow landing and lied, "Sorry, the place is a mess." He closed the door behind him.

Apparently too close for Samantha's comfort, she took a small step back to the railing.

Mike shrugged. "I was telling Ms. Kaminski here that you're part of our single-manned first response unit pilot program."

Deidrick nodded. Where was this going?

Mike said, "Since you were first on scene, Ms. Kaminski has some questions for you." Mike turned toward Samantha.

Samantha nodded to Mike and observed Deidrick with a blue-eyed focus that made him want to squirm back inside and lock them out.

Was she a telepath? It was illegal for them to use powers without a warrant. Fuck! Did she have a warrant? Deidrick tried to clear his thoughts, but meditation wasn't his thing. His mind went right to the prayer he had said with the sole purpose of getting the gauze.

She said, "You responded to the Federal Reserve."

That wasn't a question. Deidrick nodded.

She asked, "How'd you get there so quickly?'

Deidrick glanced at Mike.

Mike motioned his head to Samantha.

Deidrick looked at her while pointing to his department-issued Ford. "Instead of being at the firehouse, I roam in my unit."

As though she could've missed it on the way up the steps, Samantha took the time to regard the vehicle.

Deidrick snuck another glance at Mike.

A bit more subtle, Mike motioned his head to Samantha again.

Over Mike's shoulder, the slightly older Mrs. Smith, the next-door neighbor, came out onto her landing with her two German shepherds.

Mrs. Smith waved, "Afternoon, Mr. Jackson."

Deidrick waved back. "Afternoon, Mrs. Smith."

Always one for flirting and small talk, Mrs. Smith said, "Quite the cold snap we're havin'."

"Yeah." Deidrick was pleased that she only chose small talk. "Watch your step." While it looked like Mrs. Smith wanted to keep talking, Deidrick turned his attention and body to Samantha.

She was ready with a question. "And that is your unit? I mean, no one else drives it?"

Shit! Deidrick nodded. "Yeah."

Samantha made a neutral. "Hmph."

Deidrick didn't know what to do with that. Instinctively, he wanted to agree, but there wasn't anything to agree with. Was the pause for him to wonder or worry? Was she combing through his thoughts as they spoke?

She then glanced at his door. "And you live alone?"

Feeling a trap being laid, Deidrick couldn't help but nod as he fought the knot trying to form in his throat. "Well, I have a cat." Crap, he forgot about Diana. "And sometimes my ex comes over."

"Hmm." Her eyes narrowed briefly. "And this ex, what is her name?"

"Oh." Realizing that this whole talk was a way to talk about Diana, Deidrick relaxed a little. "Her name is Diana Winslow." His heartbeat began to mellow.

Samantha glanced at the door again. "And is Ms. Winslow here now?"

"No." That was an easy one, but the single word answer felt too short. He offered, "But she did come by last night to feed my cat."

Samantha looked up and made a come down motion.

When Deidrick also looked up, there were two male Power League heroes in their black SWAT-like tactical uniforms descending, slowly—light flight—from above his building.

Samantha said, "Thing is, one of our trackers says she's here." Samantha's expression changed slightly like she was listening to something that couldn't be heard. "In fact," she added, "Her scent is on you."

Deidrick's heartbeat ramped back up. "What? No." He shook his head. "She only fed my cat because I was working."

Pointing at Deidrick's left pocket, one of the heroes said, "What's in your pocket, Mr. Jackson?"

"Huh?" Deidrick reached for his pocket.

Samantha hustled down the steps.

Mike followed.

A hero dropped right in front of him and clamped on Deidrick's wrist with a grip like a hydraulic press.

Deidrick sucked a sharp sip of air.

"Easy." The hero kept Deidrick's hand out of the pocket. "Let me."

Deidrick didn't protest.

The hero reached in with his other hand and pulled out the fistful of three-inch-long bone tines that Deidrick had taken from Bob's rig. He showed them to Samantha.

Pulling out a tri-folded piece of paper, Samantha said, "This is a warrant, Mr. Jackson. We're going to search your place now."

Fear took a hard hold of Deidrick's throat. He squeaked, "But—"

"No buts." The hero kept a hold of him. "You're staying out here." He pulled Deidrick to the side of the landing that—if Deidrick resisted—would pull his arm out of the socket.

Deidrick went with him.

The second hero finished his easy descent to the landing, opened the door, and went in. A few seconds later, just enough time to get into the living room, he called for Samantha.

Knowing what had been found, Deidrick closed his eyes and prayed for mercy.

∞

On TV shows and movies, they always made psychologist offices look spacious, inviting, and comfortable. Deidrick had always suspected those rooms were dramatized. They were. Well, at least compared to the state-appointed psychologist's office he was now in.

This interior office smelled like a paper storage room and faint second-hand smoke. It might've been twelve-by-twelve at the most. The left wall was lined with mismatched four-drawer filing cabinets, and the desk in the center of the room was one of those wood-laminate-topped, double pedestal black steel jobs; not expensive oak like on TV. The circle clock on the wall mildly ticked seconds as—somewhere out in the halls—a floor buffer whirled.

Deidrick sat quietly as the surprisingly young-looking, but already balding, black-haired doctor looked over his court files. There were three degrees in expensive-looking frames on the wall behind him.

When the heroes had fully searched his place, they had found various stashes that Diana had hidden around his place: in the ceilings, in the walls, even under the floorboards. Deidrick had submitted to telepathic scanning. The combination of him not being involved and his scent not being on the loot had cleared him of aiding and abetting.

However, there were Volumes One, Two, and Three that only had his scent on them.

Because of Deidrick's stellar performance and his ample community service, a judge had ordered the photo albums confiscated and adjudicated Deidrick's would-be sentence. Further, Deidrick had been suspended pending psychiatric evaluation. If the doc could fix him, he could go back to work. Of course, per the sentencing, he'd never be able to ride solo again.

In truth, though, Deidrick didn't think about the future. While he wanted to get back on the job, he wanted to get well more.

So, he waited and prayed to God that—in time—this doctor could help him.

Ω

SECOND-HAND CASKET

Kate Pavelle

A story about an obsession is one thing. But a tale of two obsessions that meet is quite another.

That's one of the things I quite like about Kate Pavelle's story.

Kate writes crime, espionage, thrillers, recent historicals, humor, urban fantasy, and weird fiction. She also writes under another name, Olivette Devaux. That pen name is dedicated to over thirty works of LGBT fiction and hot romance. You can find out more about her at www.olivettedevaux.com.

When I asked her about the origin of "Second-Hand Casket," Kate tells me that it had come after her daughter had introduced her to the OfferUp app, which people use to trade or sell household goods.

"As I browsed it," she says, "I found a 'Luxury casket, lightly used' listing for three thousand dollars. We giggled over it, we sent out some juvenile texts to the owner, and I began to

wonder who would buy a casket like that, and why, and whether it was comfortable."

Naturally, a vampire story was born.

But not just any vampire story.

As I mentioned early, this is a most curious tale of two obsessions.

What happens when an online classified posting introduces a man obsessed with saving money and getting the best deal to an undead man whose vampiric curse leaves him with an uncontrollable compulsion for human blood?

Kate has the eerily delicious answer that you'll sink into in a way that is both compelling and yet surreal, like that soft and comforting silk lining of the coffin you're about to be introduced to.

The casket's lining was smooth and lush and *padded*. Henry pressed its cushioned bed with his hand again and again. He tried to imagine what aunt Rose would've felt like if she could have, indeed, experienced the deluxe memory foam and the careful pleats of slinky, luxurious silk.

Some dead slept better than most of the living, he reflected as he allowed his thoughts to stray to his days on the street. Back then, he'd have slept in this lovely thing and shut the lid on himself just to keep the rain out. His place under the highway overpass had never been as nice as this.

Still stroking the cool, smooth silk, he looked around to reassure himself that those days were now long gone. He had so much.

The inherited two-bedroom fixer-upper, a living room filled with second-hand furniture. A previously loved laptop on a scarred office table in the corner.

A kitchen, one with a working refrigerator, and a stove with two still-good electric burners. The scent of simmering summer vegetable stew reassured him that yes, this was his.

Clothes on his back, too. A bed. A wardrobe.

A sunny patch of soil where he grew food.

And all those things, with the exception of his toothbrush, were second-hand because Henry Holling knew better than to waste good things. Even now that he could buy things all new and shiny, he was loath to throw away what was still good. He wasn't a packrat – no, he resolved not to become a caricature fit for a late-night TV show. But Henry didn't buy new unless hygiene dictated, and he sold or gave away what he didn't need.

His trash pile was enviably green in its smallness.

But now, the casket.

Its carved oak and cast brass fittings gleamed as it stood propped up against his brick fireplace. It represented value. How many hot meals? How many sleeping bags? He was loath to waste anything, as evidenced by a pantry packed with canned beans and tuna fish. He'd sell what he didn't need and hold on to every penny for dear life – as evidenced by the fact that he had only one set of tools in the garage.

He was particularly proud of his restraint when it came to the tools.

But now, the casket. Who in the world would need a second-hand luxury casket?

Now that he had decided to sell it, Henry was possessed with a weird, almost regretful curiosity. The casket was so *pretty*. And Aunt Rose never got to lay down in it. She wanted it – she had even commissioned the lavish carvings of the Green Man and of the moon, with leaves all over the lid, but...oh, never mind.

She wouldn't have begrudged him a little sampling. He wanted to know what he'd been missing two years ago as he'd cowered against a pylon of a bridge. Hoping the wind wouldn't shift, hoping it wouldn't drive the rain his way. Hoping he could catch an hour of sleep.

Slowly, carefully, Henry lowered the casket to the ground. Just as well he didn't have a coffee table, or else it wouldn't have fit. And it was heavy, so heavy it landed with a thump.

He toed off his thrift store sneakers. He paused, then rushed into the kitchen and turned off the burner under his stew.

Just in case.

Tomorrow he would take pictures and post the casket online. Tonight, though – tonight he'd give it a try.

He lowered himself into its space, thankful that his aunt had been a large woman and that he was a slim man. He wiggled down, taking pleasure in the comfortable give of the padding under his shoulder blades. He would've never guessed there was a pillow under the satin, either. His neck was ergonomically supported, and his arms fit by his sides with an inch to spare.

His room looked different from this vantage point. The lamp he had salvaged from a trash day heap one block over shed just enough amber light to make him think of candles. The ceiling needed paint, too, which displeased him. Funny how things looked different if he only changed his position.

But he could hide the time-worn ceiling. The casket did, after all, have a lid. Henry sat up, reached for it, and closed it.

The darkness that surrounded him was soft, soft as silk. His breath bounced back from the silk-lined lid. Maybe a bit more air would be a good investment.

He wiggled his hand into his jeans pocket and pulled out his pocketknife. Then he propped up the lid with it, so only a half-inch gap of light made its way in. Just enough to let in some air, and to remind him that he was still in the land of the living.

Henry closed his eyes and smiled. Aunt Rose would've been pleased.

∞

Lucien Honoré Martel had scant and scattered memories from his living days. The days before he allowed himself to be turned. He didn't know whether his memory loss was the result of the brain tumor he chose to escape, or whether the living past grew diaphanous for his kindred.

He never talked about it. Likewise, he never fessed up to his impoverished state. Hollywood had been selling a lie all along, a lie of glamorous undead lifestyles, of mansions and haunted castles. Never did they mention the slight inconvenience of an undead Millennial, who escaped his illness and his staggering school loan debt only to have to flee the sun every single day.

His bathtub was not the most comfortable place to spend the day. But in Lucien's economy condo, the bathroom didn't have a window, which is why he had chosen this particular apartment.

The bathroom was safe.

Lucien wiggled in his nest of blankets and pillows as he slid down and propped his long, pale legs against the tile wall. After two months in this place, he knew not to kick the water faucet and soak his bedding. Now that had been an idiot move from the get-go.

Moving to Boston was hard on a vampire, but this job was so definitely worth the hassle. He had a boss who took his "skin condition" seriously – no UV, not ever – and that meant his night shift hours were adapted even to the daylight savings time. Even better – disposing of biohazard at a local hospital got him a source of ethical blood.

Ethical blood was the in-thing among the vampiric equivalent of hipsters, much like grass-fed beef or organic kale juice were in the land of the living. Not only did cleaning up after surgeries give him sustenance, but the job also filled him with an odd sense of satisfaction.

Where a horrid mess had once reigned, Lucien had restored tranquil order. And he had blood, lovely fresh blood that often still pulsed with the life energy he needed to continue his existence.

On his nights off, he occasionally ran into Solange or Andre at one of those all-night raves where the latest local band shook the rafters with their beat. Andre and Solange hunted those places for blood donors, from whom they would first ask consent in that "free-range, organic" way of their generation. Lucien had felt the need, too, but not chasing blood was a lot easier to do when he was almost sated after a week of hard work at the hospital.

If only he could sleep somewhere more comfortable.

The cool tile of his bath enclosure spelled relief as he planted his bare feet against it. This, too, shall pass, he reminded himself. High summer was always the hardest time with their too-long days and skimpy nights.

If he could only sleep in a perfectly dark room. If only his landlord wasn't a cheapskate who outfitted the windows with too-thin blinds that had looked adequate at first, but which let a good bit of sun through this time of the year. He could feel the hard tub through all his covers and pillows, much like the princess had felt the pea. Lucien got out, stretched a bit in the darkness of the small room, and picked up his cell phone.

For a man who was unable to shop during the day, internet deliveries made his existence a lot easier. After he killed an hour by ordering a few groceries and a pair of new scrubs, he clicked onto a well-loved little icon.

OfferUp was one of those used item exchange sites, where private sellers were often willing to bring their goods to him directly. It sure beat spending valuable nighttime shopping. Here on *OfferUp*, he often found all kinds of useful things. It was used, true, but Lucien was meticulous in his selections. He chose items that were antique, unique, or practically new. He had discovered early in his three-year vampiric existence how easy it was to get bogged down in clutter.

Daylight spectrum lamps – definitely a big, fat no. Who bought stuff like that anyway?

A plastic container of yarn, knitting needles, and unfinished projects. A flash of a memory made him smile. He used to be like that, back during his mortal days.

A luxury casket.

He paused. There was no way somebody was reusing a coffin, was there? How did a casket end up getting recycled? More importantly, it looked clean, and he could afford it. And it looked big - big enough for him to stretch out. Most modern vampires scoffed at caskets and turned large walk-in closets into safe-rooms with a bed on the floor. Lucien, however, had not found an apartment with the right kind of a walk-in closet just yet. He couldn't afford a house, and he didn't want all the outside upkeep a house entailed.

Surely a casket, a proper daytime resting place of his ancestors, would be more comfortable than this ill-conceived bathtub nest of his?

It sounded like such a good idea at the time until he found the shades would positively leak light.

Hoping to find out more, he opened the chat window.

∞

A chime announced the arrival of yet another *OfferUp* message. Henry grimaced. Had he known that his message of *"A luxury casket, lightly used"* would've brought all the asshole jokers, he would've posted an ad in a regular newspaper. The paper kind, the one which old people read. At least he'd be aiming at his target audience. Why the hell had he advertised a coffin to a bunch of twenty-somethings? And why had he called it "lightly used?"

He knew why. He had, after all, spent the night in it. Its cozy, silent comfort had him out like a light. He'd slept so well he almost didn't make it to work the next day.

Spending the night in the casket, even as a living person, made it used, didn't it? Wasn't there a rule for these things? After all, when he saw a wedding dress posted for sale, the seller had always specified whether it had been used or not. He also noticed that the used ones were bought a lot faster than the ones of brides whose dreams didn't pan out, so…hmm. Maybe his reasoning here had produced some unintended consequences.

He swiped the screen and read the post anyway.

I like your casket. Is it comfortable?

Henry rolled his eyes. Another prankster who'll make stupid vampire jokes, no doubt.

Yes, I tried it out myself, he replied.

Another ding, fast. Ah, a fast punster. Just what he needed.

When you close the lid, does any light leak inside it?

He was tempted to tell the guy off in the rudest possible way. This was Aunt Rose's casket, though. He had to be polite for her sake.

Aunt Rose had been his staunchest supporter. Not once had she tried to talk him out of buying something used and go to a regular store because he was "worth it." No, she only smiled, and complimented him on his excellent and unique taste, and told him what chore to do next in her garden.

Now he had to sell her special casket.

No light, he wrote. *I checked.* His chest filled with pride when he'd thought of asking the other person if they had a garlic allergy, but didn't. It had taken a lot of self-control not to write those few little words.

Do you take PayPal?

Holy shit. Yes, yes, he did take PayPal, and cash, and no checks, because those might bounce, but nobody was going to bring three grand in a paper bag, so PayPal made all the sense in the world.

Yes. When will you pick it up?

A pause. Long beats of stillness passed as Henry sat on his second-hand sofa with his feet propped up on his slightly-used casket. The carvings were digging into his calves, but he didn't care. Three thousand bucks was enough to pay for that coding boot camp and learn something more marketable than making a sandwich.

I wonder whether you could deliver it?

Well. A casket as heavy as that would be a bitch to move. Henry thought hard and fast. How much did that pickup truck rent for? He could ask his neighbor to help and pay him a little. But he really hoped he wouldn't have to.

$300 for delivery. That ought to do it.

Another long pause, another unexpected request.

I'd like to see it first. Can I come over tomorrow night?

Hell yes. He or she could come over no problem. His casket issue might be solved in a way aunt Rose would've approved of after all.

∞

Lucky that Lucien had Tuesday nights off! Thrilled and a little self-satisfied with his find, Lucien pushed his vintage Honda from the communal garage. Despite the balmy summer evening, he wore his black biking leathers. Not a square millimeter of his skin showed, a precaution he had acquired after an unfortunate party when he had to drive home extra fast. His helmet was equally protective, equipped with a tinted UV-blocking visor that covered his eyes.

Better safe than sorry, even if it made him a little hot.

He kicked the bike alive and zoomed down the street. His errands were simple.

Get gas.

See the luxury casket, even though it happened to be slightly used.

Go find a party for a few hours.

Or maybe he'd get ice cream. Even though he didn't need food for sustenance, he loved its cool smoothness and the explosion of flavor on his tongue.

∞

Now that his doorbell rang, Henry looked around his living room, feeling a little self-conscious. He didn't want to come across as too desperate. That would drive the price down, no doubt. Yet he had to juice every penny out this, just like he had to buy his grocery items only when they were on clearance.

His security depended on it. Besides, being cheap was a matter of principle.

The doorbell rang again, and Henry forced himself to quit obsessing whether he looked too rich or too poor, or just too weird.

He opened the door and froze. "The black Power Ranger?"

"Oh, sorry. Sorry!" A male voice, slightly accented, came out a bit muffled from under the helmet as the guy struggled it off his head. His hair stood up in wild spikes, all matted and sweaty. "I'm so used to this thing. I didn't mean to startle you."

Feeling a bit foolish now, Henry looked at him a bit closer. This was the potential buyer for his gorgeous, hand-carved luxury casket. He rocked back and forth a bit, floundering in uncharted waters. "So," he said after a moment, "I'm Henry. Would you like to see the casket?"

"I am Lucien Honoré Martel," his visitor replied, and yes, he did have just a hint of exotic music to his voice. "Yes, may I have a look?"

Henry waved in his direction and turned. "So this was my aunt Rose's casket..." He glanced over his shoulder, but Lucien was still standing on the stoop. "Are you coming in or not?"

"Do you want me to come in?"

"Yes, I want you to come in. It's not like I'll be dragging the coffin to the sidewalk!" Then he paused. "Wait. You're one of those vampire weirdos, right?"

"Yep. How did you guess?" Laugh lines crinkled around Lucien's eyes, but he did step over his threshold and followed him into his living room. He set his helmet in the corner of his sofa. It looked like a shiny, black bowling ball.

"Are you allergic to garlic?" Henry just couldn't help himself. He had to say it. If he didn't say it in a mean way, it was okay, wasn't it?

Lucien filled the space around him with darkness as tiptoed gracefully in his kickass biker boots. A languid, magnetic darkness. Despite the oncoming negotiations, Henry found he was warming up to the fellow. He seemed…nice, in a way Henry had never experienced before.

"May I try it out?" Lucien's voice was a hypnotic purr.

Purr or no purr, the wanna-be-vampire wasn't soiling the satin lining of his luxury casket! "You'd have to get out of that biking gear. The material's kinda delicate. And it's, uh, clean." He hated saying the last part. It could cost him the deal, implying that his customer was unclean in any way, but Lucien only nodded and pulled off his cuffed, black leather gloves.

"No problem whatsoever. Trust me, I understand."

He kicked off his boots, undid the numerous buckles and zippers necessary to get him out of his jacket, and then he slithered out of his leather pants. He folded his garments carefully and set them next to his helmet. Then he turned to Henry and smiled. "May I?"

Henry nodded. The surreal quality of a man having stripped down to his boxer shorts, a black T-shirt, and white tube socks in his living room was compounded by the fact that he was climbing into the casket. As far as Henry could tell, he was doing so as though it was the most natural thing in the world.

∞

So far so good, Lucien thought as he lowered himself to the soft surface. The satin cooled his overheated skin. The owner, Henry, apparently thought he was one of those extreme LARPers or just plain crazy. He didn't give off a scent of prey in the presence of a vampire. He looked anxious, though.

As Lucien made sure the casket was long enough and wide enough, he stretched out his mind toward Henry. If he knew the cause of his anxiety, negotiations would be so much easier. Mind-reading was a fine skill to master, though, and Lucien barely caught a glimpse of Henry's thoughts. A fragment not unlike the ones he had of his own past.

Maybe it was his tumor. Maybe the structural anomaly would never allow him to read minds to his fullest potential.

He sighed.

"What's wrong? It's not soft enough?"

"It's fine," Lucien replied. He inhaled in search of the casket's history. His mind-reading skills refused to materialize, but he had other weapons in his arsenal.

His enhanced scent didn't reveal a recent presence of a human cadaver in the casket which he now occupied. No, it smelled like thyme, and sweat, and dirty socks.

He sniffed again.

It smelled like Henry.

"I'll close it now," Lucien said mildly, and did so. To his satisfaction, not a photon of light got through. The lack of circulation didn't bother him, for he didn't breathe in the true sense of the word anymore.

He pushed the lid up, noted it was heavy, and climbed out.

"So, what do you think?" A needy gleam shone in Henry's eyes now, a need of approval, a need for – and now he saw it – money. The thought almost made him laugh. If everything could be solved by money, Lucien would count himself lucky.

"It's okay, and I'm sure the odor can be removed."

"Odor? Like, it smells bad?" Henry's alarmed expression made him feel a little bad, but also a little predatory. Henry's adrenaline spike had caused his skin to heat, and the heat spike made Lucien acutely aware of his increased blood circulation.

Of his blood – real blood, live blood. Powerful blood that still sang to the sun which Lucien was denied, blood that was fresher and more wholesome than what Lucien could salvage when cleaning an operating room.

"No," Lucien said. Then he got dressed all the way to his boots. Only his helmet and his gloves remained on the sofa. "No, it smells like a living man had used that casket and not a dead one. Tell me, how did it come to pass that a casket could be lightly used?"

∞

Henry didn't want to talk about it, but there was something compelling about Lucien's voice. It tugged on his soul, it drew him out of his shell, and it threatened to spill all his secrets on his second-hand rug. If he wanted to walk away from this with cash in hand, then he better tell the story his way.

Yes, he was controlling this dialogue. No matter if this madman thought he was a vampire, no matter whether he was imagining flashes of red in his dark eyes, Henry knew one thing for certain. He was in control. "My aunt Beth took me in when I ran away from my crazy family," he said. "A bunch of Baptists, women-wearing-long-sleeves, men-in-charge kind of Baptists? A cult. And…well, I didn't fit in with all that, so I ran off and found I had a relative who got away too." He paused, thinking back. Thinking to the grief, and to the knowledge that she would leave him without her counsel and her company. "But she happens to have an estranged husband, my crazy uncle Eddie, and he claimed the body. He wouldn't let me bury her, let alone in this," he said. Then he closed the casket and pointed at the carvings. "She had her own way of being spiritual, I guess. All plants and stuff, and the moon."

"A Wiccan?" Lucien said after the silence stretched too thin.

"She said no. She just liked to do things her own way." Henry looked up at his guest. "Like you do things your own way. Don't think I can't tell!"

Lucien's voice hardened. "How much did you want for this casket?"

Henry straightened up and met his gaze head-on. "Three grand, plus three hundred for delivery." He wasn't backing down on the price, not for anything.

Slowly, Lucien strode to the casket and stroke the carved wood. Then he met Henry's gaze. "Three grand plus three hundred for delivery, plus a bite."

∞

The call of the blood was too strong. Lucien knew he was losing halfway through Henry's story, and as he listened, he kept wondering how to make this bite "ethical blood." He had bitten donors before, and he never forgot a single one.

He had basic sustenance, sure – but that was like humans eating rice and beans. Henry, all excited by the transaction, was a gourmet meal in a fine restaurant.

The "...plus a bite" slipped out unbidden.

Anything could happen now.

Henry could reach for a gun. He probably had more than one, judging from the rest of his belongings. He could try to drive a piece of wood through his heart. He could tell him to go away, 'cause he won't be selling his auntie's casket to some basket case.

To his surprise, Henry laughed. "A bite? Seriously? What's in it for me?"

"You get to sell a luxury casket, lightly used," Lucien said amiably. "And you might enjoy it. All the blood donors do."

"What, you won't just wrestle me down and try to suck my blood dry?" Henry's pitch rose to an alarmed shriek.

"No, of course not. That would be medieval. In this day and age, consent is everything." A troubling thought crossed Lucien's mind. "Wait. You don't think being bitten by a vampire would turn you into one, do you? That's werewolves. Those are entirely different. Sorry." He tried to project calm as best as he could.

"Really?"

"Yes, really. I chose to become a vampire, and it took a whole ritual to make it stick." Hoping he wasn't telling too much, he showed the palms of his hands. "Well?"

"Will it hurt?" Henry was getting into the specifics – an encouraging development.

With two steps, Lucien reached the sofa and stuffed his gloves into his helmet. Then he set it on the floor, sat down, and patted the cushion next to him. "Come have a seat. I'll tell you all about it, and if you decide not to go through with it, we can just lower the price on the casket. No big deal."

As the cushion dipped under Henry's weight, Lucien's heart sang with glee.

If this went well, he would get his own blood donor.

Maybe a friend, too.

As well as a luxury casket, lightly used.

Ω

PINK PILLBOX HAT

Julie Strauss

Take virtually any street you walk down, and you can almost guarantee that the tranquil front of each home that is a façade of some sort of interpretation of "The American Dream." They harbor secrets, hidden family histories, and buried emotions beneath the apparently normal surface.

That neighbor who smiles at you over the backyard fence could very well be masking some dark undisclosed pastime; the one who greets you on their daily morning walk might be going home to a private engagement akin to a mad scientist at work on some covert experiment in a hidden basement lab.

These clandestine operations aren't always known. At least not until something goes down, the police arrive, and all the neighbors say: "He was quiet," or "She was friendly, but usually kept to herself."

Julie Strauss explores such details in "Pink Pillbox Hat," an excerpt from her forthcoming book Everything We

Wanted, *which explores many of a particular neighborhood's hidden secrets and closed-door obsessions.*

Julie is a writer and editor who lives with her husband and four children in Southern California. The author of multiple novels, including Prosecco Heart, Goodbye Yellow Brick Road, *and* Almost Blue, *she is also an avid reader. She hosts the podcast "Best Book Ever," where she engages in impassioned discussions about great reads with a different guest each week. You can learn more about Julie, her podcast, and her writing, at www.juliewroteabook.com.*

When asked about the inspiration for the story, Julie tells me that on one bright Saturday morning, she saw her neighbor step out of his house in casual clothes and tennis shoes. From inside the house, the man's wife had been yelling something indistinguishable. At that, the man turned to her and shouted: "I told you I don't know, goddammit. Leave me the fuck alone!"

After a minute, the wife joined him on the front porch. They loaded their toddler into the stroller and walked away toward the park, with his shout still echoing off the bay windows in the suburban street.

"I come from a family of silent, angry people," Julie says. "Public emotion always shocks me." But it also made her wonder what else went on behind their highly polished front door.

"I've always been fascinated by the hidden workings of suburban neighborhoods. My desk faces our street, and I watch people come and go — not only neighbors, but also visitors, workers, and delivery drivers. I invent stories about all of them. My kids call it "nosy" and "spying," but I prefer to think of it as research."

Julie is especially fascinated by myths that spring up around solitary people; the way children will invent stories and adults will gossip. (Or worse: forget about them entirely.) "The less I see of a person on my street," she says, "the more likely I am to invent wild, complicated inner lives and dramatic plotlines for them."

"Many people assume the elderly shut-in neighbor who never attends parties is shy, feeble, or standoffish. But what if the least noticed person on the block has a secret obsession? What if she knows more about the neighborhood dynamics than anyone else guessed? What if she is being taken advantage of? What if her sadness is so profound it has changed how she sees reality?

That became Jane Hanson's story."

Somehow that was one of the most poignant sights – that immaculate woman, exquisitely dressed and caked in blood.
– Lady Bird Johnson

Jane Hanson lost her Volvo, along with everything else she owned, when the full extent of Howard's criminal activity was exposed. She was surprised at how much she regretted the car's repossession. It had remained in her garage, polished and tuned up, waiting for her in case of emergency, even though she wasn't allowed to drive it for years.

She and her sister Willa were in a car accident in 1957. The Twomey girls were both sixteen at the time, and it was the one month a year they shared an age. 'Irish Twins' was what people called siblings like the two of them back in the old days. Daughters of good Catholic fathers who didn't even wait a year before knocking up their wives again. Everyone expected their parents to become one of those families with seven, eight, nine children, wide smiled and glossy haired. They'd stopped after Jane was born; but whether that was fate or intent, Jane never knew. Her parents were left with only a pair of Irish twins, only eleven months apart. Willa was just slightly taller, just slightly curvier, just slightly prettier, just slightly smarter. Not a lot. Enough to always be proving a point. Jane looked forward to the one month they shared an age after her birthday; it was the one time every year that she and Willa were equal at something.

Willa had been driving them in Daddy's car, a '55 GM with a wraparound windshield that Willa said suited her hairstyle. She wasn't wrong; every time they drove somewhere together, Willa arrived looking tousled and pink-cheeked, as if it was a snowy day in Switzerland, instead of a sticky hot day in Los Angeles. Jane, however, always arrived wrinkled, mussed, with splotchy skin and dry, itchy eyes. No matter how much she adjusted the seat or rolled the windows, she couldn't achieve the natural elegance her older sister commanded.

Not that it mattered. Jane was grateful to be near Willa, even if it was just to fade away in her presence. Willa had started smoking, a habit Daddy didn't know about. Jane would never tell. It only made her prettier, in Jane's eyes. Long streams of smoke issued out of Willa's mouth as she drove, trailing out behind her and mimicking the long scarf she wore around her neck. Willa carefully wiped out the car's ashtray as soon as they got home, so Daddy wouldn't find out.

It was because of the smoking that they crashed the car. More precisely, Willa crashed, though she blamed Jane for it. She'd asked Jane to hold the wheel while she lit a cig. That was the type of thing Willa said – *lit a cig*. Jane had never driven before – never sat on Daddy's lap and steered the way Willa had been allowed to do.

Daddy said Jane was too squirrely and couldn't concentrate, and cars were too dangerous.

Jane froze when Willa took her hands off the wheel and reached into her pocketbook. She had a moment to observe a thought that took a long time to form: her sister wanted to kill both of them. Willa hadn't bothered taking her foot off the gas, and when Jane saw that the car was veering toward a tree on the right side of the road, she reached over and shoved the steering wheel to the left. In her panic, she overcorrected, barreling them straight into a car in the oncoming lane.

Time stopped as the other car approached, yet it also seemed to move incredibly quickly. She wanted to open her mouth to warn Willa, but her jaw was too heavy to speak, even as her brain was screaming. The squeal of the other car's tires repeated in her memory, though she didn't recall hearing them until later. She'd marveled, even as it happened, at the speed and the slowness. She listened to the impact before she could open her mouth to say, "Oh!"

Much later in life, she heard that was how it felt to fall in love – very slowly and then all at once. The comparison nauseated her. She couldn't imagine anyone wanting that feeling, or promising their future to someone else because of it. Neither of the girls had been seriously hurt in the accident, though Willa's ankle had broken pretty badly. For the rest of her life, she had the slightest limp.

The girls, like all young ladies of their age, were enamored with Jackie Kennedy. Daddy was born in Brookline and still considered Boston his real home, though he wound up in California. "A real lady," he called Jackie. "That's what a *real* lady looks like." Mother, though she looked nothing like Jackie, nodded in agreement. They all agreed with him. That's what a woman did in the Twomey house.

"She didn't love him," her sister had confided after they watched John's funeral. It was the only time they had seen Daddy cry, watching Jackie stone-faced under that shimmering black veil. "What kind of woman doesn't cry at her own husband's funeral?"

Willa could pull off all of Jackie Kennedy's looks – the capri pants, the smart suits, the large glasses. If she'd ever gotten her hands on a tailored pink wool boucle suit like the one Jackie wore in Dallas, Willa would have looked even better than Jackie did. Willa walked in grace, their mother used to always say. Jane just walked. Though they looked similar, Jane felt coarse and ungainly next to her sister. Too plump and clumsy. Oafish.

Now, at the age of 72, Jane was thin as a rail. She didn't avoid mirrors like other women her age did; in fact, she was fascinated by them. Strange, really, how aging worked. How her loose, crepey skin dripped down her bony legs, and her stomach had gone concave. She had moved through her life quickly, and now it was slowly melting away. And yet she had so much to grasp on to.

For one thing, she had a pink suit. Most news stories called it a pale pink suit, but Jackie had always called it raspberry. Few women could get away with a color like raspberry, and it was no small feat to find the right shade of fabric. Jane wore hers in her darkened house when all of the drapes were closed, and she could stare at herself in the narrow bedroom mirror. The sharp collar jutted out to her shoulders, etched with delicate quilt stitches to soften the angles. The navy piping made the raspberry less cloying, as did the squared-off pockets and the neat rows of gold buttons lined up in military formation. Jane's dress was identical to Jackie's, down to the last tiny stitch. She had hand sewn the dress many years ago when she still had the eyesight for that kind of precision.

Jane had two of them, in fact. Indistinguishable from each other, except the second one had been carefully daubed with red paint on the skirt, bodice, and gloves. It was, as far as Jane could tell, an accurate match. She'd paid very close attention to the splatter pattern. She'd saved hundreds of magazines, books, and newspaper clippings. She knew the position of every drop of John's blood. How it caked thickly on Jackie's gloves.

The pink suit draped loosely on Jane now. She missed the way her hips used to press against the fabric, giving the illusion of a tiny waist. Now her body was a rectangle, with no hips to speak of. Wooden. But the matching pillbox hat, when she arranged her silver hair right, still looked pretty and feminine, showing off her slate-grey eyes.

On the days Jane wore her suit – the clean one, not the stained one – she kept the windows closed so no one caught a glimpse of her. Most of her neighbors had added giant bay windows to their perfectly serviceable ranch-style houses, as if they were looking out over Cape Cod instead of a common California suburb. They spoke of this feature as a benefit, as if their existences were so compelling that they weren't lived unless they were on view. That was the world today. Everyone needed to be seen, and Jane's closed house looked old fashioned in comparison. But Jane knew the truth. Living rooms were the least exciting part of any house. That was where you entertained the guests you didn't care about. That was where you sat and made small talk with home health care workers and relatives you hadn't spoken to in years. Only real family was invited into the intimate corners of a house. The kitchen or the bedroom.

But her neighbors here didn't understand that. They lived their lives on full display and thought she was strange for minding her own business. As if she couldn't hear what they called her. The Witch of Jacaranda Terrace, she'd heard them say. The Crazy Cat Lady, which was unfair as she only had one cat and didn't even particularly care for it. She saw children intentionally steer their bikes to the other side of the street, and teens walk faster when they crossed her property. Adults peered curiously, boldly, unashamed of their own insolence.

Jane watched them back. Odd how they didn't know it. They gossiped about her, assuming she didn't listen or was too feeble to pay any attention. All the while, she saw everything. The only difference was that she knew how to stand at the side of her window, in a perfect spot to see everyone without them seeing her. She watched it all. The parties, the children playing, the women running across the street to borrow and lend and take and give. She watched the couples move in and out of each other's orbits in a perfect quadrille, always maintaining balance even when partners changed. She knew who snuck out at night, who gazed at other people's husbands, and who should have never gotten married in the first place. She wondered why no one ever noticed that falling out of love was also very slow and then fast. It always started with an annoying habit or a single unkind remark. He only had to stray once, and suddenly you couldn't bear the sight of him anymore.

Her husband Carl Hanson had died of cirrhosis of the liver many years before. They'd only been married for seven years when Carl died. Not even as long as John and Jackie, who had ten years together. To be fair, the Kennedys had two children who lived, so they deserved a little more time. But who could say if Jane and Carl wouldn't have had children if they'd been given more time? It was impossible to know.

Most of the current residents of Jacaranda Terrace had never even met Carl. They had all moved in once people of her generation started dying, moving to condos in Palm Springs, or shuffling around in assisted living. Cirrhosis was unusual in a man so young, but it didn't surprise Jane at all. It happened very slowly, then all at once. During his final days, she would gaze out the hospital window and marvel at the people walking down the street to the store as if nothing at all were different. She sat in that chair next to his bed for what felt like an eternity, and within seconds, he was gone. She lost track of minutes and hours and days. It left her breathless.

Carl's last words had been about Willa. "Where is she?" He asked. "Willa. *Willaaaaaa.*" He was jumbling his words by that point. Had stopped making sense years ago, truth be told, but by the end, in the hospital, it was all a mess. The attending nurse looked at Jane with big, sympathetic eyes and said that terminal patients often got their loved ones' names confused. At his funeral, Willa sobbed as if she'd lost a limb, while her own husband Howard looked stunned next to her.

Jane did not shed a single tear.

Willa was the next to die. It was cancer that took her. A particularly unfair death, in retrospect. Willa's hair might have stayed jet black forever, had she lived that long. Instead, she only lived to the age of 64 and died without any hair at all. She died enraged by the indignity of the pale, jagged dome of her delicate head. Willa got much more time with Howard than Jane got with Carl. Decades more. Another injustice.

Howard visited Jane about once a week after they were both widowed. He went over her bills and checked that her refrigerator was stocked and made small talk for a few minutes. Then he went to check her computer. He brought files in a briefcase, scanned them on her scanner, and e-mailed them to someone – she never figured out to whom – and then put things back in a particular order. She didn't quite understand why he wouldn't just retire like everyone else. Or why he used her computer when he had a better one at his house. He used to work in finance; Jane could hardly believe the numbers were that compelling that he needed to continue filling his life with them. Constant columns of them, adding, subtracting, analyzing. It all made Jane's eyes cross, but when she asked him about his work, he told her he was taking care of her retirement.

The internet had its uses, even for old ladies. Jane was not completely oblivious. She found Jackie on the internet. She found pictures of bullets and frame 313 of the Zapruder film. She went down wormholes of conspiracy and counter-conspiracy theories and debunkers and policy analysis and style observations. She studied John's autopsy photos. After all, they were right there for anyone to see. It occurred to Jane that she was closer to John than Jackie had ever been. She had seen inside his head, into the crevices of his brain. For hours she had studied the curves where his thoughts had once formed and the scorched path that bullet took through them. Jackie had only ever known his body.

She would never know his final words.

People argued about whether the Kennedys were great successes or colossal failures. Jane once read that 61% of Americans believed that silly little Communist did not act alone when he shot John. But she watched that percentage change throughout the years, depending on what was going on in the country. People needed a conspiracy theory about his murder because if they ever figured out the whole truth, John would be dead forever. It was too much to bear. Titans cannot be taken down by nobodies. Goliath's followers must have felt the same way.

Women grieve, men replace. Her mother used to say that. She'd thought maybe Howard would remarry after Willa died. Even now, at the age of 75, it was not that uncommon for men like him to find another woman immediately. He was still handsome, in an average way. But Howard remained fixed in his place in life. He stayed in the house he used to share with Willa. He came to Jane's for weekly check-ins and holidays. It was as if he'd been glued down in a scrapbook. He was always a nice man, though. He was older than her by just a bit, but he treated her like a frail old lady who didn't understand things. He rolled his eyes and sighed at her if she mentioned Jack or Jackie.

Once, Howard showed up when she had the pink wool suit on – the one without the red paint stains – and studied her for a long time. She thought about acknowledging the fact of the dress. But then she decided to sit across from him on the couch and just chat as if it were a normal outfit to wear inside her house when it was ninety degrees outside. She tried to ask Howard that day if their spouses even mattered anymore. Did it diminish a person to find something out about them after they died? Did it change who they were when they lived? Oughtn't they, Jane and Howard, remember Carl and Willa based on what they had experienced when they were alive together? Or should the opinions of those who are left change as their understanding changed? These were the questions Jane wrestled with.

"I'm just tired of this," he said. "The talk of constant affairs."

"Carl and Willa had more than one affair?" Jane asked, too surprised to feel hurt.

Howard looked at her for a long time before replying.

"We were talking about John Kennedy," he said. "We've been talking about John Kennedy all afternoon, Jane."

"My mistake."

"All these affairs that he had," Howard continued, reassured that she was always a few steps behind him. "John and Robert and Martin, and all of them. Men we used to admire and wanted to know and wanted to be. Now we know too much, and they aren't any good anymore." He put his hand over hers. "The second

Oswald fired that gun, everything started to go downhill."

Sometimes, when Howard checked her mail, he pulled some envelopes out and slipped them into his pocket to bring home with him. Jane always saw this, though she pretended not to. He could get mail here; she didn't really care. He could take home whatever he needed to take home, back to Willa's house.

Jane made a separate pillbox hat to go with the stained dress, though one would most likely have been enough. As far as Jane could see, there were no bloodstains on Jackie's hat. She'd once read that when Jackie pulled her own hat off her head – no one was quite sure exactly when she did it – the hat had wound up in the possession of her personal secretary. The secretary found a hank of black hair dangling from the attached hairpins. Jackie had yanked it out so hard, she forgot what pain meant.

For her version, Jane yanked the hairs from her own sister's head. Willa had only just been diagnosed. It was a perfect match.

The last time Jane wore the stained dress was when the FBI showed up at her house. Rude, ungainly men, overloaded with bulky suits and not so well-hidden body armor.

They filed all over her house like silly little Communists, and they tore everything apart while she waited silently. Things that had happened on her computer, they told her, and a lot of people were out of money, including her. The agents asked her about lawyers, about embezzlement, about where she got money for her fancy clothes. For a horrifying moment, she wondered if studying autopsy photos on the internet was illegal. It was a shocking thing to do, and the memory of the hours she had spent looking at John's corpse shamed her.

John was another woman's husband, after all.

They had burst in – she would never have opened her door to them in either dress, but especially not this one. No one else had ever seen this dress. They stared at her in confusion, their gazes traveling up and down the nubby pink fabric, at first embarrassed to meet her eyes. The moment moved both too fast and too slow for her to explain the situation, to fix things. The older agents – none as old as her, of course – seemed to suddenly understand something about Jane.

She needed help. She didn't know who else to call except for Howard, and he was already in custody, according to the agent who seemed to take pity on her.

"We're going to get you some help, okay, Mrs. Hanson? We've got social services on their way over. We're going to get you some help." She saw him put his hand over his mouth and speak into his phone in a low voice.

"Twomey," she said. She stood up and pulled off the pink pillbox hat and flung it across the room. "My name is Jane Twomey." She followed the men out of her house and was escorted to the back of a shiny black car. She fingered a tiny bald spot on her head as she gazed out the window.

Ω

FOR LOVE OF RONALD STURGIS

Michael Kingswood

There is something so captivating and intriguing about celebrity.

Perhaps because the media presents these seemingly larger-than-life people to us in generous regular helpings, we can sometimes feel as if we personally know them.

Of course, for some, that perceived intimacy can go beyond the familiar, beyond a simple passion, and into an all-consuming infatuation.

The intensity, when looked at by others, can be inexplicable and curious.

Julie Strauss revealed that type of fascination with JFK held by an elderly lady in the story we just finished. Michael Kingswood explores an older woman's celebrity obsession, but in her case it's with a movie star rather than a political icon.

Michael mostly writes science fiction and fantasy and is best known for The Pericles Conspiracy, *an alien first contact novel, and the* Glimmer Vale Chronicles, *a sword and sorcery fantasy series. He also, as evidenced in the tale you're about the read, writes contemporary fiction. He has previously appeared in the* Fiction River: Spies *Anthology, and stars in a weekly podcast and YouTube/BitChute channel,* Story Time with Michael Kingswood, *where he reads excerpts from his work. You can find him at* www.michaelkingswood.com.

Michael said that there wasn't any specific inspiration for the writing of this story. He said that, while thinking about this anthology concept, he considered that a lot of people have favorite screen actors. Some take that fannish affection past the line into obsession.

"I then wondered," he says, "what if there was a good reason for that obsession, and the story flowed from there."

A man of above-medium height, with broad shoulders and a gut that pressed the front of his white uniform shirt noticeably outward, held the door to Mother's new home open. He smiled broadly, his white teeth gleaming beneath the bushy black mustache above his lips, and his brown eyes warmly welcoming.

"Welcome home, Grace," he said.

His name was Hank, and he had introduced himself as the supervising nurse on Mother's wing. And though he seemed kind and pleasant, Jenny could not help resenting him a bit.

The right breast of his uniform shirt had the name of this place: *Pleasant Springs*. And the grounds certainly lived up to the name. Rose bushes lining the flagstone walkway from the drive to the entrance with its Romanesque pillars, pure white paint, and wide, welcoming double doors leading into a warmly furnished interior. Plush red carpet in the corridors. Peaceful landscape paintings on the walls and softly glowing natural-light LEDs in the overheads.

But on a day like today, without a cloud in the late-spring sky and the scent of pollen carried on the same breeze that seemed alive with birdsong of all kinds, it seemed almost blasphemy to be bringing Mother here.

This was a place of ending, for all the designers and staff tried to put a comfortable face on it, and Jenny couldn't square that with the flourishing life outside its walls.

"Thank you, Hank," Mother said, and she smiled a cheerfully warm grin at him.

She had insisted on moving in here, despite Jenny's protests, and had dressed up for the occasion, donning her favorite dress: red with white flower petals embroidered at the neck, cinched with a white cloth belt. And though she couldn't move very fast with her hip as it was, she had set a new record for cane-assisted speed walking from the minivan to her new rooms.

Mother turned her smile toward Jenny. "Let's see what we have, dear," she said, and the hand that had been resting on Jenny's arm during their walk into the complex gave a strong but gentle squeeze, as though Mother were trying to comfort her.

Jenny had not seen the room before. Mother had made the arrangements herself as if she had known Jenny would object and had wanted to lay it all out to pre-empt her arguments ahead of time. She could be shrewd that way when she wanted to be.

It was actually not too bad. The door opened into a sitting room with a matching blue-upholstered love seat and reclining chair positioned around a round coffee table that looked to be made from stained oak. A TV set hung from the wall opposite the seating, between two bookshelves stained to match the coffee table. Further back was a little kitchenette with a breakfast table of the same coloring. From there, the rooms bent to the right into the sleeping area, where a full-sized bed that was obviously a more comfortable version of an adjustable hospital bed sat against the far wall, framed by a pair of matching oak nightstands. Monitoring panels, dark at the moment, hung on the wall above the head of the bed, and a small stuffed chair sat in the corner, the way it would in a hospital. Opposite that stuffed chair was the door to the bathroom. It was closed, but no doubt the bathroom was spacious and equiped with assistance devices just like in a hospital.

The place was painted a pinkish beige that felt warm, and there was the faint scent of rosemary in the air.

Mother's bags and a trio of boxes sat on the bed. Steve, tall and handsome as he had been on the day Jenny married him fifteen years ago, was bent over one of the boxes. He had on jeans and a navy blue t-shirt and had come over ahead of them with Mother's things to get a head start hanging up her pictures on the walls and stocking the bookshelves with her books. When they entered, and Jenny looked around, he looked up at her and grinned, his blue eyes flashing in the lamplight.

"Glad you made it," Steve said, and Mother chuckled softly.

"Of course we did. Isn't it nice, Jenny?"

Jenny shrugged but had to concede it was much better than she feared it would be.

Steve pulled a group of framed pictures out of the box and placed them on the nightstand closest to the stuffed chair. Jenny and Steve on their wedding day. Mother and Father on theirs. Ben and Kara as babies, and another with them from just last year. All the people that Mother loved most. Except -

"You didn't forget Ronald, did you Steve?" Mother asked. She had been watching him place the pictures, and her voice carried a sudden intonation of worry.

Hank stepped up next to Mother, drawn by her tone of voice, but before he could say anything, Steve chuckled and shook his head briskly.

"I know better than that." He stepped back to the box and pulled out another picture. This one was a black and white picture of a young man in his late 20s or early 30s. He was dressed in a suit and fedora like a person from the 1930s and wore a crooked grin that spoke of a roguish nature.

"That your husband?" Hank said, and Mother quickly shook her head.

Jenny laughed. "That's Ron Sturgis, from when he starred in *The Long Goodbye*." She looked over at Hank and raised an eyebrow. "Mother's had a crush on him as long as I can remember."

"Posh," Mother said. "He's a wonderful actor and a fine gentleman."

Jenny couldn't help but tease. "And Mother's secret love."

Mother's cheeks went crimson, and she looked away, feigning embarrassment. But Jenny knew better; they had played this game many a time in the past.

"I remember when they remade that movie," Hank said, nodding slowly. "I love Philip Marlowe, but," he gave Mother an apologetic look, "I didn't care for it much. Hard to outdo Bogart."

Mother sniffed.

Jenny gave Mother's shoulder a gentle squeeze. "Well, I grew up loving it," she said, and Mother's expression, which had begun to turn cross, brightened again.

"Come on, Mom. Let's get you unpacked."

∞

Jenny helped Mother take off her jacket, then turned to hang it up in her little closet.

"My, but that was a lovely party," Mother said, her tone almost whimsical as she maneuvered herself over toward the reclining chair in her sitting room. "I cannot believe how big Ben has grown."

Jenny turned back from the closet and nodded. She hated to admit it—it made her sound like an old fogey—but she constantly found herself astonished at how quickly he and his sister were growing. It seemed just yesterday she could practically hold him entirely in the palm of her hand. Today, he had turned twelve and stood nearly to her shoulder.

His birthday party had been loud and boisterous, an unavoidable combination when you bring a dozen boys that age together in a single space, and it had taken two full weeks of preparation and work to put together. But the joy on the boys' faces made it all worth it.

She sighed contentedly. "Soon he'll be wanting to take girls out on dates."

Mother shook her head with a knowing smile. "He won't have any trouble getting them to say yes, handsome as he is." She paused for a couple breaths, then added, "I think he looks a bit like Ronald. Don't you?"

Jenny's mirth faded a bit, and she looked sidelong at the old picture of the actor on Mother's nightstand. He was much older in that picture than Ben was now. And of course, Ron was even older now, two and a half decades later. But...she pursed her lips, then shook her head. "No."

Mother leaned back in her chair and half-shrugged, half-spread her hands almost in defense. "Well, I could be mistaken, I suppose." Her grin returned, self-deprecating this time. "Old woman can't keep her best men apart, I guess."

She giggled in amusement at herself, and Jenny found herself joining in.

∞

Christmas came and went, then Jenny saw a news article that she knew would set Mother to quivering with anticipation. She picked up the phone and called.

Mother answered on the second ring. "Hello, Jenny. Did you hear?"

Jenny shook her head in amusement. Mother was nothing if not predictable. But she decided to let her have her moment. "No, what?"

"Ronald got nominated for Best Actor! Isn't that wonderful? All these years and he finally gets the recognition he's due."

She couldn't help but laugh. Predictable, indeed. Mother sounded almost as proud as she had when Jenny graduated from college.

For a second, and not for the first time, Jenny felt a flash of jealousy, but she shoved that aside. She had no illusions about Mother's affection, and who was she to stomp on her little crush, or whatever it was?

"You'll come over to watch the Oscars with me, won't you?"

Jenny winced. She hated awards shows.

"Of course, Mom. Love to."

"Oh, good. We'll have so much fun."

∞

Ronald won, of course. And Mother let everyone know about it.

∞

The phone call came in the wee hours of the morning, and it took a moment for Jenny to get her brain to work enough to answer it.

The voice on the other end of the line jerked her to full wakefulness. She sat bolt upright, causing Steve, who had just begun to drift back off again, to come fully awake as well. She thanked the caller and hung up, and Steve pushed himself up onto his elbows.

"What is it?"

"Mom's had an episode."

"What does that mean?"

She shook her head and pushed herself out of bed, then began getting dressed. "Something medical I couldn't understand. I'm going. Let you know if you need to bring the kids over." He met her eyes, and she saw the same dread she felt mirrored in them. He nodded and reached out to take her hand.

"I'm sure it'll be fine."

"Hope so."

Jenny made record time getting to Pleasant Springs. She hurried through the entrance and down the hall toward Mother's rooms. The night nurse supervisor, Karen, was waiting outside her door, a smile that Jenny imagined was supposed to be reassuring on her face.

"The doctor just left," Karen said. "He was able to rule out a heart attack, but now we're not sure exactly what happened. He's ordered tests, and we should know more in a few hours once we get the results." Her professional comfort smile widened a bit. "But for now, Grace is stable and doing fine. She scolded us for making a fuss, actually."

Jenny shook her head. That sounded like Mother, all right. "Is she awake?"

Karen nodded. "Go on in."

The lights in Mother's room were out except those above her bed. Under that illumination, she looked haggard. She wore her pink pajamas and was sitting upright, pillows shoved behind her back to give her support, a paperback in her hands. There were dark spots beneath her eyes, and her hair was disheveled. But then, it was getting on toward four in the morning. What did Jenny expect, for her to be all done up for a ball?

Mother looked up as Jenny approached and smiled tiredly at her. "Jenny dear, you didn't need to come all the way in here. It was nothing. Just a silly spell."

Jenny moved over to the stuffed chair in the corner and maneuvered it closer to the bedside, then sat down. She looked at Mother and did her best to put on the scolding expression that had used to work so well on her children. "It was more than that, and you know it." Mother gathered herself as though to retort, and Jenny continued on quickly, to diffuse the argument before it really got started. "Besides, I wanted to make sure you were alright." She reached out and took Mother's hand in hers and gave it a gentle squeeze.

Mother didn't speak for a few seconds, then she let the book drop onto her lap and patted Jenny's hand gently.

Silence reigned for a while, and they sat there just looking at each other. Then Jenny caught sight of the book's title, and she couldn't help but roll her eyes. "Ronald Sturgis' biography? You didn't know all there is to know about him already?"

Mother flushed and glanced down at the book on her lap, then shrugged. But she didn't answer. She kept her gaze on the book for a while, and finally, she drew a deep breath. When she spoke, it was softly, barely above a whisper.

"There's something I never told you, Jenny. A mistake I made a long time ago."

Suddenly it all made sense: Mother's obsessive focus on Ronald Sturgis, the way she seemed to long for news of him. "You had an affair with him."

And, strangely enough, Jenny couldn't be angry at her. It was a betrayal of the worst kind. But it had obviously happened a long time ago, and there had been so much good between Mother, her father, and the rest of the family since then. A one-time fling could be forgiven, or even looked back on with amusement over the span of decades.

But Mother recoiled as though smacked, and her hand left Jenny's. She turned to look Jenny straight on, and there was righteous anger in her eyes. "How dare you even suggest such a thing! I loved your fath—"

She stopped mid-word, and the anger faded from her face, replaced by puzzlement, followed by terrified realization. "Jenny," she breathed, and then her body began shaking. She flopped back onto the pillows, the tremors making her body rigid even as her eyes went wide.

Jenny sat frozen for a moment, unsure what to do as her stomach went to ice. Then Mother coughed out a groan and arched backward, and Jenny sprang into action. She leaped out of her seat and punched the emergency nurse call button built into the wall above Mother's bed. Then she placed her hands on Mother's shoulders and tried to still her.

"Easy, Mom," she said, knowing somewhere in her mind that the words were useless, "help is coming."

Mother continued to shake, but her eyes were steady, and they locked onto Jenny's. The green of her irises contracted, then expanded, as though she was trying to say something through Morse code.

Then strong hands were on Jenny's shoulders, and she was flung away.

She staggered backward, colliding with the stuffed chair, and had to grab onto it to avoid going over.

Orderlies and nurses, Janet among them, swarmed Mother's bed. Janet shouted orders, and one of the others flipped a series of switches, turning on the monitors above Mother's bed.

Another orderly, a thin young man, turned away from the bed and opened a storage cabinet near the bathroom door. He turned back and pulled two paddles out of the package he had retrieved. The other assistants backed away, and the young man placed the paddles on Mother's chest. An electronic beep rang out, then Mother jerked violently. The medical personnel closed back in.

A steady tone rang out, and above Mother's head, one of the monitors displayed a line that just a few moments earlier had been jerky. Now it was straight, not varying in the slightest.

Karen's shoulders slumped, and Jenny felt her world dropping away beneath her feet.

∞

The doctors gave a medical-sounding explanation for the cause of Mother's death, but it was lost on Jenny. For three days afterward, she sat in stunned grief, unable to come to terms with what happened.

It wasn't just that Mother was gone. She had been preparing for that since before Mother checked into the nursing home.

No, what had her back on her heels was their interchange in the moments before Mother passed.

The look on Mother's face when Jenny made the accusation. She hadn't meant it as one, but Mother clearly had taken it that way. And then the desperate way she had stared at Jenny in her last moments, as though she had been trying to deny what had happened.

Because Jenny had no doubt about the fact that Mother had a relationship with Ronald Sturgis.

She just wished she'd had time to talk it through with Mother better. As it was, she had passed away presuming that Jenny thought ill of her for it. And had she come to the realization when Dad was still alive, maybe Jenny would have. But now, with him six years gone…she couldn't bring herself to judge Mother.

But now it was too late. She would never be able to have the heart to heart that would clear the air between them.

And it crushed Jenny's soul to realize that.

She passed through the funeral in a daze, going through the motions of courtesy to the multitude who came to pay their respects but not really registering anything.

A week passed, and she was only just beginning to come through her funk when Steve approached her in their living room. He had an old cardboard box in his hands and a gently hopeful look on his face.

"Jenny," he said. "I came across this as I was sorting through your mom's things." He paused, cleared his throat, and bent over to set the box down on their metal-and-glass coffee table. "You probably want to look through it."

Jenny looked at the box curiously, and only after a few seconds did she realize that he was waiting on a response from her. She looked up at him and flashed a smile his way. "Thanks," she said.

He reached out and gave her shoulder a squeeze. "I'll get started on dinner for the kids. Let me know if you want to talk later." Then he walked away through the doorway leading back to the kitchen.

She scooted forward on the couch and pulled the box to the edge of the coffee table, then slowly opened the box and looked within.

Shocker, the contents were all about Ronald Sturgis. Newspaper clippings and magazine articles going back to when Jenny was a kid, announcing his various movies and shows. Critical reviews of his performances. Gossip columns about his two marriages, and the goings-on of his two daughters' lives. On and on the clippings went, in roughly reverse-chronological order: the further down in the box, the older the records.

Mother could probably have written at least as detailed a biography as the one she had been reading.

Not that it would ever have been published. Mother was not—

At the bottom of the box, Jenny came to an old manila envelope, the kind that was fastened shut with a built-in waxy string that could be wrapped around a little button on the envelope's main body.

What was this?

She lifted it out and, carefully, unwound the string, opened the flap, and removed the envelope's contents.

The pages were old, yellowing. They had obviously been written on a typewriter, not printed on a modern computer printer. First was an official-looking letter on letterhead from a company Jenny didn't recognize. She glanced at it, then flipped to the next page.

It was a certificate of live birth from Dane County, Wisconsin. The baby was an unnamed male, born March 25th. No father listed. The mother's name had been crossed out.

Below the certificate of live birth, another official form. Documentation of consent for blind adoption. The birth mother had given up all rights to ever see the baby again. It was issued to and signed by…

Grace Cooper.

That was Mother's maiden name.

A shiver ran down Jenny's spine, and she felt her eyes widen. What was this?

She flipped back to the cover letter and looked at the company letterhead more closely. Preston Smith Detective Agency. It was dated almost thirty years ago. Jenny's eyes lowered to the text of the letter.

"Dear Mrs. Horowitz. Enclosed please find the results of the investigation you retained us to conduct. Though most records have been expunged, we have high confidence that your son was adopted by-- "

Jenny dropped the letter and flipped to the last page that had been enclosed in the envelope. It consisted of another record, this one detailing the adoption of a male baby. The adopting parents were...Jenny swallowed, then read it aloud.

"Rene and Stacy Henderson." The names rang a bell in Jenny's mind, and it all came together. Statistics that she had heard countless times before came back up from the alcoves of her mind before she read them on the rest of the sheet.

His real name was Matthew Henderson. He had been born on March 25th, one week and eighteen years before Jenny had been, in Madison, Wisconsin, where Mother had grown and lived before she met Father.

Mother hadn't had an affair with Ronald Sturgis.

He was her son.

At some point, she must have wondered what had happened to the child she had given up for adoption when she was little more than a child herself and hired the detectives to find him. And ever since, she had followed his life and career, taken joy in his exploits, and shared the pain of his disappointments from afar, the only way she could.

Jenny's cheeks were wet with tears. She wiped them away with the back of her hand and sniffed. Her thoughts went back to that first day she had brought Mother to Pleasant Springs, and what she had said to Hank.

Ronald really had been Mother's secret love, but it was a far deeper love than Jenny, in her teasing, could ever have known.

Jenny slipped the documents back into their envelope and covered them with the clippings that detailed Ronald Sturgis' public life. She closed the box and walked upstairs to hers and Steve's bedroom. She slid it into a space in the back corner of their closet, then went back downstairs to join him in making dinner.

As she went, she redoubled her resolved to love her kids and Steve the way Mother had loved her...and Ronald.

It was the best tribute she could think to give.

Ω

EVERYTHING GOT COLDER

A Bryant Street Story

Dean Wesley Smith

"Subdivisions scare me to death," Dean Wesley Smith tells me when I ask about the eighty or so Bryant Street Stories he has written. *"It's my series of stories coming from my hate and fear of subdivisions."*

Considered one of the most prolific writers working in modern fiction, New York Times and USA Today bestselling writer Dean Wesley Smith has published well over two hundred novels in forty years, hundreds upon hundreds of stories, and has over twenty-three million copies of his books in print.

In addition to the numerous books and series he has penned in his own universes, including the time travel Thunder Mountain novels set in the old west, the galaxy-spanning Seeders Universe series, the cold case mystery series, Cold Poker Gang series, and the superhero series starring Poker Boy, Smith has written a few dozen Star Trek novels, the only *two original* Men in Black *novels, Spider-Man and X-Men novels, not to mention the dozen or more pen names he has written for comic books and movie novelizations.*

Dean writes, co-edits, and publishes with his wife Kristine Kathryn Rusch, and the two are executive editors in the Fiction River *anthology series from WMG Publishing. Smith took over the acclaimed editorship of Pulphouse Publishing in 2018. You can find out more about Dean and the multitude of writing, editing, and publishing projects he is involved in at www.deanwesleysmith.com.*

When I mentioned to Dean that this story reminded me of some parts of my favorite novel, George R. Stewart's Earth Abides, *he informed me that it was also one of his all-time favorite books and that he has a first hardcover edition of it on his bookshelf in Nevada.*

I shouldn't have been surprised. Because Dean is one of the most avid collectors of pulp fiction, classic science fiction, and pop culture speculative memorabilia I have ever known. We have spent hours together when I have marveled in the vast depths and richness of his collections.

But this story is not about obsessive collecting, despite the main character, Jason, engaging in that behavior.

This is a story that speaks of the overwhelming power of nostalgia; and how it can over-ride all other drives in a person's life.

Dean tells me that the story was originally written in 2018 when he took part in an ongoing Half-Title writing challenge.

The challenge is where Dean would go to one of the thousands of his digest magazines from his collection, titles such as Galaxy, F&SF, Hitchcocks, Ellery Queen, Asimovs, *and others, and would write down half of a title from the stories published there that seemed interesting. He would* collect them onto a yellow legal pad in two columns with about sixty half-titles per sheet.

To kick off a writing session, he would typically then combine one of the half titles with another half title from the list, or make up his own start or end of the other half of a title.

And he would write.

Dean says that he likes to think of Bryant Street as the place where The Twilight Zone lives in suburban USA.

I like the fact that, even though it was written a few years ago, it speaks so brilliantly to things that are going on in the world today. And that's not to mention the "Twilight Zone" kind of year that 2020 has been so far, but the obsessively crafted silos we create and shelter ourselves within, along with the obsessive denial of some very real facts that we're not yet ready to deal with.

They turned off the electricity on a Tuesday in October. It was actually a warm and bright fall day.

Jason didn't care about the electricity. He had been surprised it had remained on as long as it had. He didn't have the money to pay it anyway. He had enough to buy some beer and groceries, basics, things like a jar of peanut butter, crackers, and stuff that would keep just fine without electricity.

When the stores were open.

Today, one of the close stores just about fifteen blocks from his home had been open, and he had been their only customer.

And as long as his small unemployment checks kept coming, he would have enough for that every week if he could find a store. Eighteen weeks was what they told him was the maximum amount of time for unemployment when he had started on it. But that had now been extended four times.

Things were that bad everywhere.

He put the two sacks of groceries his week's money had bought him on the kitchen counter and put them away as if things were normal, the only light in the room coming through the window over the sink looking out over what had been a beautiful backyard, but was now nothing but weeds.

He could drink the beer warm, but he didn't like it, so he dug out of the garage his old fishing cooler from back when he and his family used to go fishing together. He put it in the middle of the garage.

A few months before, he had bought some bags of ice to put in his freezer in his garage, where he used to have steaks and supplies but now was empty. The freezer would hold bags of ice just fine and keep them from melting until he needed them.

He then put half a bag of ice in the cooler over two six-packs of beer. He would last just fine for a few days that way.

The weather was no longer hot, but it also wasn't cold, so his house didn't get that cold at night.

Yet.

He knew it would in the rough winters this area had, so he was already preparing by shutting off some rooms, stuffing blankets around doors, and stocking firewood for his living room fireplace. He had cut down two of his own trees in the backyard and three neighbors' trees so far to get the firewood.

He had no hot water without electricity, but he had a solution for that as well. Back when the power had gone out five years before, his wife Sheila had forced him to stock up on the small canisters of propane and buy a small propane camping stove that he had to use outdoors on the back patio along with some indoor propane lanterns.

A month before the power was cut off, when he knew it was coming to that, he used the last credit left on one of his credit cards to buy a hundred more of the canisters and another stove and two more lanterns. He could cook and heat water and have light for a long time.

He had no intention of ever paying that credit card. He had been surprised it even worked in this economy.

And it was the last time he had driven his car. It had very little gas left. He would leave that for an extreme emergency.

Jason thought of himself as a survivor.

And he had no intention of leaving his home on Bryant Street. This was his home, his family's home. No matter how little money he had, he was staying.

Eventually, he would find some sort of work.

Eventually, he would bring back his home to the shape that Sheila and the girls would be proud of.

The October sun was shining and making the orange and gold leaves on all the trees almost glisten. Up and down Bryant Street, every house he could see had a For Sale sign in the front yard. For a time, he had had one as well. But then he knocked it down, and the weeds of his lawn soon covered it.

Bryant Street had been the perfect place to live in his mind. Beautiful, well-maintained, friendly.

Of course, since the collapse of the economy and the President declaring Marshal Law, no house had sold anywhere.

Even though every house on the street was in foreclosure, the banks were mostly out of business and could do nothing. They were holding on with government help, but no turnaround was evident in the near future. When he had power, he used to watch the news. All it did was depress him, so he wouldn't miss that now.

He looked up and down the street. As far as he knew, no one lived in any of the homes on Bryant Street besides him. He had no idea where everyone had gone. Some of the refugee camps that had food, he supposed.

At night, the street was dark, and no cars except the postman's van seemed to ever drive the street.

Of course, no one could afford gas.

After the initial collapse in the spring, riots had been so bad as to shut down entire cities. But at that point, everyone, including him, thought it would recover like it had before.

The US economy was too big to fail is what all the experts said. He wondered where those experts were at now, which refugee camp.

Sheila and the girls had gone to visit her mother in Washington State, driving and hoping to bring her back with them to live with us. I still had a job, so I stayed and worked.

They went missing with millions of others when a nuclear bomb exploded just a mile from where Sheila's mother lived.

Three other bombs went off around the country, all set by domestic terrorists, men angry at how much money they had lost in the collapse.

That had been over a year ago.

That's when everything spun down, and the economy collapsed completely, along with the banks.

Jason lost his job five months later. He was surprised he had lasted that long, and without Sheila and the girls, he hadn't cared.

Everyone lost loved ones in the bombs. Jason still believed in his heart that he had not lost Sheila and his girls.

He believed they would find their way to him if he stayed put in their home.

So, he prepared for a long winter without electricity, living on Bryant Street.

As the fall days went past and leaves left the trees, Jason settled into a routine of drinking a few beers a day, reading from paper books, and chopping even more firewood for his fireplace.

Over the two months since they turned off his electricity, he had managed to stay warm, taking only two baths a week with heated water and keeping bundled up.

His diet was of peanut butter, crackers, and some canned vegetables. And beer.

He had enough money by cashing his shrinking unemployment check from the government every week at the one bank that was open to buy beer, peanut butter, and at times some ice. But he had started leaving his cooler out on the back porch as it got colder and that helped the ice last a lot longer for his beer.

And the store each week seemed to have fewer and fewer supplies on the shelves. The distribution system in the country was clearly having issues.

Sheila would be proud of how much weight he had lost and the muscle he had gained by chopping and hauling wood.

On Christmas, the second Christmas without Sheila and the girls, he hung out ornaments on their fake tree and just sat in front of the fire and thought of the good times they used to have.

He dreamed that night, sitting in his lounge chair, covered in a blanket, that they came home.

He woke up the next morning alone in a cold house.

He took down the tree and stored it in the garage.

Three weeks later, when his unemployment check did not show up in his mailbox, he went to the post office to find out what happened.

It was closed down.

He went to the bank to talk to them.

It was closed down with a simple note on the door. "Good luck to you all and God Bless."

The grocery store that was often open was shut down, and he could see through the door that the shelves were stripped bare.

No one but him was moving in the cold morning air.

It looked like civilization was over.

At least any kind that he knew.

He walked slowly back to Bryant Street. No sign at all that anyone lived in any of the houses along the street.

He decided that before anyone else got here, he needed the supplies left in every one of those homes.

That day was the first time he broke into a home, going into the backyard and breaking a window to get in. He found some food in the cabinets, including two jars of peanut butter, some jam, and some bottles of wine.

He also found a kid's wagon in the garage that he used to carry the stuff to his home.

He went back to that place five times that day, pulling the wagon and with a pack on his back. He took blankets, jackets that would fit him and Sheila and the girls, and two guns hidden in a closet with ammunition. He was not a gun type of guy, but he had a hunch he might just need them. He sure hoped not.

He searched the house carefully, making sure he hadn't missed anything he might use, including matches and lighters and a new ax from their garage.

That night he used the tools he had brought from his raid to hang blankets on all of his exterior walls. Two blankets thick. That would help keep the intense cold out.

The next day broke clear again, so he went back to the next house in line with his wagon and broke in and found no more food, but a few supplies. So, he went to the house across the street.

More wine, more basic supplies like crackers, chips, peanut butter, and blankets.

Lots and lots of blankets.

For the next week, he raided every home within two blocks in either direction from his house. By the time he was finished, he was set to go through the rest of the winter.

And he had even found some cases of beer and more wine than he could ever drink in one winter.

Not only did the collapse of civilization want to stop Jason, but so did the weather. But Jason figured he could beat them both until Sheila and the girls got home.

The first week of February, the weather turned bitterly cold, so cold he didn't even dare walk outside.

He kept layers and layers of blankets nailed over the windows and doors and all the walls. He stayed only in the living room and kitchen and the fire going.

He fell asleep that evening in his recliner near the fire. He was covered in blankets and reading Sheila's favorite book, thinking of her and the girls.

At some point, a spark from the roaring fire got out of the fireplace, caught the top blanket on fire.

Jason was having a wonderful dream of being warm for the first time in a very long time. He was with Sheila and his girls on a beach, and times were good, and life was happy.

Their laughter echoed everywhere.

The smoke took Jason in his sleep as he and Sheila and the girls played in the warm sand.

On Bryant Street, the burning house was met with no response.

The house just burned through the cold night, and by morning was nothing more than a smoldering pile blackness.

Later that night, a cold snowstorm covered it in white and ice, leaving a scar on what had been a perfect neighborhood back in the good times.

Ω

THE TOOTH FAIRY

David Stier

There are different types of collectors. Just as there are different types of obsessions over collections. And, when you take it a step further, to include gamification and scoring, it can become more macabre in nature.

David Stier tells me that he has been a collector since the third grade. He started with comic books and baseball cards and, more recently, has moved on to first editions and newspaper front pages of historical events like the end of WWI and Pearl Harbor.

Stier also tells me that he plays "though not very well," he insists on adding, a 1933 Selmer alto saxophone. Considering his dedication to craft, I'm sure he plays far better than he lets on.

David Stier is a US Army veteran who served in Germany during the Cold War. He has traveled to many battlefields and historical locations in the United States and Europe. Stier studies world and US History with a focus on 19th, 20th, and

21st-century warfare. He graduated from UCSC in 1988 with a BA in Literature and Creative Writing. He currently resides in Twin Falls, Idaho.

Dave was also a runner up in the University of North Georgia's 2019 Military Science Fiction Symposium for "Prisoners of War." His short story collection, Final Solutions, Stories of the Holocaust is available on Amazon and Kobo.

Some of Dave's short stories have appeared in the following volumes of Fiction River: Visions of the Apocalypse, Pulse Pounders Adrenaline, Hard Choices, Spies, and Doorways to Enchantment. I have had the pleasure of publishing his stories in the Feel the Fear and Feel the Love volumes, as proud trophies in my own collection of "war conquests" I have tracked.

When asked about the inspiration for the story, Stier says that originality is very important to most collectors. "So, when I thought about writing an obsessions story, I figured you couldn't get more original then collecting gold teeth from dead enemy soldiers."

This tale is set during the Korean War, where he takes Private Harley's obsession to a whole new disturbing level.

Chipyong-ni, South Korea, 14 February, 1951

PFC Mark Harley scanned the terrain in front of his position. Dawn was closing in and now was the best time to get to prospectin'.

In the lightening dark he looked past the dead commies he'd nailed in last night's three human wave attacks. Most likely there weren't no live surprises left, hiding behind the few scraggly pine trees or hunkered down in the shell craters that dotted the field between Chipyong-ni—the town his regimental combat team defended—and Hill 345 to the northwest.

Making sure's the smart way to keep living, though.

His left hand itched but he clenched his teeth, stopping hisself from reaching inside his field jacket pocket to feel for the presence of his tooth pullers. He waited a little longer till the light was just right then crawled from his foxhole and got to work.

He hit pay dirt after the third corpse, used his bayonet to pry open the mouth—no gawd awful stink this time. Not usual that, since most dead'uns died with mouths agape and they almost always had at least a few rotten ones. He carefully clamped the gold front tooth in his incisor pliers and pulled with increasing pressure till the root popped free.

Gotta love that sound, heh. Like a cash register ringing up a sale.

He slipped the prize into a fatigue shirt pocket for now. He'd put it in his special canvas bag after soaking it and the others he collected today in rubbing alcohol to cut down on the stench. The stink, more'un anything, was what pissed off his buddies. Next he took out his notebook and marked the find inside, using his special code. Then he moved to the next and the next, finding treasure in some, but not as many as he'd hoped. For now, he just had to use checkmarks since he only had dead'uns to deal with. Live'uns could be a little messy and needed an "X" to keep track of. Had to stick 'em first to finish 'em off and sometimes blood flowed over his bayonet and the hand clamping the mouth shut to keep the commie quiet.

The extra points was a bonus though.

Just when he was ready to turn back to his foxhole, he caught a glint from the half-risen sun shining on a dead'un's open mouth 'bout five foot distant. He crawled that-a-way, staring in awe at the five-tooth gold bridge then hurriedly took out his molar pliers and wiggled each of the five teeth in turn till the bridge broke free with a sucking pop. He placed the find in his fatigue shirt pocket then turned back to his lines.

Come up with a higher score on this baby? Maybe a 4-pointer? Need a new code mark too.

And with that comforting thought he slipped back into his foxhole.

∞

Harley cleaned his M1 Garand with vigilant and studied care. But occasionally he'd weaken and look toward the killing field—especially the *crop* not yet gleaned in front of his position.

It had snowed some more after sunrise, the white powder dusting the dead, reminding him of salt sprinkled on a long pork feast for the local hogs— something he might experience again if'n they ever got free.

He'd need care should he go out in the daylight, but them who'd survived the night were back at Hill 345 and their artillery was most like out of range too. If he was careful it should go okay. Biggest threat was keeping Sgt. Howe, his squad leader, from not knowin'. Damned dumb of Harley, fighting Nazis during the last go, afore he'd come to know the treasures just waiting to be had now. His family could a used the gold improving the farm. When the Army had first called him back up, he'd cussed to all get out, but then he remembered how some of the Joes in Italy and France had mined Nazi gold, so as soon's they landed at Pusan, he'd a-started prospectin'.

Won't make that mistake again in the next war neither.

The hills in the distance was covered in more snow now. The pine trees scattered on the slopes gave off a white and green glow from the sun, reminding him of Christmas back home in the Pennsylvania hills. Damned cold now too, but one nice thing 'bout that was it kept the dead-stink away. It mostly froze open the commie's pie holes too, which meant he didn't have to use his bayonet to force open as many clenched dead jaws. He chuckled to hisself.

Mouthwash sure might help with all them rotten teeth.

His left hand itched again and once he reached inside his field jacket pocket to feel the presence of his prospectin' tools. Those had been a lucky find while on R&R in Tokyo.

Worked right nice compared to the mechanic's pliers I used afore that.

The three human wave charges last night had proved once again that steel was stronger than flesh, but the third Chi-com wave had come close to an upset on that there old saw. He cussed hisself again for a lack of control and with a final caress of the tooth pullers he went back to cleaning his weapon.

He refused to look anywhere else except at the cleaning rod, oil-soaked rag and the parts lying in precise order across his poncho. He counted slowly while cleaning every part, coating them with gun oil as he re-assembled the rifle. He worked the bolt twice then slipped in a clip, the solid clunk of the first-round slamming home sounding like what he thought of as a commie dirge. Mining gold after a fight passed the time and added to his treasure, but a clean rifle after a fight was the best way to keep livin' during the next go.

His buddies had gave him a hard name to cotton to, calling him "The Tooth Fairy" and joking about his *hobby*, but pulling commie teeth weren't all he was good at, as the pile of dead in front of his foxhole showed, so they mostly let him be—especially since he was always the first to volunteer to go out on patrol.

A grand way to get gold and add to the score, was that.

With his weapon all set, he took out his notebook and pencil. It had been a week since he'd been able to add to the tally. He drew a line across his last entries then wrote down the date and town's name, then drew three columns—adding a fourth when he remembered the 5-tooth bridge. Then he numbered them from one to four.

Three of the commies had been nailed by his buddy Jacky-Boy in the next foxhole so those teeth was only worth a point each, but five had been nailed by him which meant two points apiece. No live'uns to kill so no 3-pointers yet today, but the 5-tooth crown was his first 4-pointer.

"Hey Jacky-Boy," he said across the five-yard space between their foxholes. "I'm a-goin' out fer some more prospecting. Keep yer eyes peeled okay?"

Harley and Jack Lawrence had been in Korea since the 2nd Division had shipped out from Fort Lewis Washington last year. Other GIs could make that claim too, but as time passed there was fewer of them—especially since the 23rd Regimental Combat Team had been turned into a kind of fire brigade, tasked with putting out Chi-com fires like the one last night.

No doubt more dead Joes today now too.

Lawrence took off his steel pot and rubbed his short kinky hair then scratched his stubbled black face. He studied the pile of dead in front of his and Harley's positions.

"Better hurry, Mr. Tooth Fairy," he said with a nasty smile. "Word is we're bein' pulled off the line. Some Joe in 2nd Battalion'll be jumping your claim after that."

"Just doing my part to fight Communism," Harley said with nasty smile of his own. "I'll buy us some beers tonight fer your trouble."

∞

All in all it had been a good day on the line. Harley had gotten hisself more gold afore the word come down to head back to Chipyong-ni while the 2nd Battalion took their place. No one else in the squad had bought it neither.

Now, after a shower and shave, Harley and Jacky-Boy was comfortably seated in the dusky smoke-filled haze of Mamasan Lee's Bar and Grill, each with a bottle of ice cold Black Label in their mitts, and the juke box playing Dinah Shore to beat all. If they had to, Korean beer would do, but Mamasan's was the place to go for American brews—plus the best chicken skewers and noodles. A far piece from Pennsylvania chow, but good eatin' fer all that.

Harley took out his notebook to recheck the day's score. Just twelve nuggets today, but that wasn't counting the 5-toother. Since he'd got the tooth pullers on R&R his take had definitely went up. He ran a finger down each page total to compare the tally afore with regular pliers and now.

Mamasan personally came to their table and bowed, so he slipped the notebook in his fatigue shirt pocket.

Best to keep this here business to myself.

"Food okay, Joe?" she asked with a perfect white smile—no gold to speak of there.

"Great grub, Mamasan," Harley said while Lawerence nodded, hoisting his bottle her way. Harley handed her a US dollar bill. "Just keep the brews a-comin', *arasso?*"

As expected, Mamasan's eyes widened at the US money, which was the point. He didn't know how much a buck was worth in South Korean dough, but he did know it was a lot. Now they'd have all the beer they could guzzle and every time the bottles got low another would magically appear.

"Okay, Joe." She bowed lower this time and retreated to her position behind the wood plank bar, standing to the side of the red neon Pabst Blue Ribbon Beer sign. PBR was a fair-to-middling brew, but he'd take Black Label over that every day of the week.

He reached for the notebook again, but at Jacky-Boy's head shake and rolling eyes he took a swig of brew instead.

"Go on Harley, lotsa Joes take gook teeth. You're the only one that keeps score, as far as I know. Everyone in the platoon knows it, too, but they also know you're one damn fine ground pounder with two wars under his belt. And you don't try to hide nothing neither, which makes it just peachy in my book."

"Aw, shucks, Jacky-Boy. Thanks." Harley said. "Just don't be askin' me fer no kisses."

They both up-ended their bottles, and finished them off while two more appeared on a tray held by a real looker with deep dark eyes, long straight black hair and a pair a right nice *gazobas*. She smiled at Harley. He winked and she looked down while Jacky-Boy guffawed. As the bar maid headed back for more brews, she looked back once more.

"Think I know where you'll be in a while, Harley, my man."

"A regular mind reader, are ya?" Harley said. "Well, mayhap you're right on this 'un."

They finished their beers and just as The Looker brought two more, Harley spied Sergeant Howe, their squad leader, headed to their table.

"Uh oh," Jacky-Boy said, then took a huge swallow. "Looks like bad news."

"Afraid so," Sgt. Howe said. "Anyone ever say you whisper like you're in a boiler room, Jacky-Boy? Maybe you shoulda joined the Navy."

"The Navy?" he said. "No way, Sarge. Remember the boat ride from San Diego to Pusan? I puked my guts out the whole way."

Howe took Lawrence's bottle, wiped the top with has hand and finished the brew off.

"Here's hoping this is the only dead soldier we'll see tomorrow, boys. I figure you've got time for one or two more before the MP's arrive to clear you all out. At 0600 we're headed up the line to Hill 345."

Harley checked Howe's blocky phiz, looking to find the joke.

"Afraid it's true Mr. Tooth Fairy," Howe said with his usual mean look that was all Harley ever got—not that it bothered him none. "But the scoop is there's hundreds of dead Chi-coms up top on the summit, so I'm sure your *prospecting* won't suffer none."

"That's alls I need to hear, Sarge and I'm-a volunteering for the first patrol, right now," he said. And as Howe turned away, a faint look of disgust on his face, Harley finished off his beer and headed toward Mamasan and The Looker, two more dollar bills held where they both could see them, real easy-like.

∞

Hill 345 weren't that high-looking, Harley thought as his company approached the snow and scrub brush sprinkled brown slopes. Like most hills in Korea—least where they'd a-been so far—they looked like lumpy brown and white pimples dotted on a mean and nasty giant's face. But one thing he knowed for sure, was that commies was up there and the only reason they weren't firing down on 'em right now was the US Air Force jets just a radio call away and the spotter plane he knowed was there too, keepin' a look see.

Yup. Napalm was a right fine persuader, that's fer sure.

As the middle platoon in the company column, he could relax some and think on last night with The Looker. Now that they was gone from Chipyong-ni, there'd be no more happy times like that till they was pulled back and maybe not then, neither, depending on where the brass sent 'em next.

But he did have that hilltop to look forward to, as Lt. Conway, their platoon leader, said at the short briefing he'd gave just afore they set out.

"A patrol from the 24th Division reconnoitered the summit two nights ago during the Chinese Communist attack on our position," he'd said. "Intelligence estimates at least 600 dead atop that hill, but the Chi-coms may have left them there as a decoy so tonight we'll be sending up a patrol to reconnoiter and make certain." And at the muffled groans, the Lieutenant gave one of them fake officer smiles—what Harley sourly thought of as *morale-building crapola.* "But if we're lucky, they've already headed north, so there is an excellent chance tonight's action will be nothing but a cake walk."

Well, mayhap they had skedaddled and mayhap they hadn't. Harley—and the rest a' the platoon, company and battalion he was sure—would bet on them being there just to be safe. So, as his grand pappy who'd served in the Civil War used to say when Harley was a young'un, he'd keep his powder dry and eyes peeled.

And first chance he got, he'd see for hisself if there was 600 dead commies up there or not. He and his tooth pullers sure hoped so.

And if there is I might break my all-time 1-day record.

The problem now, was to make sure he was on that there patrol.

∞

Harley crouched behind a boulder about half way up Hill 345. Behind him, Jacky-Boy, Sgt. Howe and what was left of the rest of their squad was hunkered down behind what cover could be had. The weather was near freezing and the wind drove it lower, but the thought of 600 dead'uns helped keep Harley warm. Wind was blowing down slope too, so's he'd most like smell the live commies afore bein' smelled hisself. But all's he smelt now was wet dirt and rotted wood. No dead-stink yet so's probably they'd been a layin' up there long enough to freeze.

The hairs on the back of his neck rose up some. When that happened it most always meant enemies was near. He checked his bayonet, making sure it was secured to the rifle's muzzle. Once back in France he'd nearly bought the farm when it fell off. He'd got lucky over that rookie mistake and while he'd checked it afore they'd left their lines tonight it was a good habit to keep close.

Better safe-n-sorry.

Orders was to reconnoiter up the hill as far as they could get, and to Harley that meant getting to the summit. About a quarter ways up they started spying corpses, but there weren't no time now for any prospectin', so to speak — least not yet. Maybe on the way back if he got assigned as tail end Charlie. Now, at the point of the patrol was where he wanted to be. Howe usually give him the honor since his night vision was better than most a' the Joes in the platoon.

He squat-crawled from behind the boulder to the bit of scrub brush he'd spied about five meters further up slope.

Just afore he reached it, a dark silhouette appeared up trail, headed for the same spot.

Harley rushed forward, stabbing upward and into the commie just below the breast bone. The stuck pig sorta pop told him he'd hit pay dirt and the warm blood gushing down the rifle onto his hand told him that too. Harley covered the commie's mouth just in case he had any last words to say.

Someone grabbed his shoulder, flung him sideways, his rifle still stuck in the dead commie's chest. Harley rolled to the right, felt a burning stab in his upper arm. He clamped his teeth together to hold in the cry of pain as he rolled again and struggled to his feet.

A break in the clouds cast moonlight over the slope which reflected off the snow. The expanding pool of blood and Harley's rifle—angled into his chest—looked like black water surrounding the roots of a spindly tree. The second commie rushed him, knife raised over his head. He tried to pull out his back-up knife with a blood slicked hand, but afore he could, a rifle's bayonet magically appeared in the commie's throat.

The gook stumbled and fell face first onto the ground in another pool a blood. Harley fell to one knee as Jacky-Boy yanked his M1 Garand free. Harley pulled off his field jacket, then Jacky-Boy slit Harley's fatigue shirt sleeve and wrapped a battle dressing around the wound.

"Sure saved my bacon that time," Harley whispered in the cold wind. "Beers and hookers are on the house,

Jacky-Boy, soon's we get the chance. Thanks!" Then he tested his arm.

A mite stiff, but good enough for the work ahead.

"Want me to take over for a spell?" Jacky-Boy asked.

Harley looked up toward the summit. The moon appeared again from behind clouds, showing a passel of cover up ahead.

Maybe fifty meters till the top?

"Think I kin manage, buddy. But maybe stick a little closer now. We're almost there."

The tooth puller's weight seemed to increase with each step upward and Harley forced hisself to slow down, keeping his eyes peeled for fair. He checked his watch—0300.

Still plenty a time.

∞

The 24th Division sure weren't blowing smoke over the number a' dead.

Harley moved far enough away from Howe so's he could work in peace, remembering to keep his eyes peeled for any live surprises like there was down slope. He also remembered the mission and kept his eyes peeled for any intel that Regiment could use.

The moon was a real pal this night too, showing just enough light to reflect off the dead'uns' gold teeth. He knowed Howe would only stand for so much, so Harley worked fast, not even keeping score for now, figuring that could wait. Most of the pie holes was froze open too, so he just prospected the slack-jawed corpses.

All 1-pointers too.

As time passed his spirits started to fall. Lotsa missing teeth—already took by 24th Division's *on-tra-pineers*, it seemed. But they hadn't took all and he even found another 3-tooth bridge. Plus, up ahead there looked to be an outline of some kinda hooch—maybe an aid station.

He popped a gold molar free, then swung round fast-like at the sound of approaching combat boots.

"Come on Mr. Tooth Fairy," Jacky-Boy said as he tucked a Chi-com pistol in his cartridge belt. "Sarge wants us to head back to the rally point 'cause there's no gook surprises." Then he rolled over a facedown officer and cut off his collar insignias. "Lots of souvenirs here, Harley-my-man. Not just gold teeth."

For some reason, Harley didn't like Jacky-Boy's tone, which bordered on a sneer, but he kept it to hisself, pointing to the hooch instead.

"I reckon we should check that hooch out first. Might be some intel in it."

"Yeah,' Jacky-Boy said. "Might be some gold nuggets too."

Harley tilted back his steel pot so's Jacky-Boy could get a real good look at his eyes, which he most like did since the nasty smile he used when Harley's *prospecting* came up vanished.

"Might be a Chi-com officer's sword in there too, so's you comin' or not?"

The wood hooch—unlike the hill top—had a real stink to it since it was out a' the wind and closed up and the windows was all unbroke. It had all the looks of an aid station and smelled full of ripe corpses too—something they'd not had to reckon with since winter had set in. Harley and Jacky-Boy both took out flashlights to get a better look.

With the light came the squeals and scampering of rats that rumpled beneath tunics and raced out of pant legs. Noses was chewed off and the eyeballs was mostly gone with maggots crawling in and out of the blood-filled sockets.

"Don't know about you," Jacky-Boy said as he took out a rag to cover his face, "but I've had enough of this shit."

And for once Harley had to agree. Not for all the gold in Ft. Knox did he want to add to his collection from this here place.

Just as they turned to leave, though, they heard a faint voice. Harley shined his light in that direction and it hit the face of an old mamasan—maybe the oldest he'd seen since his grand mammy's just afore she'd passed on. The wrinkles across the mamasan's pale forehead looked to have been chiseled in as was them around her neck and face. Her mouth was closed, drawed tight, but she hiccupped in constant pain.

"Damn," Jacky-Boy said. "How could she still be alive and why ain't the rats got to her yet?"

At the sound of Jacky-Boy's voice, the old mamasan opened her eyes, then she tried to speak.

And when she did that, Harley's flashlight beam shot back into her face from the reflection of what looked like an entire mouth full a gold teeth. He kept the beam focused on those gold nuggets. Without thinking he felt for his tooth pullers.

"I can see what you want, *buddy*," Jacky-Boy said as he yanked Harley's hand away from the pocket. Then he took out his flashlight again and swung it around till he found a stretcher. He opened it up and set it in the open space by the door.

"Come on Harley. Lend a hand here." Jacky-Boy said. "Maybe we can get her down the hill before she dies. Least we can get her out of this God-awful dead house."

His Grand Mammy's ghost face appeared above the mamasan's. He shook the image away. Together he and Lawrence carried the stretcher to the rally point that Howe had set up. The squad took turns carrying the mamasan down slope, but Jacky-Boy wouldn't meet Harley's eyes no more. Harley was able to keep his mind blank when it was his turn to take one end of the stretcher, but when it wasn't his hand kept feeling his field jacket pocket for the cold comfort of his tooth pullers.

Wonder when the mamasan's gonna die?

Ω

EXECUTIVE DECISIONS

Rebecca M. Senese

Have you ever wondered where obsessions come from? Or what drives a person to actually obsess about something?

Rebecca M. Senese has. And the story she crafted about it is one you're going to quite enjoy.

Rebecca, who can be found at www.rebeccasenese.com, weaves words of horror, mystery, contemporary fantasy, and science fiction in Toronto, Ontario. She is the author of the contemporary fantasy series, the Noel Kringle Chronicles *featuring the son of Santa Claus working as a private detective in Toronto. She garnered an Honorable Mention in* The Year's Best Science Fiction *and has been nominated for numerous Aurora Awards. Her work has appeared in* Fiction River: Superpowers, Fiction River: Visions of the Apocalypse, Fiction River: Sparks, Fiction River: Recycled Pulp, Imaginarium 2012, Tesseracts 15: A Case of Quite Curious Tales, Ride the Moon, *'Hungar Magazine,' 'On*

Spec,' 'TransVersions,' 'Future Syndicate,' and 'Storyteller,' amongst others.

I had the distinct honor of publishing her beautiful story "The Language of Dance" in Tesseracts Sixteen: Parnassus Unbound and am delighted to be able to share this story, about a decidedly different type of dance, with you today.

Rebecca tells me that she came up with the idea when she started considering the nature of obsessions. "Often obsessions feel like they are something outside of us," she says, "some other kind of force separate from our own personality.

"What if our obsessions weren't our own?

"What if someone guided them or pushed us even deeper into them?

"Where would that lead, and what would be their purpose for doing it?

"Maybe the answer is something as simple as climbing the corporate ladder?"

A simple answer, indeed, and yet shared in such a brilliant and creative tale, which I'm sure you'll agree with as you take my hand and follow Raymel, Rebecca's main character, as he takes those initial rookie steps on the bottom rung of that corporate ladder on his first day of work.

The office wasn't like anything Raymel had pictured. For some reason, he'd thought of dark wood paneling and plush carpeting, a whiff of sharp pine in the air. Something that denoted importance and seriousness. But when he stepped off the elevator onto the thirteenth floor, he saw cubicles. Beige, fabric cubicles stretching away to a set of windows in the distance. An almost subliminal hum came from the vent above his head. A slight breeze tickled the hair on the back of his neck.

The air was moving. It wasn't stale or anything, but it certainly wasn't pine.

And there certainly wasn't any dark wood paneling.

Instead of importance and seriousness, these cubicles suggested everyday routine.

Nothing special or important at all.

Kinda disappointing.

Raymel kept his expression carefully neutral as a form coalesced around the corner, taking the shape of Ms. Braydon, one of the panelists who had interviewed him.

She smiled as she stepped forward, holding out her hand to him. Her light brown hair was swept back from her face and fastened into a swirl of a bun that almost, but not quite, threatened to be a beehive. She wore a light grey suit that looked almost designed to fade into the background.

Forgettable. Unobtrusive. Designed to let the eye fall away.

Just like these cubicles.

Raymel tugged on his own navy jacket. Single-breasted, stylish cut. Designed to be noticed.

Damn, he'd forgotten himself. As an account advisor here, he was supposed to blend in. But this suit definitely did not match those cubicles.

Ms. Braydon's smile didn't indicate anything wrong. She shook his hand.

"Welcome to the pit," she said. When he raised an eyebrow, she chuckled.

"It's just a little joke," she said. "We like to keep things light here, especially with the work we do. Let me show you to your desk, Raymel."

"Just Ray is fine," he said.

He followed down the left aisle. Cubicles flashed by out of the corners of his eyes, each the same size, the same bland beige. The rhythm of walking and the unending sameness made him almost sink into a stupor. He had to jerk himself awake as Ms. Braydon suddenly stopped.

She held her hand out as if presenting a prize on a gameshow.

"Here's your spot," she said. "I'll let you settle in. There are a couple of files on your desk. Just a little bit to get your feet wet, so to speak."

"I'm ready to dive in," he said. It was always good to appear eager at a new job. He'd read that on a job-hunting site.

"Trust me, it's better to take it slow. The work here can be a little much for some. It's best to take your time and acclimatize yourself." She smiled again. "I'll let you get yourself sorted."

She turned away before he could say anything more. After a moment, she had slipped away, disappeared among the rows of cubicles.

Raymel sat down at his new desk. The top was beige, except for the inlaid keyboard, which was taupe. A set of two manila file folders had been set just to the right of the keyboard.

He took a deep breath, smelling nothing. Not dust, not any kind of furniture polish or carpet cleaner. Nothing in the air but air.

How could anyone work like this? How would he?

"Howdy neighbor, welcome to the pit!"

Raymel spun in his chair at the sound of the voice. A man's head poked around the left side of his cubicle. Thinning black hair was brushed back from the man's high forehead. A friendly grin crinkled his face. He wore a white shirt and brown pants with no crease. Other than the enthusiastic grin, the man could have melted into the background with no trouble.

He held out his right hand.

"It's been a long time since someone has moored alongside me. Good to have ya here," he said.

Raymel shook the man's hand. A firm, but not overly so, grip. One decent pump and release.

Forgettable. Just like everything else in this place.

"Thanks," Raymel said. "I'm Raymel. You can call me Ray."

"I'm Marlinovik. You can call me Marlin," the man said. "Or even Mar. Whatever floats yer boat." He chuckled. "I like boats. Savin' up for one. A nice little two sleeper for me and the missus."

Raymel nodded. "Have you worked here long?"

Marlin chuckled again. "Seems like ferever. I was one a' the originals, along with Ms. Braydon. A lifer, you might say. You got any questions, just ask. The work can be a little confusing at first."

"Thanks. I might take you up on that."

"See that ya do. We all gotta look out for each other here. Remember, any questions at all."

"Thanks," Raymel said.

"I'll let ya get to it," Marlin said. "Coffee break's at ten. I usually walk down ta the cart in the lobby. You wanna come stretch yer legs? Or, I can just get ya a cup."

"I'll let you know," Raymel said.

"Course, course. I'll let you get on it." The smile drained from Marlin's face. He instantly looked older, more serious and intense.

"Remember, any questions…"

"I'll ask right away," Raymel said.

"Good man." A quick smile brightened Marlin's face, and then he disappeared around the cubicle wall.

Raymel spun back to the keyboard. Other than the quiet hum of the vent, he couldn't hear anything else. No typing on keyboards, no voices on the phone. Nothing. Not even from Marlin's cubicle.

This was the strangest office he had ever been in. Suppressing a shiver, he flipped open the first file.

And felt himself fall in.

The cubicles fell away, and he felt himself floating through the air, disembodied. Below, he saw a young boy standing in front of a sporting goods store, peering in the window. A breeze ruffled the boy's brown hair, tickling across his eyes. The boy gave a reflexive swipe with his hand. He wore baggy shorts that hung below his knees and a dark blue t-shirt emblazed with the number forty-seven. His feet were shoved into high-top sneakers.

Some kind of sports shirt, Raymel surmised. He focused a little deeper and grabbed the boy's name. Danny. Good, easier to stick with him when he knew the client's name.

He felt his attention shift away from the boy toward the store window. What was the boy looking at?

Several pieces of sports equipment hung in the window. A baseball bat with a glove was arranged on the right. A basketball with a hoop rested against the left side. In the center, hanging on a diagonal, was a long, black skateboard. Painted flames raced from the front to back.

The boy sighed and glanced back along the street. At that moment, Raymel knew he was killing time, just waiting for the bus.

The bus stop was just past the sports store. Already Raymel could feel the boy's attention waning from the store. His sneakers shifted in the dust on the sidewalk. He was about to head back to the bus stop.

Raymel felt a warning flash in his head, like a jab of pain in his forehead. How could that be when he was disembodied? None of it made sense, but this was his first file, and he couldn't screw it up.

He was supposed to do something.

The boy took a step away from the store. Although Raymel was disembodied and couldn't physically touch the boy, he could affect him. If he concentrated enough.

Raymel focused. He knew if he'd physically been there, he would be sweating. Beads dripping down his forehead.

Focus.

Which item had the boy been looking at?

An image flashed through his mind, so quick he barely saw it. The boy gliding past.

Gliding.

The skateboard!

Raymel sent the thought pulsing toward the boy. The image of him on the skateboard, flying over the ground. Doing spins and twirls. Getting cheers at the local skate park. Gaining recognition for his skill. Leaving this hick town and riding all over the world. Endorsements. Money. Fame. Girls.

Raymel pushed it all into the boy.

The boy stiffened, pausing with one foot lifted off the ground. Then he stamped the foot down and spun back toward the store. He pressed himself against the glass, staring at the skateboard.

The bus blew by, sending dust swirling into the air.

Swirling.

Raymel felt himself swirling, spinning, higher into the air. The sunlight brightening to a blinding white. Making his eyes water.

Spinning.

His chair squeaked as he spun to the right. He lashed out with his left hand, catching the edge of the desk, stopping the spin.

Tears from the white light blurred his vision. He blinked them away. The beige cubicle. The beige desk. Plain, boring.

Comforting.

Raymel got it now. Why this place looked so boring.

It was grounding after working on a file.

He took a deep breath. His heart was pounding as if he'd physically exerted himself. He swiped at his forehead, and his hand came away wet with sweat. Was it like that for everyone? Would it be this tiring for him all the time?

He knew one person he could ask.

∞

"Took me about a month to get the hang of it," Marlin said. He dumped four sweeteners into his coffee. They stood on the first floor beside the coffee cart. The overpowering aroma of coffee extended through the entire lobby, with just a hint of burnt beans underneath.

Raymel had opted for herbal tea. He didn't need any more stimulants. Not right now.

"Are all of the files like that?" Raymel asked. "Simple pushes toward what they want?"

Marlin shook his head. He took a sip of his coffee, grimaced, and then added another sweetener.

"They always start you off with the little obsessions, get you acquainted with how it works. Later you'll get into the more sophisticated ones. Files you work on for days or weeks." He glanced around and then leaned closer to Raymel. His breath carried the scent of sweet coffee.

"Some of the senior account execs have a few files that they've worked on for years."

"Have you ever worked on any for that long?" Raymel asked.

Marlin shook his head. "The longest for me was six weeks. A woman obsessed with her ex-husband. Could have gone longer, but then she met a guy in her cooking class. My subject got removed and transferred over to the Love Department."

Six weeks on one file, then having it transferred. Raymel couldn't imagine the disappointment, but Marlin didn't seem bothered.

He clapped a hand on Raymel's shoulder, turning him toward the elevator.

"C'mon, let's get back to the mines," he said. "We should be able to push another half dozen between the two of us before the day is done."

Raymel worked on three more files that day. One a woman obsessed with some kind of coffee syrup, another a man obsessed with a national sports team, and finally a young girl obsessed with the latest boy band.

Each was a minor tweak, mostly him pushing them toward the thing they were obsessed with. Nothing major, yet he was left feeling exhausted after each one, sagging in his chair, arms limp on the surface of his beige desk.

A whole month to get used to this? That probably meant a whole month of boring little jobs like these ones. Minute tweaks driving people toward their obsessions. Nothing to really sink his teeth into.

Raymel wanted more.

Those senior executives who worked on a single file for months or years, that's what he wanted. He had to figure out how they did it and do that himself.

Time to get started.

∞

Over the next few weeks, Raymel came to work early, trying to meet and talk to others on the floor. Most people gave him polite, but limited, greetings. A clear indication that they didn't want to be bothered. But he made sure that Ms. Braydon noticed that he was early and trying to socialize, trying to fit into the department.

He also started to spend a little extra time at the coffee cart in the lobby, especially during the morning break. Although the intense stench of slightly burnt, roasted beans started to give him a headache, he stuck around, sipping a plain black coffee as folks from the office wandered by. He greeted them, and if they gave him more than a nod, he ended up buying them coffee.

That at least got him more than a plain hello.

Carefully, he asked each about their work, using the excuse that he was new and trying to learn as best he could. Most were working on transient obsessions like he was, but usually following a client for a few days, maybe a week. Over time, he started to piece together how people moved up in the department.

It wasn't just sticking with the tried and true method of tweaking the client's obsessions.

He would have to do something bold.

It was a Friday morning when he decided it was time. He'd been working for three weeks, getting better and better at handling the transition of moving into the client's world and back to his own. Now he only got the occasional headache or dizzy spell.

Time for the next step.

Raymel sat at his desk, reviewing the latest files. The same Manila folders with the same plain white papers inside. Minor obsessions, nothing of note. Nothing for him to really dig into, nothing for him to shine.

Did he have to work on these? Hadn't one of the women he'd talked to last week mention something about checking up on previous cases?

He leaned back in his chair and took a breath. Yes, that was right. He remembered now. She'd ordered a vanilla latte with extra whipped cream. The cream had left a mustache film on her upper lip when she took a sip. She'd had blonde hair cut into a short, pixie style that just made her round face look even rounder. Her voice had had a slight squeak to it when she talked.

"Yeah, sometimes I go back to one of ma previous jobs, give 'em a bit of a nudge," she said. "Followin' up always looks good on your reports. Shows initiative." She winked. "They don't tell ya that, but they like it."

Initiative. That's what he had to do. Show them he had initiative.

Raymel spun his chair to the left, toward the drawer with all his previous cases. There had to be one he could nudge. Maybe even more than nudge.

He spent half an hour going over the files before he came to the boy with the obsession for a skateboard. Really minor stuff. But what if he could take something so minor and make it big? Wouldn't that show initiative? Wouldn't that show that Raymel had what it took to move up?

He grinned at the bland, beige cubicle wall before him.

He had just the idea, too.

∞

Melting back into Danny's consciousness was easier the second time. There was a familiarity to it, a comfort that Raymel didn't feel from the new files. Of course, it made sense, but he'd never thought of it. It was easier to connect to a client he'd worked with before. Probably why having the same client for a long period was so coveted.

He settled in and did a quick review.

When he'd pushed the boy toward the skateboard in the store window, the boy had missed the bus going home. He'd been late for dinner, causing a big blowout with his father. Grounded for two weeks. Simmering tension lingered in the boy, even to this day. It almost overrode his obsession with the skateboard.

Perfect. Raymel knew exactly what to do.

Danny was on the way to school. Feet trudging along the sidewalk. Backpack heavy on his back. It was late spring, almost the end of the school year, and an especially hot day. The sun beat down on the boy's bowed head. Even this early in the morning, his hair was damp with sweat. Sticking to the back of his neck.

Walking? Walking was so boring, so slow. There had to be a better way to get to school.

Raymel faded back after he planted the words. He felt the boy's simmering anger sharpen. Just then, the sound of wheels crackled over the concrete. Danny glanced back over his shoulder.

Another boy was fast approaching, riding a skateboard. It wasn't exactly like the one Danny had seen in the store. It was smaller. A regular board, while the other one had been a longboard.

Raymel plucked the information from Danny's mind. Could see how much he really wanted a longboard. But he couldn't afford it, and his dad sure wasn't gonna get it for him.

This was it. This was Raymel's chance. He could almost feel his heart quicken, a strange sensation when he was disembodied. Then the image before him started to blur.

No! He was being pulled back to his office. He couldn't let that happen, not yet. This was the perfect moment to tweak Danny's obsession. He couldn't miss.

Relax. Focus. Breathe.

His focus sharpened again. He reached for Danny, slipped back into his mind. Easy. Easy does it.

The other boy was almost upon him. Gave a kick with his right leg, propelling the skateboard forward. Aiming to pass Danny on the right.

All he had to do was let the boy pass. Then he could keep walking to school.

Slow, boring walking. Sweating in the heat.

Wasn't there a better way to go to school?

The wheels churned on the sidewalk. A breeze brought the scent of dust and stale grease from the diner on the corner. The sun beat down on Danny's head, like a relentless, hot throbbing.

Slow, boring, hot walking.

As the boy drew up beside him, Danny shifted, turning toward the right. Just a little.

Just enough that his backpack hit the boy in the shoulder.

The boy wobbled on the skateboard. He flung his arms out to steady himself, but the board hit a bump, destabilizing him more. For a moment, he seemed to balance on the board, arms spread. Then the board zipped forward while the boy fell backward.

Backward.

His rump hit the ground first. Then he cracked his right elbow.

Then his head came down. Slamming on the concrete curb.

His limbs flopped down, and he lay still.

The skateboard slowed and stopped about five feet away.

Danny stood halfway between the boy and the skateboard. He stared down at the boy. His hands squeezed the straps of his backpack. His breath was short and shallow and fast.

Had he done this? Was the boy alive?

Raymel could feel the panic begin to spread in Danny's mind. The boy's legs began to tremble.

Not your fault. You just happened to shift, to bump him. Shouldn't he have been wearing a helmet anyway?

Right, a helmet. Shoulda been wearing a helmet. Everybody knew that.

Raymel felt Danny grab onto the excuse, clutch it to him.

His legs steadied.

Good. That was good.

Step away. One foot, then the other. Slide along the pavement. Watch the little dust particles rise around the sneakers.

A moment later, Danny's foot bumped the skateboard.

From here, Danny could see that it was a little worn. Needed some paint as some had worn down right to the wood. Would have to sand it down, probably repaint the whole thing. He could do that in his garage at home. His dad liked doing stuff like that. Would probably even help him. A project they could work on together. Maybe it would help get Danny out of being grounded.

But how would Danny explain having it? He couldn't afford a skateboard.

Found it. Just found it.

Yeah, found it. In the grass along Maple Street, right by the empty, overgrown lot where they were still squabbling over building a strip mall.

Danny turned, far enough that he couldn't see the boy lying on the ground. Not even out of the corner of his eye.

He put one foot on the skateboard.

Pushed off with the other.

The wheels clattered on the pavement, then smoothed out as they picked up speed. Danny bent his knees, kicking at the sidewalk with one foot. Gaining speed.

And never looked back.

Raymel felt giddy with delight. He could feel Danny's obsession solidify and strengthen. This skateboard would do for now, but he really wanted a longboard. Raymel would make sure the boy did whatever it took.

No matter what.

If Raymel could have laughed in his disembodied state, he would have. Instead, he basked as he watched Danny turn the corner and pick up speed as he headed for school. Still not bothering to look back.

Then something yanked Raymel away, sending pain slicing through his mind.

Until he landed back in his desk chair with a gasp.

"What do you think you're doing?"

Ms. Braydon towered over him, hands on her hips, her face red and glowering.

Behind her, he could see Marlin and the others. Even Miss Vanilla Latte.

All of them witness to his chewing out.

The beigeness of the cubicle pounded into his brain, making his temples throb. His mouth was dry, his tongue felt swollen. His limbs trembled, even his hand as he lifted it to push a few stray hairs back from his forehead.

The motion gave him a chance to breathe. He swallowed, trying to work up some saliva to speak.

He cleared his throat.

"I was following up on a case," he said.

"You were doing more than that," Ms. Braydon snapped. "You were deliberately interfering."

"No, ma'am," he said. "I allowed the subject to keep focused on his obsession and follow it through to its logical conclusion."

She glared at him. Behind her, he could see the others turning to each other, their mouths moving, but their voices too low to hear. Probably didn't want to incur Ms. Braydon's wrath the way he had.

Less than six months and Raymel was going to be fired. His dreams of moving up, of getting to deal with clients long term was evaporating. But he was doing his job, couldn't she see that? He was doing better than his job.

He had to make her understand.

He cleared his throat again. His heart pounded. Adrenaline burned through his system, making him want to yell at her, defend himself, but he had to remain calm.

"In section twelve of the manual, previous focus of the subject upon the obsession is deemed appropriate and desired."

"Don't quote the manual at me," she said. "You overstepped, and you know it."

He pressed his lips together. Breathe. Focus.

"The subject's obsession was already growing," he said. "I allowed the subject full expression of his obsession."

Ms. Braydon's eyes narrowed. She tilted her head. The tall, almost beehive-sculptured bun on her head shifted. If she nodded her head at him, would it slide off and crush him? The thought almost made him giggle. A panic response. He clenched his jaw, trying to hold in the giggle.

If she wasn't going to fire him, laughing at her would sure make it happen.

"And you're sure the subject had a strong enough obsession to justify this? You didn't force it in any way?"

Her tone dripped with sarcasm. Had she been monitoring him? Even if she had been, he hadn't overstepped. Sure, he'd focused the boy's obsession on how hot it was walking to school, how much easier it would be with a skateboard. But the motion to turn had all been the boy's decision. His act had set the whole thing in motion. Raymel hadn't forced it upon Danny.

Had he?

He thought back, trying to sort it through. If he could review the record… but he knew without even asking that such a request was the wrong move. The look on Ms. Braydon's face told him.

He had to be sure.

Was he?

He took another breath, trying to slow his galloping heart. The boy had been walking along, and Raymel had tweaked his misery. Then the other boy with the skateboard had come along. Danny had turned just enough to knock the boy off.

Raymel hadn't told him to do it. The boy had done it on his own.

Raymel lifted his chin and focused on Ms. Braydon.

"The subject was ripe to take this action," he said. His voice rang out over the cubicles, strong and clear. "I focused his obsession and allowed him to express it fully. Just like my job intends."

He could feel the air still around him as if the entire floor held its collective breath. Ms. Braydon studied him, eyes narrowed, her expression unchanging. No one moved.

This was it. Make or break. He would probably be fired.

Raymel felt peace descend on him. He'd done his best, everything he could think of to do to get better, to move up, to achieve a higher rank. Even if they did fire him, it was okay. He'd done a good job, and he knew it. Even if they didn't.

Ms. Braydon lifted her chin as if she'd been reading his mind. A slight smile curled the corners of her lips.

"Well done," she said. "That was a masterful job. You set the subject down on a path that will allow us to claim his soul without deliberate interference. That is a real gift."

Murmurs rumbled through the crowd behind her. Ms. Braydon took a step back, gesturing for Raymel to stand.

He did so, surprised to find his legs held him without trembling.

They weren't going to fire him after all! A flash of heat surged through him. His heart began to pound again, this time from excitement and not fear.

The smile widened on Ms. Braydon's face.

"Come with me, Raymel," she said. "I'd like to introduce you to Mr. Fox and the executives on the sixty-sixth floor. I think you've got the makings of a real Demon."

She took his elbow and began to steer him down the hall toward the elevator. Raymel wanted to skip along beside her but forced himself to take measured steps.

The sixty-sixth floor! It was what he had always dreamed of but never let himself really believe it was possible. Would he be able to twist his client's obsession further? Would he be able to even plant new obsessions? Would he be able to twist a client's soul?

Would he even, maybe, one day meet the Boss, Mr. S.?

The Underworld was the limit.

As Ms. Braydon pressed the elevator button and a deep, solid bong sounded, Raymel let a smile cross his lips.

He was on his way.

And he would be damned if he was ever going to stop.

Ω

EDITOR'S OBSESSIVELY THANKFUL AFTERWORD & ACKNOWLEDGEMENTS

Our walk, dear reader, is now drawing to a close. I hope that you not only enjoyed the tales that these brilliant authors had to share, but that they gave you something to think about, to ponder, to reflect upon.

One of the things I appreciate about gathering together stories on a theme is the manner in which the authors all take that common thread and craft so many different and unique things with them.

The uniqueness isn't just in genre, but in tone, voice, perspective, and atmosphere.

And while I, and the authors whose stories you have just read, are honored to have been able to take you on this journey, I would be remiss not to mention all of the other amazing people and patrons without whom this anthology would not exist.

First, Kristine Kathryn Rusch and Dean Wesley Smith, whose "Denise Little" style workshops inspire, teach, and inform so many writers. Thank you for allowing me into those workshops. Thank you for believing in me enough to invite me to join you along with so many other amazing editors on the stage, including Denise Little herself. I have learned so much by listening to and collaborating with every single editor I've had the honor of working alongside all these years.

I have learned more about writing, and about editing, in these past seven years than I have in all the previous decades on writing and editing I have done. And I continue to learn from you.

This anthology would not exist without you, and the work you have done for the writing community. And, it would most certainly not exist in this format without your support of this book, and of the Kickstarter, through the most generous offer of a custom course designed to support it.

I will likely never be able to repay your kindness, your generosity, your support, the endless wisdom and advice you have bestowed upon me, as well as your unwavering belief in me. My only hope is that, like you, I can share the things I have learned with other writers and perhaps pay you back by paying it forward.

Thank you to Julie Strauss, whose masterful work as a line editor, and whose constant support as a friend helped me through those tough parts along the way.

Speaking of tough parts, thanks to Liz Anderson, my Love, who sees all those behind the scenes bumps, hears about all the scrapes and scratches, who listens patiently to my various foibles and frustrations, enthusiastically supports me in my obsessive dreams and visions, and who is always there for me and always has my back. Every single part of my journey as a writer and as a person is made better by her incredibly powerful presence as my partner.

And, finally, a thank you to the amazing patrons who supported this anthology on Kickstarter. You helped make this happen. Your support, your belief in this project, your willingness to step up, truly does warm my heart and reminds me of the goodness and compassion that exists in the human spirit.

Kevin Aldrich

Michael Anderle

Stacey Anderson

Joy Auburn

J.J. Austrian

Natasha Bajema

Robert B. Battle

Danny Bell

Alexandria Blaelock

Zach Bohannon

Mike Bray

N.M. Browne

BUDDYH

Harley Christensen

James G Connolly

Jamie Davis

Roland Denzel

Geoff Emberlin

Valerie Emerson

Joshua Essoe

Jana Fedoriska

Karlita Gesler

Tina M Noe Good

goodideafactory

James Gotaas

Nancy D. Greene

G Hardie

Tara Henderson

David H. Hendrickson

Laura M Holt

Jonathan Evan Hudson
Ilja Isphording
Robert Jeschonek
Juliana T Johnson
Jean Kilgore
Kari Kilgore
Barbara Klein
Mia Kleve
Dakota Krout
Christie LeBlanc
Sam Linton
LMBPN Publishing
Camille Lofters
Celine Malgen
Rick Massel
Todd McCaffrey
Kathryn Mcloskey
Mountaindale Press
Aaron J Moxcey
Dr. Tanner Lee Nash
James Nealon
Juanita J Nesbitt
Jared Nelson
Juak Cher Ng
Luanga A. Nuwame
Joanna Penn
Charlene Perry
T.W. Piperbrook
Susanne Pohl
Mary Jo Rabe

Kris Austen Radcliffe
JP Rindfleisch IX
Johanna Rothman
Carolyn Rowland
Lori Ryan
DL Sackett
Diane Sayer
Ricard Scheck
MJ Silversmith
Dean Wesley Smith
Carolyn & Stephen Stein
Louisa Swann
Lori Swapp
Stephanie Tallent
technogypsy
J. Thorn
Stanley B. Trice
Aaron Turko
Suzy Vadori
Rob Vagle
Judy K. Walker
Laura Ware
Paul Weiss
Keith West, Future Potentate of the Solar System
Angie Wise
Wolfpack Publishing
Lyn Worthen
Erin Wright
Zelpha Comic

About the Contributors

Each contributor's biography appears at the beginning of their story. You can learn more about the contributors by visiting their websites.

Ezekiel James Boston
www.ezekieljamesboston.com

Stephen Couch
www.stephencouch.wordpress.com

Joe Cron
www.joecron.com

Leah Cutter
www.leahcutter.com

Dayle A. Dermatis
www.dayledermatis.com

Robert Jeschonek
www.bobscribe.com

Kari Kilgore
www.karikilgore.com

Michael Kingswood
www.michaelkingswood.com

Kate Pavelle
www.olivettedevaux.com

Annie Reed
www.annie-reed.com

Kristine Kathryn Rusch
www.kriswrites.com

Leigh Saunders
www.leighsaunders.com

Rebecca M. Senese
www.rebeccasenese.com

Dean Wesley Smith
www.deanwesleysmith.com

Julie Strauss
www.juliewroteabook.com

David Stier
www.books2read.com/rl/AuthorDavidStier

About the Editor

Mark Leslie is a writer, editor and bookseller who was born and grew up in Sudbury, Ontario, spent many years in Ottawa and Hamilton, Ontario and currently lives in Waterloo, Ontario.

When he's not writing, Mark attaches "Lefebvre" back onto his name and works as a writing and publishing coach and consultant. As Director of Self-Publishing and Author Relations for Rakuten Kobo between 2011 and 2017, Mark established Kobo Writing Life which represents between 10 and 18% of Kobo's weekly unit sales, larger than any of the major publishers.

A bookselling veteran for more than twenty years, Mark has worked at virtually every type of bookstore, has sat on the Board of Directors for BookNet Canada and also been President of the Canadian Booksellers Association. He has given talks across Canada and the United States, in London, Paris and Frankfurt on the bookselling, writing and publishing industry.

Mark can be found online at www.markleslie.ca.

Selected Works from the Editor

Non-fiction paranormal:

- *Haunted Hamilton: The Ghosts of Dundurn Castle and Other Steeltown Shivers* (2012)
- *Spooky Sudbury: True Tales of the Eerie & Supernatural* (2013) – Co-written with Jenny Jelen
- *Tomes of Terror: Haunted Bookstores and Libraries* (2014)
- *Creepy Capital: Ghost Stories of Ottawa and the National Capital Region* (2016)
- *Haunted Hospitals: Eerie Tales about Hospitals, Sanatoriums and Other Institutions* (2017) – Co-written with Rhonda Parrish
- *Macabre Montreal: Ghostly Tales, Ghastly Events, and Gruesome True Stories* (2018) – Co-written with Shayna Krishnasamy

Fiction:

- *One Hand Screaming* (2004)
- *Evasion* (2014)
- *I, Death* (2016)
- *A Canadian Werewolf in New York* (2016)
- *Nocturnal Screams* (Short Fiction Series) (2017/2018)
- *Stowe Away* (2020)

Editor:

- *North of Infinity II* (2006)
- *Campus Chills* (2009)
- *Tesseracts Sixteen: Parnassus Unbound* (2012)
- *Fiction River 23: Editors' Choice* (2017)
- *Fiction River 25: Feel the Fear* (2017)
- *Fiction River 31: Feel the Love* (2019)
- *Fiction River 32: Superstitious* (2019)
- *Obsessions* (2020)

www.ingramcontent.com/pod-product-compliance
Lightning Source LLC
Chambersburg PA
CBHW032238010726
47494CB00002B/541